I0524363

Persuasions

VARIOUS DISTRACTIONS

AE LISTER

Various Distractions
ISBN # 978-1-83943-762-5
©Copyright AE Lister 2021
Cover Art by Kelly Martin ©Copyright December 2021
Interior text design by Claire Siemaszkiewicz
Pride Publishing

Published in 2021 by Pride Publishing, United Kingdom.

VARIOUS
DISTRACTIONS

Dedication

To my devoted readers, whose consistent engagement with me through The Braided Crop Ranch Facebook group keeps me motivated and inspired!

Prologue

I don't know how I'd ever lived without Vincent in my life, to be honest. He spent more and more time at my place, and I began to contemplate asking him to move in with me.

The fact that he enjoyed being of service to me in ways beyond the sexual was eye-opening. Vincent found peace when he cleaned and cooked, or played the piano — now that his skills were improving. When I wasn't teasing him and using his piano practice as the lead-up to a session, he could concentrate and enjoy making music for its own sake. It delighted me to watch him there, whether it was deliberate foreplay or a simple rehearsal.

I never grew tired of his beauty.

I'd thought him cute when we'd met, with an ass just right for putting in lace panties. But he'd blossomed into something more stunning and ethereal under my care. He seemed more confident with himself in public, even as he submitted willingly to the most humiliating ordeals in private — as if the more debased I made him there, the more he felt fulfilled and able to function in the real world. His submission, specifically at the hands of *my* domination, seemed to satisfy something so basic and primal in his psyche that it seemed the key to Vincent as a person.

I felt more confident in my dominance now. Observing the way Vincent responded to me and my whims, watching him unfold over a couple of hours on the spanking bench until he was wide open and ready to explode with satisfaction, fulfilled a part of me I'd ignored for too long.

But at times we made mistakes.

Sometimes Vincent wasn't completely honest about whether he enjoyed a particular game or tool. Usually, I figured it out. But I wanted him to let me know if something didn't work for him. We were in this together, and I couldn't enjoy doing something to him that made him less than happy. Not telling me that he didn't like something felt like a betrayal, and I had finally made him see that.

Because the last thing I wanted was to cause him distress. I was after his pleasure, his need, his desire. I wanted to break him out of the societal prison we lived in so he could fly free in the world of his submission.

I felt comfortable being naked with Vincent more of the time. The dysphoria my female body posed to my masculinity didn't affect me as much, at least around him. He knew who I was as much as I did, and my physical parts didn't present an issue to either of us.

Having him in bed with me almost every night made me happier than I'd expected. I had become addicted to his long legs and arms that seemed to want to enfold me, his softly curved belly and perfect ass, his sweet neck and rough cheeks. He was like a limpet in bed, always finding ways to embrace me, even though I was happy just to be near him. Soon I found it difficult to sleep without him touching me in a way that reassured me of his presence in my life.

My stubborn idea that Vincent had betrayed me by misguidedly searching for domination from Zane before we'd been introduced and the fact that it had almost caused me to lose him, made me sick to my stomach. Vincent had only been obedient to Daphne's request to keep quiet about Zane, for reasons she'd failed to tell him. And when I'd discovered the photo with Vincent *and* Zane in it, I'd flipped out and almost lost the one thing that meant anything anymore.

Vincent.

I was lucky he'd been so persistent, lucky he'd sat on my front step in the pouring rain for over an hour, waiting for me to come to my senses and let him in, lucky he'd insisted I give us another chance.

We'd taken that second chance and run with it.

Vincent was upstairs folding laundry when I got a text that the package had arrived. I collected it from the mailbox and called him down.

I smoothed my hand over the small box holding the anklet I'd selected for him. We had discussed the idea of him wearing something to represent my collar but hadn't settled on a specific timeline. I hoped he would be pleased with the surprise and that he'd like what I'd chosen.

The anklet was constructed of stainless steel in a simple chain-link style, and I'd made sure it would be large enough to fit. It wouldn't be locked, but he could wear it as a symbol of his submission to me whenever he liked.

He came slowly down the stairs, carrying a basket of clean kitchen towels and dish cloths that he set down on the sofa before padding over to me in bare feet with curious eyes and a puzzled smile. He was wearing a soft pair of gray sweats and a purple T.

"What's that, Sir?"

I grinned at him. "A gift."

His delicate eyebrows shot up and his eyes widened. "For me?"

"For you," I said softly. "Kneel."

He stared at me for a few seconds, then went gracefully to his knees on the carpet, his eyes on the floor, hands behind his neck — ever the obedient servant. I took a moment to admire his beauty before speaking.

"I picked something out for you," I said, taking the delicate jewelry from the box and dangling it from my fingers. "Look."

He lifted his eyes and fixed them on the anklet. "A bracelet?"

I shook my head. "It's for your ankle...if that works for you."

He smiled as his blue eyes twinkled with interest. "Like a collar? For my ankle?"

I grinned. "Exactly. I thought it would be less obvious than a bracelet or a collar. If I want you to wear one as part of a scene, it will be the usual. But this is something you can wear day-to-day if you want."

"I want to. It's beautiful," he said, reaching out to touch the cold metal.

"May I put it on you?" I asked.

"Yes, Sir. Please."

"Stand."

He stood in one fluid motion, keeping his hands behind his neck.

"Stay still."

"Yes, Sir."

I dropped to my knees, maintaining eye contact with Vincent. It seemed significant that I put it on him this way. Because even though he was my boyfriend and my submissive, I was just as much in service to him. Kneeling at his feet didn't diminish our connection or demean my power over him. I only had what power he granted me. Every time we had a session, I had to ask for that power and he had to give it to me. He was free to take it back at any time.

I smiled and bent to affix the chain around his left ankle. His feet were beautiful—strong, agile and delicate, all at the same time. When I was done, I bent to place a kiss on the top of each bare arch, before standing and meeting Vincent's gaze.

"May I see it?" he asked.

"Of course."

He sat down on the sofa and pulled up the leg of his sweatpants to peer at the shiny metal circling his ankle. He flexed his foot and craned his neck to see.

"What do you think?" I asked. It looked perfect to me, but I wanted Vincent to be comfortable with it.

"It's sexy. It makes me feel like a palace slave," he breathed, pointing his toes and flexing his arch. The steel glistened and sparkled in the sunlight coming in the windows.

I laughed. "A palace slave, huh? I can work with that."

He looked up at me. "Thank you. I'm proud to wear your collar, Sir."

"Ah, Vincent. You make me very happy."

He nodded and stood. "Shall I go finish the laundry?"

"Of course. And thank you. It makes me feel all kinds of proud that you're wearing my collar — on your pretty ankle...while you fold the laundry."

He flushed and nodded. "Yes, Sir."

I quirked an eyebrow. "Did you just get hard, Vincent?"

He laughed softly and sidelined a glance as he turned to leave. "I got hard when you fastened it around my ankle, Sir."

I laughed and waved him off. "Of course, you did."

I watched as he climbed the stairs and peeked at me with an impish grin before disappearing at the top.

Chapter One

Taking afternoon tea at Daphne's on Sundays had become a regular event.

Vincent wore a pretty pair of panties beneath his clothes, either at my direction or of his own choosing, and Daphne had him strip when we arrived. We had agreed Daphne could take charge of Vincent while we were in her home. I didn't mind. I enjoyed watching him respond to her. He'd told me it was much more exciting for him, now that I was involved.

The first few weeks, she'd made Vincent perform some relevant service in his lacy underthings, like setting up the finger sandwiches and cakes on her tiered stand or making the tea or coffee.

Now that this visit had become a weekly ritual, his duties had expanded into other, more delectable, areas.

We took turns feeding Vincent small bites of cake or bread, giving him sips of tea from our cups and otherwise treating him as our amusing and beloved pet. He grew more and more aroused, and I caught him eyeing Daphne's magnificent tits more than once. He said he didn't like the clichés of femininity but, honestly, who didn't appreciate a great pair of boobs?

As if on cue, a piece of the cake Daphne was eating fell into her cleavage, and she giggled. "Oh dear!"

I raised my eyebrows. "Vincent, did you see that?"

Daphne refrained from digging the morsel out of her blouse as her cheeks heated. The woman could set off a fake blush on cue. She winked at me with a grin.

"Yes, Sir," Vincent said, gazing at me with wide eyes.

"Would you like a taste of that delicious cake?" I asked devilishly.

Vincent made a small sound and nodded, licking his lips.

"I thought so. Why don't you snuffle that crumb out from between Daphne's tits? If you can find it, you can have it."

Daphne giggled, pulling her blouse down and leaning toward Vincent. Vincent blushed and looked at me to make sure I knew what I was asking.

I nodded. "Go ahead. It's all right." I gestured at Daphne's generous offering. "I've been there too, y'know," I whispered, as if it were a secret between me and him.

Something flashed in his eyes, and he smiled, then turned to Daphne.

"Mistress?" he asked.

His utter politeness sent a jolt of desire through me. He was so well-behaved, as if I had trained him to this, when, really, it came so very naturally.

"Go ahead, Vincent. Hands behind your back, please. You'll probably need to use your tongue."

My eyes widened as I watched my sexy twenty-four-year-old boyfriend lean forward slowly, hands behind him as requested, and gently push his face into the tantalizing crease between Daphne's breasts.

She made a small noise and looked at me over Vincent's head as his velvet tongue darted and licked to find the morsel of cake.

"Oh, goodness." She stroked Vincent's cropped ash-brown hair while he cleaned her up. "What a soft tongue you have, Vincent." She gasped. "I'd forgotten, my dear, how adorable you are."

Vincent made whimpering noises as he chased the crumbs and no doubt inhaled Daphne's particular scent of jasmine and roses.

I glanced at the black lace boy-shorts he was wearing today and noticed he was hard, which was par for the course with Vincent. The boy was a priapic miracle. *A savant perhaps?* He got hard at the drop of a hat and came on command. What more could a Dom ask for?

Lots more, it turns out.

When Vincent finally located the piece of cake and swallowed it, pulling reluctantly away from Daphne's warmth, I smiled at him, pleased.

"Good boy. I'm sure Daphne is very relieved that her little accident has been rectified."

Daphne looked anything *but* relieved. She looked like she'd like to tie Vincent to a chair and ride him for a couple of hours. But she'd had her chance with Vincent, and now the boy was mine.

I watched him stand and start to tidy the dishes, while flashes of memory came through of using the single-tail the previous evening. I'd strapped Vincent to the spanking bench and lashed his buttocks and thighs lightly, just enough to push his arousal to the brink of tipping over. Then I'd released him and sucked his cock until he'd come, howling, down my throat. He'd wanted to touch me, but I'd forbidden it, and I wouldn't forget the sight of his fingers clenching and unclenching while I worked him furiously to orgasm.

"Are you finished, Sir?" he asked, and it took me a moment to realize he was speaking about the cake and not asking if I was done reliving our encounter.

I cleared my throat. "Yes, thank you, Vincent."

He took my plate and I leaned back in my chair, checking the time on my phone. It was only four-thirty, but we needed to get home and have a light supper. We had a gallery show to attend this evening. My friend Juno was exhibiting their artwork for the first time, and I'd promised them Vincent and I would drop by.

* * * *

"Seriously? Full dress?"

"Yes, Vincent. It's a gallery exhibition. It's *de rigeur*." I gestured down the hall. "I laid out your things in the guest room."

"Oh, good, because I don't really have anything appropriate for something like that."

I smiled. "It's taken care of."

"Thanks, Nic."

"You're very welcome. I'm looking forward to seeing you dressed in what I selected."

I grinned to myself as he walked down the hall and into the guest room. I'd arranged some things on the bed that weren't exactly regular dress items for a man-about-town.

As I'd expected, he was back at the bedroom door after a few moments.

"It's not a suit. I was expecting a suit," he said, wringing his hands.

"You can wear a suit if you want," I said.

Vincent frowned. "But I don't own a very nice one."

"That navy blue one in the closet looks good on you."

His forehead creased. "I don't know."

I raised my eyebrows. "You don't want to wear what I laid out?"

He regarded me like I was ever-so-slightly insane. "But it's— I've never worn stuff like that...in public...before."

"I know...which is why I wanted to challenge you this evening." I moved in close and put my hands on his shoulders. "It's entirely your choice. Look... I'll help you pick out a shirt that will go with the blue suit. And I can dress you in those other things another time—just for us."

He seemed conflicted. He glanced down the hallway, then looked back at me. "They're very nice," he said, lifting a finger to his mouth and chewing on the nail.

"Yes. Do you know what inspired those purchases, Vincent?" I asked.

He shook his head, eyebrows raised.

I moved to the dresser and picked up my laptop. I flipped the top, opened Chrome and googled 'Tom Holland *Lip Sync Battle*', then angled it toward Vincent and hit play.

"Oh God. Really? You got me *that* outfit?" he said, turning toward the hall.

Tom Holland dancing in his gender-bending ensemble in the notorious episode of *Lip Sync Battle* that featured prominently in my fantasies. Even more prominently in those fantasies, however, was the idea of Vincent wearing something similar.

"Not the exact outfit, but pretty close," I said, smiling. I cupped his throat with my hand and drew it down his chest until it rested flat there. "I'd love to see you in it."

He stared at me, then looked back at the video and sighed. "Fine. I'll try it out. But I'm not promising to wear it to the gallery."

I nodded graciously and waved him down the hall. "I'll wait here. I'd like to see you all kitted up because, if I have to help you put those things on, we'll never leave this house."

"Promises, promises." He disappeared down the hall.

I concentrated on getting myself dressed. I had a tuxedo I saved for these occasions, in midnight blue, that showed off my trim masculinity to its best advantage. With a crisp white shirt underneath and a midnight blue bowtie, I fancied myself a classic movie star. I'd blown my hair dry and slicked it back with mousse. I contemplated putting on eyeliner but decided against it. I wanted to present as male as possible tonight, not anything in between. That was Juno's gig, and they did it better than I ever could.

When Vincent called to me from the guest room, I made sure my hair was in place and my bowtie was straight before making my way to him.

We stopped in our tracks when we saw each other.

"Oh, Nic. My God. That suit is so hot on you," Vincent said, gaping at me as I tried to make some kind of comment on a vision that would have brought me to my knees if I wasn't worried about wrinkling my dress pants.

"Me? You're the one who looks entirely edible. *Jesus*, Vincent." I looked him up and down. "Have you *seen* yourself?"

He blushed. "No. I didn't want to look before I got your opinion. And there isn't a full-length mirror in there." He smoothed his hands down the shiny PVC short-shorts with the hot-pink ruffles at the edges. "The material feels amazing, though."

I stepped into the room and took his hand, then led him down the hall to our bedroom, guiding him to the mirror.

"Look at yourself, sweetheart. And try not to get hard. It's too fucking late for me, though," I said, grinning and waggling my eyebrows.

He laughed and gazed at his reflection in the mirror. "Oh!"

"Yeah," I said, watching as he examined himself from multiple angles. "With your purple Docs, a bit of hair gel and some eyeliner... Vincent, you will be stunning."

He seemed entranced with the image in the mirror. The black pinstripe suit-vest-slash-halter-top with pearl buttons up the center showed off his trim build and sexy arms and shoulders. The PVC shorts hugged all the delicate curves of his ass and hips. His legs were shapely and divine in the fishnet stockings. The elastic pink ruffles on his wrists that matched the hot-pink trim on his shorts completed the effect.

Except for the color of his hair, Vincent in this outfit would remind anyone who had seen the infamous video of Tom Holland of that performance. He had a matching grace of movement, a similar body type and the same aura of youthful beauty.

"Okay," he smiled, gazing excitedly at his reflection.

"Okay? Meaning?"

He nodded and turned to me. "Okay, I'll wear this."

"To the gallery?"

"Yes."

I smiled so wide that I thought my face might split open. "Vincent, you will be the finest piece of art in that room, I guarantee it. But I won't say that to Juno."

"I wonder what they're going to wear?" Vincent said, cocking his head.

I laughed. "If I know Juno — and I do — it will be something eye-catching and unusual. They *are* known for that."

Vincent frowned. "You don't think they'll feel like I'm trying to upstage them at their own show?"

I shook my head. "I don't think so. I mean, Vincent, you look absolutely stunning and very unique. But Juno will make sure they are the center of attention. Don't worry. I think they'll appreciate this outfit on you more than anyone else, except me."

By the time we'd applied thick liner around Vincent's baby blue eyes, waved out his short hair with gel and laced him into his Doc Martens, he looked even more ethereal and gorgeous. I started to worry he *might* upstage Juno, but I wasn't going to say anything. I had to trust that Juno would pull out all the stops for this occasion and wear something that would eclipse even this heavenly image of androgyny.

I handed him the black trench coat I'd bought for him to wear over top of the outfit, and he smiled at me with relief. "Oh, thank God. I wasn't sure how my leather jacket would look with this ensemble."

"I've got you covered, sweetheart," I said, holding the trench for him to slide his long arms into. "This exhibition will be the safest place for you to wear such an outfit. The gallery will be filled with people leaning so far to the left they'll fall over — artists, activists, poets and dreamers, baby. That's our crowd."

Vincent laughed and I couldn't help kissing his sweet, smoothly shaved cheek.

I grabbed a black umbrella from the stand and handed it to him. "Look at that. Your outfit is complete, except for the hat."

"Is it even raining?"

"Who cares?" I laughed. "Let's go."

It took fifteen minutes to get to Sandy Hill, where the exhibit was being held on the first floor of an old Victorian townhome. Despite my urging to bring it along, Vincent left his umbrella in the car. I could tell he was nervous and that he might have regretted letting me persuade him to wear the revealing outfit to the gala. But there was no turning back now unless he safeworded, and I didn't think he was uncomfortable enough to do that.

As we approached the front door, I turned and grabbed the lapels of his coat, forcing him to meet my gaze. "You are spectacular. You look divine. People will love it."

He tipped his chin and took a deep breath, apparently shoring up his courage, and nodded. I released him and turned, stepping inside with Vincent at my heels.

"Nic Walker! And Vincent! How lovely!" A familiar voice greeted us as Carlos and his boyfriend approached. They were wearing matching purple suits and looked swanky and hip in a very urban style.

"Hi, Carlos, Leslie. You look great!" I said.

"Nic, you look awesome! Love that tux on you. Haven't seen you in it for ages!"

"Well, I broke it out for Juno. You know, gotta be at least a little fancy for their first exhibit."

I turned to Vincent and helped him slip out of his trench coat.

"Oh. My. God," Leslie exclaimed, putting a hand to his lips and clutching his partner's sleeve. "Carlos, *look*! Oh my God. Vincent, you look so hot!"

"Vincent. Jesus Christ. I think I just came in my pants," Carlos mumbled. "Nic, did you do this?" he asked, waving his hand at Vincent.

Other people were coming over now and commenting.

"He looks like Tom Holland! Oh my God!"

"Vincent, you're killing me. Fucking epic."

I raised my hands in the air. "Folks, folks, keep your hands off the merchandise. And remember, we are here for Juno and their art." I turned to Carlos. "I may have organized the outfit, yes. Does it work for him?"

"It works for me. I can tell you that much," Carlos commented, his gaze going over Vincent in a way that would worry me if I didn't know him well.

Vincent hadn't said a word, but his cheeks were flushed from all the praise and being the center of attention. He stood a little stiffly at my side, but I figured he'd relax once we got into the crowd and everyone backed off a little.

Leslie moved in close beside Vincent and whispered something in his ear, making him smile and nod. Then he bumped him gently with his hip and Vincent laughed and said, "You're incorrigible. I'm going to tell Nic you said that."

"Wonderful. Maybe he can set something up?" Leslie said, waggling his eyebrows and giving me an innocent little wave.

"Leslie, stop giving Vincent naughty ideas," I said. "Has anyone seen the artist?"

"Oh, my goodness, yes. They're in the next room circulating and impressing everyone," Carlos replied, gesturing ahead of us.

"Come on, darling," I said, taking Vincent's hand and tossing his coat onto one of the racks by the door. He gazed at it wistfully, but I wasn't letting him cover himself, because that would be a crime against everyone. I led him past the gawkers and into the next room.

It didn't take us long to find Juno. They took up most of the space in the room, with the incredibly intricate train of the ballgown they were wearing.

"Oh, wow," Vincent said, his eyes going wide.

"Amen. See? I told you Juno would be hard to upstage."

They were wearing the most luscious gown made of silk and brocade. The silver basque scooped low over Juno's flat chest, pushing up their pectorals so their rouged nipples thrust forward like tasty berries. The delicately embroidered burgundy silk skirt flounced wide and generously to the floor, making it impossible for anyone to get within a foot of them from any side. Nevertheless, they were surrounded by adoring fans. In their white-gloved hand perched an old-fashioned cigarette-holder with an unlit cigarette in the clasp.

We heard a sudden inhale of breath as Juno's gaze found Vincent. Their eyes narrowed and the hand not holding the cigarette circled their waist and opened the overskirt, flaring it out and away to reveal a fitted skirt underneath, just as elaborately adorned as the outer fabric.

"Vincent Blake, you are a vision!" Juno said, spreading the skirt like a cape and herding people out of the way as they walked toward us.

I stepped forward and stopped, opening my arms as if to call attention to my own fabulous outfit, and looked down at myself, then up at Juno.

They smiled haughtily and dismissed me with a wave of their cigarette. "Oh, Nic, you always look handsome and commanding," they said. "But *this* one."

Juno circled Vincent like a lioness sizing up its prey.

Vincent met Juno's assessing gaze with the modesty of a virgin presented at court. It was amusing to see the look on his face and the color in his cheeks as Juno took in his alluring outfit from every angle.

Finally, they stopped and held out a well-manicured hand to Vincent.

"Come."

Vincent glanced at me, then took Juno's offered hand and allowed himself to be pulled close and embraced. Juno enveloped Vincent in the vast swathes of material of their overskirt as they whispered something that was likely scurrilous in his ear.

Vincent's cheeks darkened and he sidelined a glance at me, then whispered something to Juno. Juno threw their head back and laughed loud and long while keeping Vincent in the cradle of their arm.

"Juno, can I have my boyfriend back?"

"No," they said without apology. "You think you can dress him so deliciously and hog him all night? Amateur."

I rolled my eyes. "Fine. Get him something to eat, will you? I'll be checking out the paintings."

Juno would ensure Vincent enjoyed himself. And they would get bored of him soon and bring him back to me so they could dazzle everyone else with their talent and graciousness.

I wasn't worried about him at all.

Chapter Two

I walked back to the first room and picked up a program from the young maître d'—probably Juno's latest conquest. He gazed at me hesitantly and smiled.

I held out my hand. "Hi. I'm Nic. How do you know the artist?"

The man blushed. "Hi. Well, we met recently and…they want to paint me so…I said I'd help out tonight. My name's Charles."

I raised my eyebrows. It seemed Juno's method of acquiring willing subjects-slash-sexual partners hadn't changed.

I smiled and looked the young man over. "I can see the appeal. You're lovely."

He laughed. "Thank you very much. You came with a very attractive man. He looks like Tom Holland in that music video."

"Yes, that was the intention. He's my boyfriend, Vincent."

"May I ask what pronouns I should use to address you, Nic?"

"I prefer he or him. But they or them is fine as well. Thank you for asking."

"You're welcome. Juno told me it was very important to learn everyone's preferred pronouns this evening." He frowned. "I think there might be a test later."

"If I know Juno, there will be. I won't tell you what the reward for a pass might be, but I can imagine."

Charles visibly shuddered. I winked and walked away in order to peruse Juno's artwork.

Their style was dramatic and original, using the representation of body parts in an unintuitive way that made one uncomfortable at first glance. As one stayed with the work and let the swirls of acrylic and emotion sink in, they were almost calming in their use of motion and color—like a more ethereal Picasso. Really, they were brilliant.

By the time I'd enjoyed all the paintings exhibited in this room, ranging in size and subject, with the models' names used as the titles, I moved into the second room again. Vincent stood comfortably at Juno's side while they explained a particularly colorful work to him. When they happened to see me, Juno beckoned me over.

"Do you know what this one's called, good sir?" Juno asked, grinning as they gestured to the large painting.

I focused in on the title printed on the card. "What the fuck, Juno?"

Vincent and Nic, Soulmates.

Juno laughed loudly and clutched Vincent closer, pointing their cigarette at the painting. "It's the best one here, I think."

"How the fuck did you paint Vincent and me? We never posed for you."

Juno shrugged. "An artist's trick. I had a photo of the two of you from the drag show we went to. It was perfect because it was after Vincent got wrapped up in the blue-and-purple boas and you were kissing him and laughing." They inclined their head at the art piece. "This is how it looked to me."

The painting was large and full of turquoise and eggplant hues, with some nods to our skin color thrown in, as well as a couple of spots of intense blue, which I think represented Vincent's eyes. It was beautiful.

"I love it," Vincent said, his gaze fixed on the painting, an enthusiastic smile on his face.

"Dammit, Juno. Now I have to buy this one," I said.

"No, you don't. I'm going to gift it to the two of you."

I stared at them. "What? You can't do that."

They raised their eyebrows and put a hand on their hip. "It's my painting, Nic. I can do whatever the fuck I want with it."

I groaned. "Okay, fine. But let me pay you."

"It costs three thousand dollars if you're going to purchase it," Juno said.

I paled. "Really?"

"You're not going to buy it. I'm giving it to you. Consider it a housewarming present," they said, laying a hand on my arm and taking a drag from the now-lit cigarette.

"But I've been living in that house for years," I said, uncomfortable with such a generous gift, even if it had been inspired by the two of us.

"Not with Vincent," Juno said tersely, as if they didn't want to hear another protest.

"That's true."

"Well then, I don't understand the issue," Juno said, then gave Vincent a quick kiss on the cheek and moved off, swirling into the crowd as seamlessly as their voluminous dress would allow.

Vincent and I exchanged a hopeless glance. There was no point arguing with Juno. We would never win. And it was a gorgeous painting.

"Come here. I simply must touch your bottom in those shorts. They're so *shiny*!" Vincent giggled as I pulled him close and groped his ass. "God, that's so soft and smooth. I want to spank you in these."

"Oh, Sir! Not here," he said with a flirtatious lilt, like he might consider being thrown over my lap in front of the rest of the patrons.

I raised my eyebrows and let a slow smile form on my face.

"I mean, really, Nic. I don't want to be spanked here."

My smile vanished. "Damn. For a second I thought..."

He looked down. "Yeah, for a second I did too. But no. Please. I'm not ready for that yet."

My smile slowly returned. "You said *yet*."

"Yes, I did."

"Hmm. That's very interesting."

"Let's get something to eat. A person came with a tray, but there are hors d'oeuvres laid out over there."

I lifted my elbow for him. "Shall we?"

He smiled and took it. "Yes."

* * * *

Back at home that evening, I helped Vincent off with his trench and took his hand, bringing him up to the bedroom, where I stripped off all my clothes except for the white button-down, which I left open. I stood him at the end of the bed while I grabbed my phone and sat against the pillows.

"Pose for me."

Vincent blinked. "What?"

"I want to take some photos of you in that outfit. You look fucking delectable, and I want to remember it."

He smiled. "What should I do?"

"Hmm. Put your hands on your hips and look haughty. The opposite of Real Vincent."

He did as I'd asked and put forth a strong attempt at being proud and self-centered.

"Nice!" I said, taking shots of him. "Now turn around so I can get a booty shot, but peek over your shoulder at me and smile."

He obeyed, but instead of smiling at me, he stuck out his tongue.

I clicked mine. "Vincent, you are a naughty boy. Show me how bad you can be."

He laughed and turned around, climbing onto the bed and stalking slowly toward me on all fours while I kept taking photos. I pushed myself up onto an elbow as my breathing quickened. When he got too close, I moved my phone out of the way and he was right there, up in my face with his stunning blue eyes and bowed lips.

"Hi," he said in a breathy voice. He smelled of rum and Coke. He might be as tipsy as me at this point. We had taken advantage of the open bar.

I smiled and raised my brows. "What are you after, doll?"

He stretched like a cat and moved his gaze along my body as he did, then glanced up. "You. I want you." The stare he leveled at me ignited flames in my belly. "What do *you* want? Sir?"

I sighed, circling my fingers around his wrists where they were wrapped in the ruffled bands. "I want you to fuck the shit out of me, Vincent. But I want you to keep most of this outfit on while you do it."

He grinned and took his bottom lip between his teeth. "Yeah? I can do that."

I matched his grin. "I know you can. You're very agile. And your cock is probably very hard right now."

He blushed and nodded, his breath hitching. "Yeah."

"Then do it," I said, spreading my thighs and tilting my chin up so now I was the haughty one — which was true in any case.

Vincent extricated his wrists from my lax grip and slid an arm beneath my hips, pulling me forward and flat underneath him. I gasped at the sudden change of position but smiled up at him.

"You are my androgynous angel," I whispered, drowning in the blue eyes outlined with kohl that gazed at me from beneath his gelled hair. "Now show me what you've got for me in those short-shorts."

He laughed and shook his head at my ridiculousness, then went up on his knees so he could push down the shorts and the fishnets only far enough to release his red and leaking erection.

He was such a fascinating enigma, my Vincent. So demure and delicate in public, but with a priapic energy that was always ready and willing at a moment's notice to burst forth. His penis was a beautiful, magical thing to me, and I revered it in a way that spoke to my gender-queer soul. It was like a pet that needed to be fed regularly or it would shrivel and die from hunger. Neither Vincent nor I had a silly name for it, but there was a certain affection and admiration beyond the purely sexual for such an endearing and functional part of his anatomy.

Once released, he entered me with a smoothness and unapologetic practicality that thrilled me, as if he had a job to do and he wanted to get to it.

His shiny shorts were bunched at the top of his thighs, so I grabbed onto them for purchase as he sank in all the way and began a shallow, rough thrusting that had me crying out within moments.

* * * *

One of the great things about Vincent spending so much time here was that his piano playing had come along splendidly. Because I was a stickler for discipline and routine, I made him practice for an hour every day — in lacy panties, of course — and sometimes with a steel plug in his ass or wearing a cute little crop top or the purple basque. Because — my house, my rules. And he totally got off on it. I knew it made his lessons more fun for both of us.

He'd been working as a financial advisor at Scotiabank when we'd met — a job he'd hated. One day, while coming down from an intense session, he'd confessed it was killing him to work there, but it was good money and he was loath to abandon a steady paycheck.

I'd asked if he had any objections to being a kept man, because I had no issue having him quit that job and maintain the house for me.

He'd been reluctant initially, only because of societal expectations ingrained in him since childhood. When I'd explained he would simply be my live-in housekeeper, cook and entertainment, as well as my beloved partner, he'd decided it might be an acceptable choice—especially because Vincent truly enjoyed doing those things for me, for *us*, and it would make him happy in way that organizing the financial needs of strangers would not.

His repertoire for meals had expanded as he watched online video tutorials and found recipes he wanted to attempt. He wore clothes around the house that made him feel comfortable, unless under specific instructions to wear less, but he always had on a pair of pretty panties. The boxer briefs in this house were all mine.

"I want to officially ask. Do you want to move in with me, Vincent?" I said as finished up the stir-fry he'd put together. He'd made a kale salad, too.

He smiled. "I can give my notice at the apartment."

"Really?"

He hesitated. "Are you sure you want me to move in with you? Or will I annoy you too much?"

"Vincent, you never annoy me. I want you to move in with me."

I slid out of my chair and sank to my knees beside him, gazing up at his confused and startled features. "Can you imagine how wonderful it will be to always come home to you, cleaning and cooking for me? You might even have time to relax then, because you're not always going back and forth."

He smiled, staring down at me. "Yes. I'd love to live here with you, Sir. I want to be yours. *All* yours."

I kissed his knee where it was covered by the soft material of his yoga pants. "Oh, Vincent. You are all mine. Wherever you are, you're *mine*. But you might as well be here where I can keep an eye on you."

* * * *

Vincent gave notice to his landlord that he would be out by the end of the month, and we moved him in that weekend. I hired a moving service because neither Vincent nor I wanted to spend time doing the grunt work. Vincent had more important grunt work to do at my place.

We donated the majority of his furniture to charity. We brought his books and sailboat models, his clothes, CDs and various personal objects to my place. I helped Vincent put the books in my bookshelves and place his sailboat models around the living room. I don't know why I loved them so much. He brought a number of unopened model kits and a large schooner he was working on, and I gave him the guest room to use as his crafting space.

The painting Juno had gifted us had arrived the day before, so I had Vincent help me mount it to the wall above the headboard of our bed. The vibrant colors popped against the soft gray paint on the walls.

"I want to take you out for supper, to celebrate," I told him.

I thought back to my reluctance to get involved with anyone after breaking up with Zane. I'd almost missed the best thing in my life because I'd been a coward, holding on to old resentments and fears. Now I knew how little I owed Zane and how lucky I had been to dodge that bullet, and I thanked the Universe every day for giving me Vincent—and Daphne, because she hadn't taken no for an answer and had dangled him in front of me when she knew I wouldn't be able to resist.

"That sounds wonderful," he said, tidying up the magazines on the coffee table and taking my empty mug to the kitchen.

I followed and crowded him against the cupboards when he turned. "And you won't have to cook tonight." I took his stubbled chin in my hand and softly pressed my lips to his.

When I pulled back, he smiled. "I like cooking for you, Sir."

Seriously, how the fuck did I get so lucky?

"Turn around."

He raised his eyebrows but obeyed when I gave him the space.

"Lean over the counter."

Languorously, knowing how much I liked to watch him, he wrapped his fingers on the edge of the counter and leaned forward, bending until his torso was flat against the clean granite surface. He pressed the side of his face against the cold stone, watching me.

"Good boy," I said, pulling the waistband of his blue panties down over his gorgeous ass. There were still some marks from the crop I'd used on him the day before. Nothing major, just tiny bites from the single tail that Vincent loved. I traced one with my finger. "Feeling better here?" I asked idly.

He sighed. "Yes, Sir. You'll need to fix that soon."

His voice sounded quiet because he knew he wasn't supposed to tell me what to do. But if there was anything Vincent loved more in the world than having his ass beaten, I didn't know what it was. He liked everything I did to him, really, but getting spanked or thrashed with a crop? *His. Favorite. Thing.*

Mine too.

"Yes, that's a good idea. Maybe after dinner?"

His face flushed with the thought of it. "Yes, Sir. Where are we going?"

I tilted my head, examining the pale flesh of his backside as I tickled the top of his crease, making him gasp and close his eyes. "Hmmm. You choose. My treat. Here, slick it up."

He opened his mouth, taking my finger inside and swirling his tongue around it, sucking. His breath hitched.

When I thought it was wet enough, I pulled it from his mouth and parted his ass cheeks, rubbing my finger over his hole, teasing him before pushing it into him.

"Oh. Sir," he said breathlessly, his eyes closing with the shame and pleasure of being so unceremoniously defiled in what was now his own kitchen.

I leaned forward and opened my mouth on his shoulder, pushing my finger in as far as I could, wiggling it the way I knew he liked, pressing against his prostate as he swore and gasped. I bit down as he cried out.

I smiled against his skin, licking with my tongue as if to apologize. I wasn't sorry. Vincent enjoyed some pain with his pleasure.

But I needed to stop or we wouldn't go anywhere except the bedroom or the basement tonight, and I really wanted to take Vincent out on the town — but not without instructions.

With some regret I withdrew my finger and gave his ass a slap. "Get up. Go upstairs and put on those frilly white panties I bought you last week and the dark blue skinny jeans with that nice black button-down."

He stood, flushed and breathless and wanton, and I wondered if we should stay home. But no, he deserved this special night. And so did I.

"Yes, Sir." He gazed at me longingly before turning and heading upstairs.

I swiveled to the sink and started the water running so I could wash my hands.

Goddammit, how would I concentrate on something so mundane as eating, knowing that when I got Vincent home, he was going over my knee in those white knickers?

Chapter Three

Vincent decided on Milestones for our dining adventure. Their Sussex Drive location was hip and picturesque, and we hadn't been downtown for a long time.

I asked him if he'd wear a plug while we were out and, because his deepest desire seemed to be to please me, he agreed. I had him pull down his jeans and pretty panties and lean over the sofa while I lubed up the plug and carefully inserted it.

Vincent stood and straightened his clothes, his flushed face the only evidence of the object inside him.

"You are the best boy," I told him, stroking his cheek and winking.

"Yes, Sir. I know, Sir."

"Cheeky boy."

"*Your* boy."

I grinned. "You won't be able to forget you belong to me. You'll be reminded every time you move."

"Yes, Sir." He paused before stepping out of the door. "I love this, Sir."

"I know."

At Milestones, we had to wait in the large entry space for a table. I thought Vincent looked delectable, more so because of the secret he carried under his outfit. But although that particular part of his ensemble wasn't obvious to the casual observer, he looked damn good anyway. His dark jeans hugged his slim legs and showed off his ass, while the pea coat I'd bought him gave him a casual elegance as well as tucking in slightly to show off his trim silhouette. I caught a couple of young women side-eyeing him.

I placed a possessive hand on his arm and leaned in to his ear. "You have some cute groupies."

He became deliciously awkward and self-conscious. "What? Where?"

I nodded in the direction of the two attractive girls, who were giggling and pretending to check their phones but glancing at my boy with their wide fawn eyes and winged liner. Those girls wouldn't know what the hell to do with Vincent. They'd take one look at his frilly panties and run screaming, not even waiting to see what was underneath. Or perhaps the younger generation wasn't as worried about gender-norms as mine was. I could only hope that was the case.

At any rate, I wasn't sharing. I stepped closer to Vincent and pressed myself against him—only for a second, but long enough for the girls to get the hint that Vincent was not for them or anyone else.

Only me.

When our table was ready, we followed the attractive hostess into the loft-like interior to a small booth near the back. I thanked her and slid into one side while Vincent sat opposite me.

"How are you gentlemen this evening?" she asked pleasantly, handing us menus.

"Good, thanks. You?" I replied, giving her my most rakish smile. Her sudden demureness and deference reassured me of my dominating influence. Her face flushed and she glanced at the floor, then back at me with a hesitant smile.

"I'm very good, thank you. Your server is Michael. He'll be by shortly. Have a wonderful evening."

"Thank you," both Vincent and I said.

He gave me a piercing look. "How do you do that?"

"What?"

He lifted his hands up. "How do you just…Dom everybody?"

I laughed. "What are you talking about?"

He tilted his head to the side. "I don't know. You have this thing, this attitude — a way of carrying yourself, maybe? I'm pretty sure that girl would have kneeled for you if you'd asked her to."

How delightful to be reminded of my innate confidence, which I had used to my advantage on many an occasion. I doubted the hostess would agree to an evening with me if she discovered all my secrets, however. Then again, people surprised me sometimes.

"I was sure you were going to be too soft for me," I told Vincent.

He blinked and looked down. "I *am* soft. I'm not a confident person at all."

I tapped my finger on the tabletop and held his gaze when he looked up. "That's bullshit."

His brows tightened and I knew he wanted to say I was wrong, so I continued.

"That's total bullshit. You are as brave and as strong as a lion, Vincent Blake. But you *are* soft in all the right places."

He blushed furiously and dropped his gaze to the table, fighting a smile. "Thank you, Sir."

"Now what do you want to eat, my brave boy? A steak? Something spicy?" I asked, my voice teasing enough to make him raise his gaze.

"What are you having?"

"I don't know yet what I'm going to order, if that's what you're asking. But I know exactly what I'm having when we get home." I glanced down at my menu and said, with a smirk, "A very *thick* sausage."

Vincent glanced at me shyly. "With sauce?"

I raised my eyes at his cheeky behavior. "Of course. I want *all* the sauce, Vincent."

He closed his eyes and moaned quietly. "Yes, Sir."

"Now pick something to eat so we can have supper and go home for dessert."

* * * *

With the intensity of a scientist, I watched Vincent eat his steak, my motivations far from objective. He proceeded with a deliberate attempt at seduction, so that plug in his ass was doing its job.

"Vincent, stop it."

"What?"

"You know what."

"Sir, I don't know what you mean. I'm just eating my spicy shrimp," he said, popping one into his mouth and chewing suggestively.

"Vincent. Have you heard of something called figging?"

He stopped chewing and swallowed, his gaze dropping to the table. "Um, yeah," he said in a hushed voice.

I grinned. "I'll give you some spicy shrimp if you insist on teasing me so boldly. It'll be a small piece of ginger, peeled and lodged in your impertinent bottom.

And I will really enjoy watching you suffer through *that* torment."

He swallowed the piece of steak in his mouth. When he looked up, his eyes were blue fire. "Yes, Sir."

I sat up straighter. He seemed to like that idea. I hadn't done it to anyone in a long time, but I *would* consider it.

"Are you going to keep teasing me?"

He shook his head, but that small smile returned. "I'll try to be good, Sir."

"I certainly hope so."

Vincent behaved himself for the rest of the meal, but the damage was done, and I wanted to get him home. When the server brought our bill, Vincent placed a fifty-dollar bill on the table.

I looked at the money, then at Vincent as I retrieved my wallet. "Vincent, I'm taking *you* out."

"I want to help pay."

I picked the fifty up and held it out. He shook his head and sat on his hands. I couldn't quite believe my obedient boy was suddenly being obstinate.

"Vincent, take the money back."

He looked at me, pleading with his gaze. "Please. I want to help."

"This is not helping. It's just pissing me off."

"Please, Sir. Please let me contribute. Let me pay for half."

We stared at each other, and I debated forcing him to take the money back. But I didn't want to do that, so I reached out and grabbed it, crinkling it in my fist and shoving it into my pocket.

"Fine. At least now I have something to punish you for," I said, giving him my sternest look.

"Yes, Sir," he said. He couldn't suppress a slight, victorious smile.

He had *no* idea what lay in store, but the thought of it made me giddy.

I paid the bill with my card, and we got up to leave. I simply couldn't wait until we got home to play with him. "Go to the men's room. Wait at the sink."

He blanched, opened his mouth, then saw the look I shot him.

"Yes, Sir." He glanced to the right, then the left, then at me.

"Do you know where the washrooms are?"

"No, Sir."

I nodded toward the left half of the restaurant. "Past the kitchen and to the right. Make sure you go into the men's, not the women's. It's confusing."

"Yes, Sir."

I gave him a few minutes' head start, then grabbed two cloth napkins and the little tub of aioli from my sandwich platter and followed, keeping everything hidden in my jacket. In the men's room, Vincent stood by the modern trough-sink. There wasn't anyone else in the room — for now — so I pointed to the handicapped stall on the end.

"In you go, Vincent."

"But I don't need to go to the bathroom," he said.

"Get in the stall. *Now*."

He responded to the tone of my voice and went into it with me on his heels.

"Lock the door," I told him, placing one of the napkins on the back of the toilet and the little tub of aioli on top of it. Vincent eyed it suspiciously but latched the door as instructed.

"Now put your hands on the side of the stall and keep them there." I pointed to where I wanted him.

He looked skeptical. "But it's…it's probably dirty."

"You can wash your hands afterward. It's not that bad. What I'm going to do to you is going to be *much* dirtier."

He shuddered and got into position, turning his head to see what I was doing.

I took the crumpled fifty-dollar bill from my pocket and waved it in front of his face. "You're just lucky I'm going to wrap this in a napkin before I stuff it in your mouth," I said, as the shock washed over his features. I wrapped the bill in the wine-colored cloth. "Do you know how dirty this bill is?"

"But...why?" He seemed genuinely confused about what was happening, so I filled him in.

"To keep your noises muffled while I spank you and play with you until you come—in a public washroom...with people around."

"But—Sir..." he said, desperation in his voice.

"I won't spank you if anyone is in the bathroom. We'll wait until we're alone for that. But I may not stop playing with you if someone comes in here. You'll just have to be quiet. Open your mouth, Vincent."

It took him a moment to comply, and I knew this was pushing his limits. I placed the cloth-wrapped fifty between his lips. "Bite on that and don't let go. Got it?"

He quivered with the shame and anticipation of being disciplined in a public bathroom stall, but he obeyed me.

My good boy.

I put my mouth to his ear and spoke softly, with affection, so he'd realize I wasn't actually mad. "Do you want to safeword?"

He sighed. "No, Sir."

"Do you deserve to be punished this way?"

"Yes, Sir."

I grinned against his ear and quickly kissed him on the cheek.

"There's no one but us here right now, so let's get this part over with." I unzipped and unbuttoned his jeans and pulled them down to his thighs, fixing the frilly white panties over his ass for now. But I reached around to take the measure of his erection.

"This is turning you on, no matter how much you pretend to hate it."

He made a noise, and another shudder ran through him.

"Shake your head back and forth quickly if you change your mind and want to safeword. Got it?"

He bobbed his head up and down.

"I'm going to spank your ass because I don't want you arguing with me about me paying for you when we go places. It's something I like to do for you, and I don't want you to feel guilty about it or like you owe me anything. The things I get from you, Vincent, are worth much more than any money you could give me."

He moaned as I rubbed my hand over his satiny bottom. His fingers splayed out on the stall as he pressed against it. I pulled back and gave him a slap, then another and one more, as he grunted with shame and discomfort.

"Do you understand?"

He mumbled what sounded like *Yes, Sir* and nodded his head frantically. Since no one had come in, I gave him a couple more spanks, then pulled the white panties down and unceremoniously tugged on the plug. Vincent made a noise as it slid out. I placed it on the cloth napkin and ran my thumb up between his cheeks, making him jerk and twist.

"Stay still. Don't move."

I scooped up some of the aioli and rubbed a bit on the fingers of each hand. Then I moved in close. As I palmed his dick, I slid the fingers of my other hand between his cheeks.

"This is when you really need to be quiet, Vincent."

He made a soft noise of excitement and unease as I started to jerk him off in the bathroom stall. We were still alone in the room.

Just as I'd managed to insert two fingers knuckle-deep in Vincent's ass and gotten him to the edge of an orgasm, we heard footsteps and voices.

Vincent's body clenched around my fingers as he stiffened all over. I froze and waited while the men continued to chat in the direction of the urinal trough.

"Oh, wow, Tanya is all over you, man! What did you say to her?"

The other guy laughed. "I said I wasn't interested in a relationship right now. I guess she took it as a challenge."

We heard zippers and the sound of urine hitting porcelain. "But you're gonna try to get in her pants, right?"

"Fuck yeah. If not tonight, I'm pretty sure I'll be in by the weekend."

"That's fucking genius, man."

"Works every time."

I peeked out the side of the stall door to get a read on these assholes. One of them had a fairly distinctive orange shirt on. I filed that away for later.

They finished up and left without noticing the two sets of boots in the handicapped stall. Vincent and I made sure they'd gone and we were alone again before we resumed our questionable activities.

I made good use of Vincent's prostate and pumped his cock the way he liked — rough and fast alternating with slow and steady — until I got him back to where he'd been when the interruption had occurred.

He thrust his dick into my hand and made desperate noises that would have been much louder if we hadn't been in a public place. If anyone came into this room in the next few seconds, they would probably get an earful, because my baby was ready to explode.

"Oh, fuck yes. Do it, Vincent. Come in my hand, baby," I whispered in his ear, pumping him with an alternating rhythm to the aggressive finger-fucking. I crowded him in against the stall so he wouldn't collapse when his climax arrived.

He stiffened and clamped down on me as a muffled groan tore from his throat. His semen surged over my fingers as he pressed against the metal wall, making it creak and sway slightly. His choked groans delighted me.

"Oh fuck, baby. Oh, fuck yes," I whispered, my ears on high alert for anyone coming in. As Vincent's jerky movements slowed and his muted groans turned to soft sighs, we heard footsteps again.

He shot me a panicked look. I lifted a slick finger to my lips, urging for quiet. While he watched, I licked my finger as if it were ice cream and not Vincent's jizz I was eating, while the footsteps went into a stall and the door slammed shut and latched. In a moment, rude noises from the interloper filled the space.

Making a disgusted face, I extracted the napkin-wrapped bill from Vincent's mouth, took the fifty and put it on the back of the toilet, picking up the steel plug, which I held up in front of him.

I whispered, "I can't smuggle this out in my pocket, so it's going back where it came from."

He let me insert it, since he really had no other option. I used the napkin to wipe us off and tuck him as carefully and noiselessly as possible back in his pants. The person in the stall made horrific noises that camouflaged our rustling, although the room had begun to fill with a distasteful odor. I picked up the fifty and stuffed it into Vincent's back pocket, patting his ass when I was done.

"Let's go home," I whispered, taking his hand and leading him from the stall to the sinks as two men rounded the corner into the room.

But at this point we were just two men washing our hands, so nothing seemed suspicious, although the next person to go into the handicapped stall might wonder if someone had had a dirty little picnic in there, because I'd left the other napkin and aioli.

We finished washing up and Vincent, although looking like he might pass out, followed me valiantly through the restaurant. I saw the man in the orange shirt speaking to a young woman with long brown hair in a ponytail.

"Hold on," I said to Vincent.

I walked over to the table and tapped the woman on the shoulder. She turned, regarding me with curiosity.

I flashed her one of my best smiles. "Hi there. Are you Tanya?"

She nodded. "Yeah, that's me."

I turned to the men. "Which one of you was talking about getting into Tanya's pants while you were in the bathroom a short while ago?"

Their eyes flew wide and they glanced at each other awkwardly.

"Uh —" Orange-shirt guy seemed lost for words.

Tanya stared at me for a moment in shock, then turned to glare at them. "Nice. Fuck you, Jamie. I'm just trying to be nice. I'm not fucking flirting with you."

She turned back to me. "Thank you."

"You're welcome." I smiled sweetly at the men as I swiped a french-fry from orange-shirt-guy's plate and gave him a salute.

"Gentlemen, have a wonderful day. Bye, Tanya."

I walked back to Vincent and took his hand, leading him outside. Once we got to our parking spot, Vincent collapsed against the side of my car, his head on his crossed arms.

"Jesus Christ. Jesus *fucking* Christ."

I put a hand on his back, wondering if I'd broken him finally. "Are you okay? You didn't safe signal so I—"

He looked at me, his sated blue eyes full of awe and respect. "That was… That was…"

I raised my brows. "Awful? Inexcusable? Past your limits?"

"So fucking dirty and shameful I can't even believe it."

I nodded, because it had been all those things. "And?"

"Mind-blowing. Amazing. Incredible."

I smiled and pushed a lock of hair off his forehead.

"Vincent? Vincent Blake?" A hesitant voice sounded nearby, making me turn.

A young woman with ash-blond hair and fine features stood there, confused and embarrassed, staring at Vincent with a stunned expression.

"Carol! Wow, I didn't expect to see you here," Vincent said.

"I'm…meeting a friend."

Vincent glanced at me, then turned back to Carol. "This is my boyfriend, Nic."

I looked Carol over. She was appealing—small and feminine in a way I certainly wasn't. Her coat looked expensive.

Carol stared at me for slightly longer than was polite. "Oh. Oh, okay," she said, looking embarrassed. "Hi. It's great to meet you," she said, offering her hand.

"Carol." I glanced back and forth between the woman and Vincent, wondering how they knew each other.

Vincent blushed. "Carol and I used to be in a relationship."

The ex-girlfriend. The woman he'd followed here and subsequently broken up with months before I'd found him.

"Oh, yes. You did mention that." I put on my most polite smile. "Nice to meet you, Carol."

She looked me up and down, still smiling nervously. I could tell she was trying to figure this out and wondering how to address the situation without sounding impolite. Finally, her gaze landed back on Vincent. "Vincent, you look...different. Older...or something?" She shook her head in embarrassment. "I mean, you *are* older."

Vincent laughed and looked down shyly. "Yeah."

"Sorry to bother you. Did you have a good meal?"

"Yes, we were having supper. It was excellent, especially the surprise dessert." My gaze slid to Vincent, who went even redder in an instant.

"Oh? Is it your birthday?" she asked me.

I smiled. "It sure felt like it."

Her smile wavered, but she nodded. "Well, it was wonderful to see you, Vincent. Great to meet you, Nic."

"Carol," I said, inclining my chin.

"Yeah, same. You look great, Carol. Have a good one," Vincent said, giving her a little wave.

She smiled as she walked toward the doors of the restaurant but glanced at Vincent with a frown as she reached them. He didn't notice.

"Whoa. That was unexpected," Vincent said.

"So that's your ex. Hmm."

"What?"

"I don't know. I pictured her differently."

Vincent's forehead creased. "She looked tired...and kind of depressed."

I grinned. "Well, duh. She doesn't have you in her life anymore."

He shook his head. "I don't think she was all that upset about the breakup, honestly."

"Were *you*?"

"Huh?"

"Were you upset about the breakup?" I asked as we got into the car and put on our seatbelts.

"I was at first. She's a nice person, and she tried, you know?"

"Tried?"

He looked at me with soft, liquid eyes. "She tried to make me happy."

I thought about that for a moment then pushed aside my natural feelings of jealousy toward the woman. "I'm glad."

He nodded. "It didn't work. She didn't have what I needed."

I quirked my lip and raised an eyebrow. "A drawer full of silicone penises and a God complex?"

Vincent laughed. "Exactly."

He started the car and pulled out of the parking spot as I grinned and stared out of the window.

Chapter Four

When we got home from dinner, I sent Vincent downstairs. "Strip to your white panties and wait for me by the spanking bench."

I changed into sweats and a T-shirt and headed down. Our little escapade in the men's room at Milestones had only served to whet my appetite, and now I wanted to play with Vincent at my leisure. Perhaps I wanted to reassert my control after running into his ex.

I never claimed to have lofty motives.

The first thing I did was have him lean over the bench and pull the panties down so I could see his flushed skin from an hour before, when I'd tanned his hide in the handicapped stall.

"Your ass looks lovely." I wiggled the plug and pulled it out, throwing it onto the floor. "You hard again?"

"Yes, Sir."

"Of course you are. I love that about you, Vincent."

"Yes, Sir."

"Take off the panties and lie on your front."

He did and I examined his ass with blunt efficiency. "Hmm. Needs more spanking, I'd say. But I want to frustrate you, so we're using this first." I showed him the vibrating prostate plug then fastened him down so he couldn't go anywhere.

"This is going in your ass. It's going to vibrate against your prostate while I go upstairs for an hour and catch up on some work. When I come back, I expect to see you in quite a state."

He sighed, shot me a worried look, then said, "Yes, Sir."

"And, Vincent?"

"Yes, Sir?"

"If I come down here to a puddle of your jizz on the floor, you're going to have to lick it up and I'll put you in the cock cage for two fucking weeks. You just got off at the restaurant, so I expect you to be able to control yourself, no matter how good the plug feels. Got it?"

"Yes, Sir."

Once I'd lodged it firmly inside him, I turned the prostate plug on low, gave his ass a slap and left him, knowing full well this would drive him mad with the urge to come in about twenty minutes. I'd said I would be gone an hour, but I'd come back in half that time to make sure he didn't explode, despite his best intentions, because I knew the way Vincent responded to anal stimulation and orgasm denial. The just-barely-there vibration on his prostate would have him dripping with desire in no time.

I went upstairs and tried to distract myself from thinking about my restrained sub. I found my focus eventually, and before I knew it, I'd been at it for forty minutes—longer than I'd planned to leave him.

"Shit," I said, closing my laptop and standing, listening for sounds from the basement. I'd left the door open so I'd hear him if he needed me.

It was only as I approached the top of the basement steps that I heard it. The creaking of the spanking bench and sounds of desperation from below, like someone touching a hot burner again and again. Little cries of dismay at the intensity of the small bursts of pleasure he was getting from the plug by now.

I couldn't stop a smile from forming on my face as I descended the stairs and saw him, his muscles taut against his restraints, a sheen of sweat over him, his pelvis making unconscious thrusting motions before he willed himself to stop with a plaintive, soft whine and delicious shudder.

He looked ripe for a ravishing.

With no preamble, I walked up and wiggled the prostate massager out of his ass, throwing it to the floor with a thud.

"Good boy. You held off. I'm actually surprised." I grabbed the penis gag from the cabinet and approached him. "Open your mouth."

He did, his eyes a dark, blown blue as I placed the rubber penis between his lips and fastened the gag behind his head.

"You remember your signals?"

He grunted.

"Good." I glanced at him as if he were as insignificant as a worm in the dirt. "I'm going to paddle you now. And when I'm done, I'm going to flip you over and fuck you until you lose your mind. Got it?"

He whimpered and nodded, a pained expression on his face.

"Yeah, it's gonna hurt. Your ass is gonna be red when I'm done, but that will help you keep yourself from coming until I've satisfied myself with your fat, leaking cock."

He groaned.

I gave him twenty hard swats with the leather paddle before I decided that was enough and tossed it to the floor.

He trembled as I undid his restraints and fastened him on his back, crooning over how well he was doing and how beautiful he looked like that—desperate and hard and ready to explode.

I blindfolded him then straddled the bench and rubbed myself against his straining cock until I shook with my first orgasm.

"Oh, Vincent," I sighed, "that felt so good. But you need to stay hard for me, baby. I want two more while you're inside me."

He groaned and thrust up so I could feel how desperate he was. As I lifted his erect cock off his stomach and guided it into me, he made a strangled noise as he fought the urge to spill prematurely. The legs of the spanking bench creaked again as he pulled on his restraints and inhaled huge gulps of air.

"That's it. You can do it. Hold off for me. This won't take long."

I leaned forward and gripped his strong shoulders as I rubbed back and forth on him, rolling my eyes as his rock-hard length hit my G-spot and thrust me over the edge again.

"Oh fuck! I'm coming again," I stuttered as I was quaking atop him and a sudden, mournful noise came from his throat.

His cock jerked as he stiffened and spilled unexpectedly. His body went rigid and his eyes wide as he spurted in a paroxysm of physical ecstasy and mental agony.

He was magnificent in his failure, resplendent in his distress and disappointment. I was so proud of him.

But I didn't tell him that because I knew he expected disapproval, and I didn't want to disappoint my little slut boy. As he continued to thrust involuntarily, I made a clicking noise in my throat.

"Oh, Vincent," I said, with dismay and sadness, "you're such a naughty, naughty boy."

He stopped moving, his head lolling to one side as he made a sad, sorry sound in his throat. I pulled off him, feeling some of his release dribble out, and leaned forward to disengage the blindfold and gag.

"That was very naughty, Vincent. I don't understand why you couldn't just hold off for a few minutes. I thought you were more capable," I said with mock seriousness as I gave him a wink to let him know I was only playing. He seemed relieved but kept up his part, evincing embarrassment and shame.

"So now you're going to clean me up and make me come a third time," I told him, straddling the bench again, closer to his face.

His eyes widened and he licked his lips as I rubbed myself on his chin, spreading my juices and his spunk all over him.

"Understand?"

"Yes, Sir," he gasped, opening his mouth as I lowered myself onto his face, grinding against his lips, teeth and tongue.

He rose to this challenge and ate me like he was starving—or desperately trying to absolve himself of his sins. I recalled the moment he'd lost control. It had made me feel omnipotent. The pleasure rose in me from his enthusiastic technique, along with the knowledge that he was licking up all the spunk from his untimely release. It seemed a suitable punishment.

I leaned forward, curling my hands over the bench, and rubbed against him as I closed my eyes and came again. Vincent stabbed his tongue inside and slurped over me, his nose rubbing my clit. I hoped he could breathe.

When my orgasm waned, I pulled off him. He gulped at the air, shuddering and shaking with excitement. Vincent lived for this kind of debasement. His eyes were wide and vibrant, his face shiny and wet. He looked so happy that I couldn't help smiling.

"Good boy. I suppose you think you've vindicated yourself?" I said, raising my brows and wiping myself with a small towel I'd placed nearby.

He knitted his brows and said, "No, Sir. I'm sorry, Sir."

I wiped a dry section of the towel over his chin and cheeks, cleaning him like a child who'd made a mess of himself. Then I rubbed it roughly over his half-hard cock.

I tossed it to the floor, pulled my pants back on and placed my hands on my hips. He watched me, waiting for me to let him know if he was still in trouble or if I was satisfied.

"Well, I'm going to unfasten you and you're going to stand in the corner until I come get you, so you can think about what happened and how you might do things better the next time."

"Yes, Sir," he said, sighing with regret.

I left him standing naked in the corner of the basement, his hands flat on the wall so he'd keep them off his dick, and went upstairs, secretly thrilled at his unquestioning obedience. And I knew that for someone like Vincent, ignoring him and leaving him alone, unless he was actively engaged in some sort of domestic service, was the worst sort of punishment. He lived for attention, whether positive or negative. He craved it—and ignoring him completely was the only way to effectively chastise him.

As I puttered around upstairs, happy and sated, the sounds of *Sympathy for the Devil* playing from my phone on the kitchen counter pulled me out of my reverie. I couldn't wait to tell Daphne I'd put Vincent in the corner.

"Hey, Daphne," I said cheerily as I answered her call.

"Nic, I've got a problem," she said, distress in her voice.

I went on high alert. "What's wrong? Are you okay?"

She sighed. "Yes, I'm fine. It's only my livelihood that's at stake."

"What's going on?"

"You remember how I was having that shower stall put into my dungeon space? For watersports and enema play and all that fun stuff?"

"I seem to remember you telling me about it, yeah."

"Well, it was only supposed to take two days, but they found mold in the walls. So now it's going to be a full abatement. They have to tear everything up, go in with protective gear, the whole shebang. It's a complete gut job now and it's costing me a fucking fortune, Nic!"

"Oh shit."

"Yeah, you better believe it. I didn't plan for this. I don't have anywhere else I can meet my clients. Unless..."

"Unless?" A sense of uneasiness filled me.

"Nic, you know I wouldn't ask, except I have no other option."

Oh boy. "What? Wouldn't ask *what*?"

"Well, I was wondering if I could use your dungeon for a week. Only a week, Nic. I swear I will find another space by then."

"Daphne, I don't have a dungeon."

"Oh please. I need to use your basement."

I took a deep breath because I wanted to tell her no. That space was for me and Vincent.

"My sub is standing in the corner down there right now," I told her, mostly to delay a definitive answer.

"Oh my. What did Vincent do?"

"He came too soon."

Daphne chuckled. "Naughty, selfish boy. I hope you teach him a lesson. I always deal very strongly with those kinds of infractions."

"I'm handling it. He hates being ignored." I put my hand to my forehead. "Would you bring your own gear? I don't want you to use my stuff for your paying clients."

"Oh, Nic, thank you!"

"I haven't said you can yet."

"Okay, fine. Of course, I'd bring all my own equipment. You could put your things upstairs for the time being, couldn't you? Your bedroom's quite large." She waited for me to say something. "It would only be afternoons and evenings."

"Vincent's here in the afternoons. And we're *both* here in the evenings."

Daphne used her wheedling, persuasive voice. "*Please*, Nic. I promise it'll just be for a week. And I'll make sure my clients know it's a temporary space. They're very well behaved generally."

I couldn't help laughing. "Oh, I know. You'd better clean up after every session, Daphne. I swear to God, if you make a mess of my fucking basement, I will *kill* you."

"Oh, Nic, you are the *best*! Thank you so, so much!"

"At least Vincent's already aware what you do with people, so he won't be shocked when he sees the parade of subs or hears the sounds coming from down there."

"True. Maybe I'll hire him as my assistant. He might enjoy that. I'm sure my clients would."

"Daphne."

"Kidding. I'm kidding."

"You'd better be."

"Nobody's going to touch your precious boy, Nic. Even if he were my assistant, I wouldn't let anyone touch him."

"He's *not* going to be your assistant, Daphne."

"Fine. Okay. What about general eye candy? I could pose him in the living room when I'm expecting clients."

"You'd better be joking."

"I'm joking…maybe."

"Maybe I'd better take the week off work."

"Don't be stupid, Nic. It'll be fine."

"If you say so."

"I do. Anyway, gotta go. But thank you so, so much! I'll bring my stuff over tomorrow. Don't forget about your naughty boy in the corner."

After I hung up with Daphne, I immediately regretted saying yes. Daphne was definitely in the right line of work. She had a way of getting people to do what she wanted.

I walked downstairs, wondering what Vincent would think about this unexpected development. He was, of course, standing obediently where I'd left him. But as I approached, I heard sniffling and saw that he was shaking.

"Hey, hey, Vincent, it's okay," I said in a comforting tone as I placed a hand on his back. *Dear God, have I broken him?*

When he lifted his face to me, it was wet with tears. "I'm so sorry, Sir. I'm so sorry. I didn't mean to."

"Didn't mean to what, Vincent?"

"You felt so good and when I felt you coming, I couldn't stop myself."

"Oh, sweetheart, you already made up for that little mishap. I only had you stand in the corner for fun, not because I'm actually mad at you."

He didn't seem to believe me. "But I *disobeyed* you."

"But it wasn't your fault."

"But I should have held back."

"Vincent, stop it. You are *perfect*. You are *lovely*. I didn't think standing here would be so hard on you."

He looked at the ground, shuffled his bare feet.

A ray of understanding dawned. "Did you have to stand in the corner a lot as a child, Vincent?" I asked softly.

He nodded. "Yeah. But I'd kind of forgotten…until this. And I just started feeling like I'd done something really, really bad and that you might never forgive me."

I leaned against the wall beside him, giving him a very serious look. "Vincent, there is nothing you could ever do that I wouldn't forgive you."

He raised his eyebrows. "Nothing?"

"Well, maybe if you murdered someone. But it would probably depend on who." I crooked the corner of my lip.

He smiled, and it was the sweetest thing. Then he went serious again. He whispered, "What if I, like, betrayed you or something like that?"

I stared hard at him. "Is that something you're likely to do?"

"No," he breathed. "But anything's possible."

"No, I don't think that's true."

"What do you mean?"

"I mean, Vincent, that I don't think you're capable of that kind of obfuscation. You're too genuine, too honest, about everything to ever be able to hide something like that."

"Okay. Maybe."

"Plus, you know I would beat your ass if you ever did — and *not* for the fun of it."

He laughed. "Yeah. Okay."

"Oh, by the way, tomorrow we have to move the spanking bench, the straight chair and the stuff from the cabinet upstairs to the bedroom."

"What? Why?"

"Because, Vincent, our dear, dear friend, Daphne needs to use our basement as her dungeon for a week."

He blinked. "Oh."

"Yeah, I'm about as thrilled as you are."

Chapter Five

Saturday morning, we moved most of our stuff out of the basement. I should have had Daphne help, because the spanking bench was fucking heavy and there was a lot of shit to get out of the cabinet. I used some space in the linen closet upstairs to stash our toys for now. It wasn't ideal, but it would do for a week.

Vincent seemed fascinated with all the items we brought up. He pointed out several that he wanted to try. I formulated a 'lesson plan' for the next few weeks.

Luckily, Vincent was stronger than he looked. I wasn't exactly a wimp but moving that damn spanking bench up two sets of stairs nearly killed me. When we were done, we collapsed on my bed, staring at the ceiling, and I wondered how we would get through the week.

"Daphne is going to owe me big time for this," I told Vincent. "I'm a little nervous to have her clients parading through my home."

"Well," Vincent said, "most of them will want to keep a low profile. Right? I know I did."

"True. I feel like most of Daphne's clients are government workers, so, yeah. So funny that a government town like Ottawa fuels the Dominatrix business so well."

Vincent snaked his fingers across the bedclothes to entwine with mine. I turned my head to meet his gaze.

"I can't wait to use the spanking bench up here," he said.

"Vincent, I'm fucking exhausted. Unless you want to spank yourself, you're gonna have to wait a bit."

He moaned in frustration, and I laughed. "God, you are insatiable. Why don't you strip to your pretty panties and go practice your piano? Then you can make us lunch, okay?"

He smiled. "Okay... I mean, yes, Sir."

I leaned up to watch him strip out of his clothes and whistled when I saw the burgundy lace boy-shorts he had on. "Oh, sweetheart, those are so pretty."

"Thank you, Sir." He crawled onto the bed toward me. "May I?" he asked as his face hovered close to mine, his lips parted and ready.

I nodded. "Of course."

He leaned in and kissed me, soft and tentative at first, then bold and passionate, until my breath caught, and I felt the telltale pulling sensations in my belly. But I had stuff to do, and he needed to behave.

"Vincent," I mumbled against his mouth, "go practice your piano."

He sighed, giving me one more deep tongue kiss, then pulled back with regret. "Yes, Sir."

Later, as I fed Vincent bits of the lunch he'd made us from my fingers while he knelt on the floor beside my chair, I said there was something I wanted to ask him.

"Of course, Sir. You can ask me anything."

I nodded and pushed my chair from the table. As Vincent began to stand, I said, "No, stay on all fours and follow me to the sofa."

I grabbed my laptop from the counter as we passed it. Then I sat and pointed to a spot by my feet. "There."

He knelt where I'd indicated, gazing at me with curious blue eyes as I called up some photos on my laptop.

"I'm going to show you something, and I want you to tell me if it appeals to you at all or if you have no desire to explore it in any way. I need you to be honest with me."

He nodded. "Of course, Sir."

I turned my laptop toward him and watched his expression. His eyes flitted to mine with surprise. But he looked at the screen again with a tentative interest.

"Well?"

"I, uh, I mean, those are gay men, right? In puppy hoods?"

I smiled. "Probably. It's something a lot of the young, gay leather crowd is into right now. But" — and I looked at him meaningfully — "not everyone into this is a gay guy. There are straight guys and women who enjoy puppy role play."

He licked his lips, looking at the carpet where he was kneeling and up at me with a desperate look in his eyes.

My breath caught with hope, and I smiled. "Is that something you'd like to explore with me?"

He still seemed hesitant. "Uh, do I have to be a *puppy*?"

I blinked. For some reason, I'd thought Vincent would jump at the chance to be a puppy. "No, of course not. It's just something I thought you might want to try, and you'd make a really cute puppy. I already bought you a hood."

"I like the idea of it. But couldn't I be...a kitten...instead? Or is that too dumb?"

Suddenly the warmth of my feelings for Vincent permeated me. *Of course.* Why hadn't I realized he might prefer a feline persona?

"Vincent," I said, cupping his chin in my hand, "of course, you can be a kitten. It's not dumb at all."

He smiled, his eyes filled with excitement. "I think I'd like that more than being a puppy."

I kissed him on the lips. "Of course you would. I should have realized. I can't wait to source some cute kitty ears and a fluffy butt-plug tail."

"Oh, Sir," he said, breathless and flushed.

* * * *

On Sunday, at tea, Daphne's effusive appreciation of our willingness to let her use the basement allowed all my resentment to melt away. I knew that if the tables had been turned, she would have done the same for me.

Vincent puttered around in his burgundy boy-shorts, tidying Daphne's kitchen while we chatted together, eyed his graceful movements and appreciated the way his ass looked.

"I've decided to explore some kitty play with Vincent," I told her.

Her eyebrows flew up. "What a wonderful idea! Vincent would make such a sweet kitten, and I bet he'd love every minute of it." She glanced over to where he stood wiping down the counter. "Dear Vincent, put down that rag and come sit at my feet."

He did so promptly, gazing up at her with interest. "Yes, Mistress?"

"Are you going to be Nic's cute kitty?"

He glanced at me as his cheeks flushed, then turned back to her. "Yes, Mistress."

"Oh, Nic, are you going to put him in some ears and a fluffy tail?"

I couldn't help grinning at her excitement, because I felt it too. "Of course. Just imagine how he'll look."

She covered her mouth with her hand as her eyes popped. "Oh my. He's going to be so sexy as a kitty."

"I found some really cute gear online. It's supposed to come by the end of the week," I told her, reaching over to ruffle Vincent's hair.

Daphne cleared her throat. "Speaking of gear..."

I closed my eyes in trepidation. "What?"

"Would you and Vincent help me move a few things into your basement? I assume you've moved your stuff out?"

I opened my eyes and narrowed them. "I thought you'd get a few of your slaves to do it."

"Oh, I will! Of course, I'll have them move *most* of the stuff in. But would you and Vincent help me with a couple of things this afternoon? Pretty please?"

"Just how much stuff are you moving into my basement, Daphne? You don't need to bring absolutely everything, do you?"

She shot me an innocent look. "Well...I have clients with varying needs, you know."

"Oh God, Daphne. You're only going to be using it for a week. Then you'll have to move it all out again!"

"I'm not bringing *everything*. I'm leaving the larger items and just having them covered. But there are a few, like...medium-sized items I'm going to need."

I glanced at Vincent, who shrugged, still in his place at Daphne's feet. "Fine. Okay. Sure," I said, wondering what we were getting ourselves into.

Two hours later, Vincent and I stood at the bottom of the basement stairs, watching Daphne admire the bondage furniture we'd helped set up. The room looked like a veritable dungeon now.

"Remember *this*, Vincent?" Daphne said, running her hand along the polished wood of a basic stocks piece and sharing a pointed gaze with my sub.

"Yes, Mistress," Vincent said as his eyes glazed over.

I remembered it from the essay I'd made Vincent write for me, detailing the time he had spent with Daphne. The stocks had been a favorite means of restraint for Vincent.

Seeing it here, in my basement, probably thrilled him. My versatile spanking bench and the various cuffs and spreader bars I owned worked pretty well for me, but I'd been meaning to invest in a couple of other pieces. Or, better yet, maybe I should have Vincent construct his own? I'd have to purchase the wood and look up some how-to videos on YouTube—surely I could find one. *IKEA should expand their furniture line.*

"You want to see what he looks like in one of these?" Daphne asked, a devilish smile on her doll-like face.

"Sure, if Vincent doesn't mind. I'm not in the mood for a scene or anything right now, but it would be nice to get a visual."

"Clothes on or off?" she asked me.

"Shirt off but his pants can stay on." I turned to Vincent. "Will you let Daphne put you in the stocks for a few minutes, Vincent? Just so I can get an idea of how lovely you look in such a precarious predicament?"

"Of course, Sir."

"Bend down, please," Daphne told him, and peeled the shirt over his head when he did so.

She deftly positioned him and closed the top, latching it to the bottom piece so Vincent's wrists and neck were snugly encased.

"Hmm. Doesn't that make him quite vulnerable?" she commented.

"Yes. That's why the medieval peasants were restrained like this in the streets for the populace to throw fruit at."

"Lovely. Vincent doesn't look like a peasant, though. More like a prince," Daphne said, stroking his hair.

I rounded the device to stand in front of him, then leaned down, bracing my hands on my knees so I could look him in the eyes.

"How do you like it?"

He smiled at me and breathed harder. "I like it, Sir."

"I know you do. One of these days I'm going to get you to make your own set of stocks. Then I will restrain you in it and use one of my biggest silicone dicks to ream you until you scream for mercy."

Vincent made a soft noise.

I stood up, carding my fingers through his light-brown hair. "But for now, since I have stuff to do, I'm just going to see how your ass looks in those burgundy boy-shorts again."

Daphne grinned and nodded. "Oh yes. Me too."

Vincent struggled in the stocks as Daphne and I moved behind him. He was decidedly stuck, though, and couldn't even turn his head. His chest rose and fell with excitement and frustration. I knew his dick was hard in his jeans.

"Are you hard, my slutty prince?" I asked.

"Yes," he whined. "So hard."

"Let's see." I slipped a hand below him to cup his jeans where his erection pressed against them. "Oh yes."

Vincent moaned.

"Quiet. I want to examine you."

I glanced at Daphne, who stood off to the side with her arms crossed and her eyes on Vincent.

"Let's see, shall we?" I undid the button on his jeans and eased the zipper down, then slid my hand inside and palmed his dick while Vincent struggled to stay quiet and still.

"Ooh, yes, my baby is hard as hell already." I pulled my hand away and eased his jeans down over his ass so they rested mid-thigh. The rich burgundy of the lace popped against his pale skin, and I took a sharp breath.

I turned to Daphne. "Have you ever seen anything so pretty?"

"Goodness, no. Nothing compares to Vincent's ass in pretty panties."

I smiled and leaned down to kiss his lace-covered bottom. "No. Nothing does compare," I said.

I stepped back and slapped Vincent hard on one butt-cheek then the other.

Vincent gasped. Frustration manifested in the parts of his body not restrained by the wooden device. He shifted his feet and wriggled as Daphne and I took turns slapping his ass and laughing.

Then I told Daphne to pull the boy-shorts down and tuck them under Vincent's testicles.

"Mmm. He looks delicious, Nic," she said.

"Yep. A feast for the eyes," I said, touching him at the top of his crack and running my finger between his cheeks, nudging against that vulnerable opening but not breaching it, as Vincent made desperate noises. I tickled his hole and stepped back.

"That's enough for today," I said. "Can you get him dressed, Daf, while I go upstairs and check on something? You can release him."

"Of course."

I went up and grabbed the mail from the mat where it had dropped. I was expecting a letter from the university updating my RRSP information, but it hadn't arrived yet. I'd have to call HR this week.

When I returned downstairs, Vincent was still captive, and Daphne was leaning down to chastise him while she held her hand for him to lick.

"What happened?" I said, walking down the stairs.

Daphne laughed but shook her head. "Well, Nic, as soon as I started trying to put his erection back in his pants, your boy came all over my hands."

"Vincent!" I said, walking over to Daphne. Vincent's pink tongue moved over her fingers more quickly, as if to make up for this embarrassment. "What do you have to say for yourself?"

Vincent tongued the last bit of spunk from Daphne's fingers and licked his lips. "I'm so sorry, Sir, Mistress. I couldn't help it."

I crossed my arms and looked at Daphne. "Let him out. He honestly can't help it sometimes. I didn't think this would do it, but..."

Daphne released the clasp on the device and opened it. Vincent carefully stood, then sank to his knees at my feet. "Please forgive me, Sir."

I ruffled his hair again. Honestly, what was I going to do with him? I couldn't even put him in a cock-cage because he'd simply have a wet dream in the night and wake up distressed.

"It's okay. I never actually forbade him, mainly because I had no idea that would be needed."

"May I speak, Sir?"

"Yes, Vincent."

"Mistress's hands are so...soft and small," Vincent murmured, then shuddered. "And she's used them in...so many merciless ways on me. I think my body just remembered all the times she —"

I held up my hand. "Fine. That's enough. I get it." I levelled a glance at Daphne. "Don't touch his penis again."

"But you told me to —" she protested, grinning at the absurdity of it all.

"I won't make that mistake again," I said with mock gravity, winking at her and grinning at Vincent, who smiled.

We left Daphne to arrange and organize her things and went upstairs — Vincent to fold laundry and me to relax.

I sat down at the piano bench and flexed my fingers. Then I started playing a classical piece I liked for its melody and rhythm and soon became lost in the music as memories of the weekend flitted through my mind.

When he came downstairs a little while later, he walked over and leaned on the piano. "That's so pretty."

I smiled. "One of my favorites."

"You play so well, Nic."

"Thank you." I kept playing and gazed at him as the soft notes floated through the room.

He stood there listening silently for several moments before he spoke again.

"So, you remember when we ran into my ex last week?" Vincent said, with a strange, forced casualness.

I narrowed my eyes at him. "Carol? How could I forget?"

He nodded, suddenly nervous.

"Why do you ask?"

"She texted me. She wants to get together for coffee."

I didn't say anything for several moments. When I got to the end of the piece, I stopped playing.

"When?"

"Tomorrow."

"Do you want to go for coffee with her?"

He shrugged. "Not really...except she sounded like she needed someone to talk to. She said things hadn't been ideal for her the past few months and she wanted to talk to someone she knew was a decent guy."

I nodded. "Well, you are that, Vincent. I'm not gonna tell you not to go. Just be careful that she's not trying to pull you back in with her." I spoke quietly, because saying that out loud was like staring one of my greatest fears in the face.

He shook his head. "I don't think so. She just needs a friend to talk to."

I nodded but must have appeared doubtful.

"Nic, even if she did try, there's no way I'd want to get back with her. You know that, right?"

"I think so."

Vincent moved to sit beside me on the piano bench. He looked at my hands splayed motionless on the keys. "Nic. I'm not going to get back together with Carol."

I stared at my hands as well. "You say that now..."

I was simply teasing, in a way. But my comments spoke to an underlying insecurity that Vincent would leave me someday for either a man or a woman—a person who wasn't a mishmash of identities like I was, for someone more conventional.

In a fluid movement, he slid off the bench and sank to his knees under the piano, laying his head on my thigh.

I stared down at him. "Vincent."

He didn't say anything. He didn't move.

"Vincent," I said again.

He lifted his head to meet my gaze. I cupped his face in my hands.

"I know," I said.

"Do you? Do you know how much I love you? How much I *need* you?"

I had to blink back my emotions and nod, because I didn't trust myself to speak.

"She just wants to go for coffee. I need to see if I can help her—because she asked me to and I'm a good person."

I blinked back sudden tears. "Vincent, you are a very special person. I'm just scared I'm not the only one who sees it."

He kissed the palm of my hand. "It's just coffee."

I nodded again and smiled. "I know. It's fine. I'll be fine."

He kissed me sweetly and pulled back. "You're everything, Nic. She's just an old friend. That's all she'll ever be."

* * * *

On Sunday, while Vincent was gone for his coffee date, I found myself pacing the house, unable to quell my anxiety, so much so that Daphne left whomever she was humiliating in my basement and came upstairs to ask what the hell was wrong with me.

"Vincent's having coffee with his ex-girlfriend."

Daphne stared at me. "So?"

"I know! I know that's how I should feel, but I can't help being paranoid. She's so —" I motioned with my hands.

Daphne looked puzzled. "Fat?"

I glared at her. "No. Just...I don't know. She's beautiful...and pretty. And obviously comfortable with her gender," I finished lamely.

"Ah. I see."

"What?"

"You know Vincent loves you because of your identity, right? At least partly."

"He shouldn't. He should just love me because I'm me."

"Yeah, okay, that's not what I mean."

"No?"

"No. Part of what he loves about you is that you don't conform to the norms just because society says you should. And he doesn't either. I don't think Vincent could have a standard relationship if he tried. And why would he? He's got everything he wants here with you."

"I know. I know I shouldn't feel this way, which makes it even more annoying."

The corner of her mouth twitched. "Come downstairs. I've got Brian in the stocks right now and you need a distraction."

I hesitated. "I don't know."

"I'm not inviting you to participate, Nic, but you can watch. Brian won't mind, and I'll make sure it's okay with him. It'll take your mind off Vincent."

"Fine."

"Okay."

For the next hour, I leaned against the basement wall at the foot of the stairs and watched Daphne torment

Brian as he squirmed and pleaded in the stocks. As with most of Daphne's clients, Brian had a killer body. Since there was no one else home, Daphne let Brian be as disruptive as he wanted, and boy, could he be vocal. When she finally let him come, he screamed so ferociously that I worried the neighbors might complain. It was entertaining, to say the least.

I left them to Brian's aftercare and went upstairs, wondering when Vincent would roll in. Why had he been gone so long? I started getting supper ready, even though Vincent was in charge of that.

And by 'started to get supper ready', I meant that I made a salad.

I was almost done when Vincent arrived.

"Hiya," he said, taking off his boots and hanging up his jacket.

"Hey. I made a salad," I said nervously. Goddammit, I wanted to be the big, bad Dom and I couldn't stop being the jealous boyfriend.

"Thanks. I'll start getting supper ready. Sorry I took so long."

I shrugged. "You two have a lot to talk about?"

He blushed and nodded. "Yeah. We did."

I didn't say anything, just started to take the ingredients for the supper we'd planned out of the fridge.

"I told her about you and how much you mean to me — that we're living together now because this thing we have is serious."

That made me feel good. "It is serious, Vincent. I've never lived with anyone before."

He smiled. "She's happy I found you. She knows she couldn't give me what I needed." Vincent started chopping up some vegetables. "She said if she hadn't run into us, she'd never have tried to get in touch. But when she saw me, she wanted to tell me what was going on with her and see if I could help. She's feeling kind of abandoned right now."

"Oh yeah? She's not with anyone?"

"Not anymore." He stopped slicing and looked at me. "She's pregnant, Nic."

My eyebrows flew up. "Pregnant?"

Vincent nodded. "It was an accident. She's not with the guy or anything. It was a one-night stand, and she doesn't have the guy's last name. She has an appointment this week to terminate. She asked if I could take her."

Well, now I feel like the biggest shit on the planet.

"Oh God. Wow."

"Yeah. I hope you don't mind, but I said I would."

"No, I don't mind, Vincent. I'm glad."

I got a knife out and helped him work.

"I hope you didn't miss me while I was gone," Vincent said.

"Of course I did. Don't you know? I'm like a fifties housewife, waiting for my husband to come home."

He laughed softly. "Pretty sure that's me. I'm the one who wears the apron around here."

I winked, feeling a lot better about things, but sorry for Carol. "And very little else. I know. Anyway, Daphne invited me downstairs to watch her torture a client, so that helped."

His eyes flashed and the knife almost slipped, but he righted it. "Oooh. Was it fun?"

"It was fun for Brian."

Vincent laughed and I shot him a grin.

Chapter Six

On Monday morning, I left a still-sleeping Vincent to have my shower and dress for work. I had been lucky enough to get a job doing what I loved — teaching music — at the local university. I only had two classes — one on the history of music and one on music theory — which were easy to manage and also enjoyable. Teaching piano to Vincent had re-awakened my interest. It felt good to exercise my teaching muscles and feel I was fulfilling the promise of my degree.

I had use of a cramped office on the second floor of the building, where I could hide between classes, and I took advantage of that, packing snacks and a lunch so I could decompress in my own space. More often than not, Vincent put something together for me after we'd cleaned up from supper. He spoiled me.

While I chowed down on the sandwich Vincent had made, I got a text from the chef. I'd changed his contact name to "b" because it could stand for *boy* or *baby* or *biatch* — and he was all those things to me. Also, *bottom*.

Hi. How is your day going?

Good. Yours?

I just had a call from my cousin, Taylor. He finally left his emotionally abusive, religious parents. They've been treating him badly for years and he's finally had it.

Oh shit. That's terrible. How old is he?

Seventeen.

Wow. Is he in town or where you grew up?

My aunt and uncle live in Gatineau. He's staying with a friend here in Ottawa right now. He's pretty shaken up. Is it okay if he comes over tonight? He wants to talk to me in person. He's acting like he's fine and I know this has been a long time coming, but I'm worried about him.

Why don't you invite him for supper?

Thanks. I will. See you at five?

Around then, yeah. What have you told him about us, if you don't mind my asking?

That your name is Nic and you're my boyfriend. Is that okay?

smiley face emoji That's perfect.

* * * *

By the time my second lecture let out, I was beat. I enjoyed the teaching aspect of my job, but the marking and prep-work could be exhausting. I'd been slogging through a number of essays from students whose ability to present their thoughts on paper left something to be desired. I hoped their practical performance skills were better than their literary ones.

As I was driving home, I remembered our dinner guest. At least I didn't have to do the cooking, but I was a little ticked that I wouldn't be alone with my boyfriend tonight.

I'd completely forgotten about Daphne.

As soon as I walked through the door, I remembered she was entertaining clients in my basement. Perhaps 'entertaining' wasn't the exact word for what was happening down there. As I took off my boots and hung my jacket, a pained yelp drifted up the stairs, followed by whimpers. Then Daphne called whoever it was a cunt and told them to kiss her feet or they'd get the cane.

Fuck my life.

Vincent came through the kitchen with an oven mitt on and a pained expression on his pretty face. "I forgot about Daphne," he said.

"Yeah, me too."

Our heads turned in the direction of the basement door at the noise of a paddle hitting naked flesh followed by the unmistakable sound of a violent orgasm and Daphne's disappointed voice. "Now we have to start all over again!"

"I guess I should have put up some soundproofing," I said, dropping my messenger bag and kicking off my shoes. I held my arms out to Vincent. "Come here, beautiful."

Vincent smiled and moved into my embrace. "Rough day?" he asked as his oven-mitted hand patted me on the back.

I shrugged. "Kind of. Glad to be home." I glanced at the basement door. "Maybe we should take Taylor *out* for dinner."

Vincent looked crestfallen. "But…dinner's almost ready. And he'll be here any minute."

"It smells amazing, sweetheart. I'm sure everything will be fine."

We heard a curse from Daphne and a howl of pain from her sub. Vincent and I exchanged a look as the doorbell rang.

Vincent's cousin, Taylor, turned out to be gregarious and sweet. He was built like a quarterback and didn't seem like a typical gay teen, but I wasn't going to make assumptions.

We'd quickly let him know about Daphne and what she was doing in the basement. He didn't run screaming out of the door. Maybe he was happy there were people farther from the cultural norm than him.

During supper, he shot curious glances at me, and I knew he was wondering what my deal was. I passed for a guy from a distance, most of the time, but up close the lack of facial hair and absence of an Adam's apple confused some people. It had been fun to keep Vincent guessing at first, but I felt like being transparent with Taylor.

"I'm Vincent's boyfriend, but I don't have a penis," I said bluntly, giving him a no-nonsense look over my fork.

"I'll get more bread," Vincent said, standing and heading for the kitchen.

Taylor stopped chewing for a second, then resumed. He swallowed and narrowed his eyes at me. "Are you trans?"

I loved that he didn't skirt the topic and smiled. "I prefer non-binary, but trans is fine. I don't take hormones. I haven't had any surgeries, not that I'm against any of that. I'm simply a very masculine person who happens to have a really flat chest and a cunt."

Taylor grinned. "I get that. You prefer male pronouns, then?"

"Yes, but if you make an honest mistake, I won't jump down your throat."

Vincent returned, his gaze flying between Taylor and me, clearly wondering how to react.

"I like your boyfriend, V," Taylor said, grabbing a roll. "It's almost like you're gay too—except that Nic has lady parts. But, I mean, who cares?"

"I'm glad you see things that way," I told him.

Taylor held up his hands. "Hey, I just came out to my stupidly religious parents. I'm not gonna judge anyone."

"I never thought of it like that," Vincent said, as he resumed his seat.

"Like what?" I said, taking a roll.

Vincent frowned. "I never thought of myself as gay. Even though I call you *Sir* and my *boyfriend*."

Taylor's knife clattered to the table as his eyes flew open. "You call him *what*?"

Vincent froze like a cornered rabbit.

I smiled, calmly chewing. After I swallowed, I said, "Vincent calls me *Sir* because I'm his Dom. And, Vincent, you don't have to apply any label to yourself you're not comfortable with."

Taylor's eyes went as round as saucers as a yell came from the basement, then a loud groan and Daphne's voice—"What a good slave. Now clean my boots and you can go."

"Oh, my fucking God," said Vincent, hiding his face.

"So," Taylor said, gesturing at me and Vincent, then toward the basement. "Are you all—"

"Daphne does her own thing. Unfortunately, she has to do it in our basement because her dungeon is undergoing extensive renovations."

He cocked his head, trying to figure us all out. "But you and Vincent…"

"I'm Vincent's Dom. He is my submissive. But we also have an equal partnership."

"Oh," Taylor said, still confused.

Vincent lifted his head and folded his hands in front of him on the table. "I don't call Nic 'Sir' *all* the time." He looked at me and blushed more, then shrugged. "Most of the time, maybe."

Taylor slowly grinned at us. "You kinky fucks. I think that's amazing."

"You do?" Vincent said.

"Yeah. I just got a lecture on how the lifestyle I'm 'choosing' is the Devil's playground and I think I'm the most conservative person in this house, because all I want is dick. Although, you've got me thinking."

"Great. You've been here all of an hour and we've already corrupted you," I said, just as Daphne led an attractive man out of the basement on the end of a leash.

"Hey, Nic. Can I get some water for Cameron?"

Cameron was six-foot-plus and stunning. I mean, cover of *GQ* handsome, with a scruffy beard and messy brown hair and a muscular build. He wore a pair of tight lycra shorts and a leather collar. I had a feeling he only had the shorts on because he was in my kitchen.

I got up and grabbed a glass out of the cupboard, but Daphne told Cameron to stay where he was and followed me, saying, "No, I just need a bowl."

I raised my eyebrows as she took a small bowl and filled it with cold water from the tap. She brought it to Cameron, who stood obediently with his head bowed by the table where Vincent and Taylor sat, frozen in place.

"There you go, you dirty dog," Daphne said, placing the bowl on the floor.

"Thank you, Mistress Daphne," Cameron whispered, then fell to his hands and knees and lapped at the water, splashing it everywhere in his haste to quench his thirst.

Daphne lifted her booted foot and pressed the heel into Cameron's bare calf. "Be more careful. You're making a mess on Nic's floor."

Cameron gasped at the pain and apologized, attempting to be neater.

All of us—me, Vincent and Taylor—tried to comprehend what was happening.

Daphne stopped torturing Cameron and looked at the table. "What are you eating?"

I raised my eyebrows at her gall. "Daphne, can I speak to you for a second?"

"Sure." She turned to Cameron. "Keep drinking. I want all that water gone. You need to hydrate."

I walked with Daphne to the entryway. "Daphne, that's Vincent's seventeen-year-old cousin, Taylor."

"Oh? He seems cool."

"He is cool, but I can't help thinking this might be more than he bargained for. We invited him for supper, not a peep show."

Daphne had a saucy grin on her face before I finished speaking. She folded her arms across her bustier, which pushed her voluminous tits even higher. I wondered if her nipples would pop out.

"I think he's okay with it." She gestured at the table.

Taylor leaned forward, petting the top of Cameron's head as the handsome man lapped carefully from the bowl on the floor. Vincent's gaze met mine and he shrugged helplessly.

"Oh, for fuck's sake, can you please get him out of here? I said you could use the *basement*."

"Oh, relax. It's good for him. And Vincent's seen it all before. Usually he's the one on his knees."

"Daphne, I had a really long day, and all I want to do is eat my supper, make Taylor feel like he's not a deviant and cuddle with Vincent. Is Cameron your only client tonight?"

She frowned. "Yeah. But he's got another hour with me."

I blinked. "Didn't he come twice already? I mean, it sounded like it."

"Oh, Nic, you're so cute. I can get this one off about six times a session. He's always so pent up and craving the humiliation." She put a hand on my arm. "But I'll gag him so he doesn't make so much noise, okay?"

"I'd appreciate that," I said, standing my ground.

"Anything for you, Nic. Come on, Cameron. Back to the basement. You've been such a naughty, naughty boy, disturbing these nice people."

She walked to the prostrate man, winked at Taylor as she grabbed Cameron's collar and pulled him to stand. "I think a little cock-and-ball torture will be a nice way to proceed."

Cameron shuddered as Taylor's eyebrows flew up.

"Yes, Mistress," Cameron said, following Daphne downstairs as Taylor gazed at his crotch and winced.

"Shit. She's a real ball breaker."

"Well, she's not going to break them, Taylor," I said, returning to my seat and trying to make light of this awkward situation. "Just twist and squeeze them a little."

Vincent regarded me skeptically. "A little?"

"Okay, a lot. You're going to hear some noises of distress, Taylor. Can you handle it?"

He shifted in his seat. "I mean…maybe?"

"Why don't we finish eating and go sit in the living room? The noises won't be so obvious in there."

Things were a little better in the other room. We heard a few groans and yells, but not a constant stream of begging and pleading or Daphne's continuous chastisement. It was almost tolerable. I tried to block it out, and I saw Taylor and Vincent attempting the same.

"So, Taylor, how are you doing? You seem to be holding up okay. But getting kicked out of the house? That's pretty brutal."

Taylor nodded and there was pain in his eyes that he tried to hide. "I knew it would happen. And I've been miserable living there for a long time, but it's scary as fuck to be out on my own now. I mean, I'm seventeen. I guess I can look after myself."

"You're still very young. Are you in school right now?"

"Well, I was. But my school is on the other side of the river. And I want to stay in Ottawa."

"I'm sure you can enroll in a school here in Ottawa."

"Maybe. But I'll need a residential address in the city."

"That's true. I'll get the names of the alternative high schools in the area, and you can call and inquire about registering. You can use my address."

"I can? Wow, thank you."

"If you need a temporary place to stay, Vincent and I have a spare room."

Taylor blinked at me. "Really?"

I glanced at Vincent and he nodded.

"Yeah. Unfortunately, we have an enthusiastic Dominatrix in our basement until the end of the week, but things should calm down after that."

As if to underscore this statement, a tortured cry vibrated from the depths of my home.

"Is Cameron…? Is he okay?" Taylor asked.

I nodded. "Daphne is a professional and my friend. I'm sure he is getting everything he wants from this session."

Taylor nodded. "If I could use your spare room for a few weeks, that would be amazing. I promise I'll be out by the end of the month." He frowned and rubbed a hand over his face. "I just have to get everything sorted out."

"Look… Take it easy. You can help Vincent around the house and figure out the school stuff in a bit. Take some time to adjust to what's going on."

"Thank you, Nic."

I turned to Vincent. "Is that okay with you?"

"Yeah. I'm fine with having Taylor here for a little while."

I realized it would restrict our Dom/sub activities for a few weeks, and that made me sad. But we could adjust.

Everything would be easier once we had our basement back.

Chapter Seven

By the time Friday rolled around, I was losing my fucking mind. Taylor had moved in and Daphne was still entertaining clients in my basement on a regular basis. She swore she would be out by Sunday, but I was starting to wonder if that timeline was realistic.

Vincent ran himself ragged making sure Taylor felt comfortable and welcomed, keeping me happy with good meals and a clean house and dodging awkward questions from Daphne's clients while they waited for their appointments and other clients finished up. It was not the ideal situation I'd anticipated when I'd asked Vincent to move in with me.

I had only wanted *Vincent*.

On Friday, I handed Taylor a fifty and suggested he go the movies with a friend, because I needed some private time with Vincent. He didn't seem offended and agreed to take off for the evening, thanking me for the financial incentive.

"What are you going to do to him?" he asked.

"I beg your pardon?"

"I mean, does he like spanking? Or just being ordered around?"

I stared at Taylor, wondering about his inquiry. "I think that's something you'll have to ask Vincent."

"Awe, c'mon." He grinned. "I bet you're good with a paddle."

Whatever line of this family gave Vincent his shy, submissive nature didn't seem to have affected Taylor. I regarded him with my most Dom-like manner. "I'll show you how good I am with a paddle if you keep asking me rude questions."

"Promise?" he said, shooting me a wink and a saucy smile, and this had become inappropriate really quickly.

"Taylor, you're only seventeen and you're Vincent's cousin. I'm not going to show you anything."

"Tease."

I raised my eyebrows. "But if you don't start treating me with more respect, I will toss you out of this house on your little ass, no matter how much Vincent wants you to stay."

He paled. "Oh shit. I just got hard. Sorry. I do appreciate being allowed to stay here. But I find your relationship with my cousin totally fascinating. I think *you're* fascinating."

I didn't know what to do with that remark. "Thanks? What's so fascinating about me?"

He gaped at me. "Are you kidding? I'm *gay*, Nic. Gay with a capital G — like, so gay I'm surprised I don't fart rainbows. And you apparently have lady parts. And I don't even care about that because you are the most masculine person I've ever met and the most capable, dominant, sexy guy... I'm, like, super jealous of Vincent right now."

I blinked at Taylor, wondering if he meant what he was saying or if he was just confused. Most of the gay guys I knew wouldn't touch a vulva with a ten-foot pole. Then again, most of the gay guys I knew were older. Maybe members of the younger generation of gay men were more open-minded. It was quite the revelation.

I cleared my throat, embarrassed now, because I did think Taylor was cute and a small part of me wanted to see how he'd look bent over my spanking bench, but as soon as I thought that my brain recoiled, and I only thought of Vincent. Taylor was only seventeen and totally off limits, besides the fact that I was fucking his cousin.

"Go to the movies, Taylor. Maybe you'll meet someone."

"Maybe. I'm going with my friend Stacy. She's usually a pretty good wingman."

"Glad to hear it. Bye."

"Bye, Nic. Don't spank Vincent too hard, okay?"

This kid was incorrigible. I laughed and shook my head, waving him away. "But then he'll be so disappointed."

Once Taylor had left, I found myself grinning with amusement and looking forward to my evening. I grabbed a small bottle of honey from the kitchen before I headed upstairs.

Vincent, in blue pajama pants and a white T-shirt, was folding laundry.

"Hi, gorgeous."

He turned and flashed me a smile. "Hi. How's everything down there?"

I shrugged, putting the bottle of honey on the dresser. Vincent tracked it, but he didn't say anything.

"Daphne's got a guy in the basement. He's a quiet one, though. It's not too bad."

"What's Taylor up to?"

I smiled, a devilish glint in my eye. "Taylor has gone *out*."

"Out?" Vincent said, raising his eyebrows.

"Yes. He's gone to the movies with someone named Stacy."

Vincent nodded, blushing, and glanced at the honey again. "Oh."

"I might have bribed him," I confessed.

"Might have?"

"Okay. I *did* bribe him. I gave him fifty bucks."

Vincent straightened, affronted. "*Fifty?*"

"He'll have enough for snacks," I explained, looking my boy up and down with lascivious intent.

Vincent put down the shirt he was folding and backed up a step. "What do you —?"

"I need to strap you to that spanking bench, Vincent, and do terrible, wonderful things to you — or I am going to lose my mind."

His eyes widened and his breath hitched. "*Oh*. Okay."

I stared at him, crossing my arms and raising my brows. I used hand quotes. "*Oh. Okay?*"

He swallowed, flushing and smiling. "I mean, *yes, Sir*."

"I hope so. Strip. *Now*."

"Yes, Sir," he said, inclining his chin.

I smiled as he peeled off his shirt and loosened his PJ pants.

"Good boy."

He dropped his pants to reveal the sweetest pair of lavender panties, with frills at the leg openings and pretty pink flowers on them. I shook my head slowly from side to side.

"Jesus, Vincent, if I'd known you were wearing those, I'd have given Taylor my VISA and told him to stay at a hotel. *Holy fuck*."

Vincent folded the clothes and placed them on the bed, then straightened up as I moved forward and fell to my knees in front of him, putting my hands around to cup his ass.

"Sir," he whispered reverently as he looked down at me. His hands went to my hair and he traced gently through the short strands.

I gazed adoringly into his blue eyes for a moment, then followed the curve of his chin, the soft slide of his throat, the planes of his lightly haired chest and the narrow trail of darker hair that led into those gorgeous panties. Closing my eyes because I just couldn't deal with such exquisite perfection, I leaned forward and pressed a soft kiss to the outline of his erect cock under the satin.

"Sir," he said again, sighing and pushing gently against my lips. "Oh, Sir."

I stroked my hand along the soft swell of his belly above the panties as his breathing became shallower and he bit his lower lip. I slid two fingers underneath and pulled the satin down over his jutting cock to his strong thighs. Before he had a chance to react, I'd wrapped a hand around it and licked up the underside, watching his chin drop in shock and his eyes roll back.

In a moment I had the head in my mouth as I sucked, licked and teased, enjoying every gasp and whimper my boy made. But I needed to stop. I had to get him on that bench.

I pulled off and gave his sweet slit a lick before I pulled the panties down and had him step shakily out of them.

"I need you to get cleaned up for me, Vincent," I said meaningfully. "Can you do that?"

He blinked, then nodded. "Of course. *Everywhere*, Sir?"

"Everywhere."

He knew what I meant by 'everywhere'. Excitement flashed in his eyes. He went into the en suite and shut the door.

I pulled the spanking bench into the middle of the room. Then I sat on it and stared at the bottle of honey while the shower turned on and my beautiful boy polished himself to a shine, inside and out. He finally emerged, his skin glistening with remnants of moisture.

"Come here."

Vincent obediently walked to me, and I grabbed his chin, giving him a deep, tongue-heavy kiss before I pulled away, breathless, and told him to get on his stomach on the bench. In a few minutes I had him fastened down and blindfolded.

"I want to restrain you completely and spend at least an hour eating your ass and edging you…maybe two."

"*Fuck*. Okay. Yes, Sir. Please, Sir."

"You're wondering why I brought the honey."

"Yes, Sir."

"It must be apparent now."

He shuddered. "Yes, Sir."

"You need to be quiet for me, Vincent. Try your best."

He couldn't see, and he couldn't move. I placed a gag in his mouth so he couldn't speak. His cock jutted below the bench and I'd bound his balls in a tight leather strap that kept them separated and pulled down—just enough that he noticed and to make it harder for him to come. I told him how incredible he looked trussed for my pleasure like this.

"Vincent. You look like Christmas, Easter and Thanksgiving dinner all rolled into one perverted package. I feel like I should put on my nice clothes."

All he could do was groan in response.

I grinned, grabbing the bottle of honey off the dresser and putting it on the floor beside me. I had deliberately bought the one with the nozzle, for purposes which were about to become clear. Even with that accommodation, though, this would be a messy business, so I unfolded a large bath towel and placed it under the bench.

I got on my knees behind him and slid my hands along Vincent's back, over his ass and down his thighs, watching as his muscles clenched in anticipation. With practical deliberation, I slid my thumbs between his cheeks and pulled them apart, blowing on his hole to see it clench and unclench. God, he was beautiful and so, so vulnerable. I planned to make him scream with pleasure—but first I would make him squirm.

The metal legs of the spanking bench creaked when I teased his hole with my tongue. He smelled clean and musky.

Vincent gasped and struggled as the bench complained.

I released him and picked up the honey. The bottle squelched as the gooey amber liquid pooled at the top of Vincent's crack.

"I'm anointing you, sweetheart. This might get sticky."

Yellow honey oozed across Vincent's skin. I used the nozzle to spread it over his crevice, then gently pushed it into him.

Vincent whined.

"Oh, fuck yeah. I'm fucking *basting* you."

I squeezed honey into his hole as he whimpered. He tried to look at me, but I'd made sure that he couldn't see anything. "I am going to fill you up and eat it all out of your ass, baby. It's going to take *hours*."

I don't know how it felt to have an ass full of honey, but I squeezed until half the bottle was gone and Vincent's moans became continuous.

With the bottle put aside, I used my fingers to play with his sticky ass. Amber liquid dribbled out of his hole, but I pushed it back in, deep. When I withdrew, globs of thick honey followed my finger out.

"Oh, this is so fucking hot," I said as I pressed two fingers deep inside him, displacing more of the amber liquid. Vincent groaned against the gag as his thigh muscles clenched in frustration.

I slid my fingers out and licked the honey off them. I would drink champagne out of his ass if I could figure out a way to get it in there. I might have to suspend him upside down. *Hmm.*

Since half of what I'd put inside him was already on the towel, I inserted the nozzle and added more. He seemed to like it, gasping and moaning as his ass filled with sticky liquid. The visual was pretty epic.

I put the bottle down and spread him with my thumbs, watching honey ooze out his hole before I bent and licked it up, lapping and sucking it out of him.

He made a muffled noise and the bench creaked. He tasted so good — sweet and pure and innocent.

I licked and sucked and poked my tongue inside him as far as it would go, slurping the honey and using my teeth on his rim gently, driving him to distraction.

He made the most wonderful, desperate noises behind the gag, and I hoped the spanking bench could hold up to the way he pulled against it. I ran my hand underneath and along his cock, spreading honey there, too.

He whimpered as it jerked against my palm. He was rock hard, but the cord on his balls would keep him that way while I took my sweet time eating him out.

Whenever my jaw got tired, I used my fingers and pumped him, adding more honey when I needed to. By the time forty-five minutes had gone by, Vincent was covered with sweat and goosebumps, as well as honey. His cries were hoarse and so desperate now. My poor baby was feeling the strain.

Good.

I gave his buttock a kiss and a nip before I stood on shaky legs and went into the en suite, washing the honey off my hands, leaving Vincent to wonder what I would do now.

I returned and moved to the front of the bench, removing the gag from his mouth and bending to kiss his drool-covered chin and lips. He opened his mouth and moaned, grabbing at me with anguished hunger.

"How does it feel to be basted like a Thanksgiving turkey?"

"Oh fuck, *fuck*," he groaned, struggling and panting. "Please…"

"You want to come? But I'm not finished."

Vincent made an anguished sound. "Oh, *please*, Sir!"

"Nope, sorry. I'm enjoying this too much to end it yet."

I stood and went to the other end of the bench. I picked up the honey and inserted the nozzle, squeezing even more into him.

"Oh *God*, oh, *Sir*," he groaned, squirming.

"So fucking sticky. I'm basting you up, baby."

He whimpered as I filled him, jabbing his hole with the nozzle, fucking him with it, treating him like the object he loved to be.

When the rest of the liquid had been squeezed into Vincent's rear, I threw the bottle aside. With my thumb and fingers, I played with my rude canvas while he groaned and begged and shuddered, pleading with me to let him come. I kept saying no, that I wanted to take my time because it was so, so good. *He* was so good.

By the time I thrust three fingers into him, most of the honey had come out and Vincent was a panting mess. The spanking bench sounded like it was going to collapse from his constant, violent struggles. I needed to give my boy some relief.

"Okay, Vincent, you've been very, very good for me. You want your reward?"

"Please, yes, *oh*, *Sir*, please, please, fuck, *please...*"

I moved the towel away, then maneuvered myself so I lay underneath the bench with my mouth near Vincent's tortured cock. He struggled wildly as I grabbed his cock and directed it between my lips.

He yelled and jerked violently in his restraints. "Oh fuck! *Oh fuck!* Oh *God!*"

I grinned and sucked him into my mouth, running two fingers along his taint and up to his still-sticky hole. While Vincent made a high-pitched sound, I shoved them deep inside and slid my throat over his dick.

Silence.

His cock jerked in my mouth while my fingers probed his ass.

When the first spurt of his release hit my tongue, Vincent screamed so loud that I wondered if Daphne would hear him in the basement. But I didn't give a damn. I kept sucking and fucking him with my fingers as he cried out repeatedly through one of the longest orgasms I'd ever witnessed.

When his semen overflowed my mouth, he jerked in his restraints one final time, then groaned and relaxed onto the bench, flopping like a landed fish and silent but for the sounds of his shallow breathing.

I pulled off his cock, making a satisfied smack with my mouth as I crawled from underneath the bench and moved to where his head lolled on its side. His mouth was open, his hands balled into fists where they were fastened to the bench.

I took Vincent's face in my hands and kissed his slack mouth, plunging my tongue into him over and over like I wanted to keep fucking him whatever way I was able.

He moaned and tried to respond, but he was so spent that he seemingly couldn't make his tongue move the way he wanted to. I licked all around inside his mouth, then pulled back and pushed the blindfold off.

His eyes were closed. *Did I kill him?*

"Vincent? Are you okay?"

His lids fluttered open, his blue eyes unfocused and blown wide. He didn't say anything—simply tried to home in on my face.

"Oh, sweetheart. You came so hard. I couldn't swallow it all. See?" I showed him my chin, shiny with his spunk. "That was so fucking hot."

He licked his lips and smiled. I returned it. I hadn't broken him. He was so strong, my Vincent—and brave, to give himself to me like this.

I released him from the bench and helped him stand. He was wobbly and probably sore as I guided him to the bed, where I'd placed some towels, knowing honey got on everything and was hard to lick up completely.

My lips and tongue felt tingly and numb from all the ass eating and cock sucking. I told Vincent and he laughed softly.

"Am I supposed to feel bad?" he said, his voice sounding rough and exhausted.

"Nope. You're supposed to feel good. It wasn't only you who suffered."

He rolled his eyes.

There was a soft knock at the bedroom door. I didn't know how much time had passed, but not enough for a movie.

I got off the bed and opened the door a crack.

Daphne peeked in at me with a strange smile on her face. "Everything okay up here? It sounded like someone got stabbed or strangled."

I couldn't help laughing. "God, Daphne, I can't believe you have the gall to complain about that."

"Not complaining. Just want to make sure Vincent is alive."

"I'm alive," Vincent said weakly from the bed. "Barely. I need a drink of water, Sir."

Daphne laughed. "You'd better look after him. I'm done for the night and going home. I don't have any clients until Monday, so you and Vincent have the weekend. Well, I suppose Taylor will be around. You could always send him to me. I'll look after him."

I raised my eyebrows. "He's seventeen…and gay."

"So? I've always wanted a pet. Seriously, Nic, I can feed him and entertain him for an afternoon or two."

I raised my eyebrows and opened my mouth to say no.

"Not with sex, you nitwit. I have video games and movies. I'm quite capable of hosting teenagers without corrupting them."

The idea was tempting, and I knew Taylor would find Daphne fascinating. He already thought she was cooler than anyone else he knew.

"I'll consider it. Thank you." I frowned. "Wait a minute. Monday? I thought you were getting your dungeon back by then?"

Daphne gave me an apologetic grin. "Yeah, I thought so, too. Unfortunately, they aren't finished. But it shouldn't take much longer. I told them I needed it done by next weekend."

"*Next* weekend?" I said, my voice too loud.

"Nic, relax. It won't be much longer."

"That's a whole extra week!"

She shrugged. "So? I'll buy you guys dinner out a couple of nights."

"Daphne..."

"It'll be fine, Nic."

I glared.

She smiled. "Now go look after your lovely boy."

Chapter Eight

Taylor was excited to spend the weekend with Daphne.

"Is she going to show me how to beat a guy's ass?" he said, alarmingly eager.

"No. Her dungeon is *here* for the time being. Remember?"

"Oh."

"I'm sure she can give you some tips, though."

He brightened.

After he left, Vincent cleaned up the kitchen. "Do you think it's a good idea? Taylor spending the weekend with Daphne?"

I walked over and wrapped my arms around him, pulling him close. "I think it's a fantastic idea, because I get you all to myself for *two* days."

He grinned. "Mm-hmm. And no indecent activities going on in the basement."

I nodded. "Only up here and in the bedroom. Maybe the shower?"

He blushed. "No more honey for a few days, though. There were *repercussions*."

I laughed, patting his bottom. "Poor thing. I'm the one who had to eat it all. I should probably have my blood levels checked."

He held his face up for a kiss, which I gave him.

"Come upstairs," I said.

He raised his eyebrows.

"All I want to do is put your pretty cock in a cage, dress you in something nice and watch you putter about the house all day—doing chores, practicing the piano and waiting on me."

He sighed, his face flushing even more. "Sounds heavenly, Sir."

"I got you a skirt," I told him. "It's purple...and very, very short."

"I want to see it." He started for the stairs.

"Strip first. I want you naked until I dress you."

Later in the afternoon, Vincent sat at the piano, wearing his cock cage, the purple miniskirt and nothing else. I bumped the heat up to keep him warm and settled on the sofa with a book.

I found it relaxing to listen to him play. Although very much a beginner, Vincent had progressed from very simple pieces to short classical excerpts that I curated for him. I'd performed several for him and had asked him to choose his favorite, then we'd worked on his chosen one until he'd mastered it, then we'd go through the same process again.

About noon, I let Vincent quit his piano practice so he could make us some lunch. I sat at the kitchen table and watched his very sexy behind sway under the miniskirt as he chopped vegetables for omelets.

I'm embarrassed to say that my first thought when I heard his sudden cry was that he'd unexpectedly orgasmed. But when he turned halfway around with his hand out and dark red blood spreading over his pale skin and dripping on the floor, I sprang into action.

"Oh Jesus," I said, rushing over and grabbing a dish towel from the oven handle. "Stay still!"

Vincent stared wide-eyed at the bleeding gash between his index finger and thumb, his mouth open but no words coming out.

"It's okay. I've got you," I said, wrapping the wound with the towel and pressing tight. "Look at me."

He didn't. Instead, he stared, transfixed, at the towel where the blood had begun to seep through. His face had turned ghostly white and his breathing was shallow. He was going into shock.

Shit.

"Vincent! Look at me," I said, squeezing his good hand so he'd pay attention.

His fingers tightened around mine, and his eyes flicked up to my steady expression.

"You're okay. It's going to be okay. I know what to do."

His gaze fluttered around searching for a landing place as the panic oozed out of him in viscous waves.

"Vincent," I said again, pouring all the confidence and reassurance I could from my composed features into his frantic eyes, "take a deep breath. It's just a cut. You're going to be fine."

He nodded, which relieved me tremendously, and licked his lips. "It hurts."

"I'm sure it does, sweetheart. But I have to keep pressure on it to stop the bleeding. I'm taking you to Emergency."

He glanced at the purple skirt. "Not like this!"

"No, of course not. I'll help you get into some proper clothes. Come on."

I led him out of the kitchen and upstairs, all the while keeping pressure on his injured hand. When we got to the bedroom, I glanced at him. "Can you hold this with your other hand?"

He swayed and almost fell. I placed his free hand on the towel, making sure he applied a strong enough pressure on the wound.

"Here… Sit on the bed. Lean over with your head on your knees and take deep, steady breaths. I'll find you some clothes."

"I'm so sorry," he said as he followed my instructions. "I don't know what happened."

I chuckled, to let him know I didn't think the situation was serious, although the amount of blood was alarming. I'd heard that hands and fingers bled profusely when cut. I hoped he hadn't severed a tendon. "You had an accident, that's all. It happens to everyone."

"I'm sorry."

"Vincent, it's okay. You didn't do anything wrong."

His voice was muffled by his position. "But I wrecked our lunch."

"I don't care about lunch. I only care about you."

When he slowly sat up, I was pleased to see color in his face.

"You look better. Keep taking deep breaths and put your head down again if you need to."

I grabbed a pair of sweatpants, a soft cotton T-shirt and a hoodie and dumped them on the bed before sitting beside him again.

"I need to look at it," I told him.

"I don't want to see it."

"Do you have an issue with blood, Vincent?" I asked, because it was obvious he did.

My brave boy tried to smile back but didn't quite succeed. "Li'l bit."

I nodded. "Okay. Well, *you* don't have to look at it but I do."

He took a deep breath. "Okay."

He focused on the wall in front of us as I pried his hand from where he'd gripped the cloth. Luckily, the entire dish towel wasn't soaked bright red—only part of it. I pulled the fabric carefully away from the wound as Vincent made a hissing sound. His hand twitched, causing some blood to gush forth. The cut itself seemed about an inch and a half across.

I put the towel back and told him to hold it again. "It doesn't look too bad, but you'll need a few stitches. I'm going to get something better to wrap it up and we'll get you dressed."

I had a first-aid kit in the bathroom cupboard. I led him to the sink, got him to turn his head and carefully ran clear, cold water over the wound, then wrapped it in some gauze that I tied around his hand. Thank goodness the bleeding had lessened.

I deftly removed the cock cage and helped him to get dressed. By the time he was sitting in the passenger seat of my car, he seemed much better. I think he preferred the look of his hand wrapped up in gauze to that of a bloody towel, and I didn't blame him.

In the car I tried to distract him by asking him questions about some of his favorite TV shows. We were deep into *The Umbrella Academy* and also watching *The Marvelous Mrs. Maizel* on Prime. He let me speak and answered my questions, but I could tell he wanted to be anywhere else.

At the hospital, Vincent was able to fill out the registration form himself, since his right hand was fine. I helped hold the clipboard steady and got his health card from his wallet for him. When we'd registered, I went to the nearby snack machine and got us each a small bag of cookies.

"Here," I said, ripping the package open and handing it to him.

"Thanks. I'm not really hungry."

"Vincent, please eat a couple of cookies. I don't want you passing out on me."

He blinked, looking about half his age, then nodded and fished a small chocolate-chip cookie out of the bag.

"Although maybe that would move us to the head of the line," I said, smiling.

He didn't respond.

I felt so bad for my poor, injured boy. My stomach clenched and my heart melted. Was this what it felt like to be a parent? It was devastating and excruciating, and I *hated* it. At least Vincent was a functioning adult most of the time, even if his accident had caused a temporary regression. But the sympathetic pain and discomfort I felt for him emphasized my feelings.

I patted his knee like a dad who just wanted to fortify his kids' failing spirits. "It won't be long. You're going to be fine."

"Thanks. I appreciate everything you're doing, Nic. I've never been good with this kind of thing."

"It's okay. It's a good thing it was you and not me. Because I would have only been mad and irritable and a pain in the ass, waiting here for some medical attention."

He smiled. "Yeah, true."

I raised my eyebrows. "Vincent, did you just admit I can be a pain in the ass?" I said in my stern Dom voice.

His eyes widened but he held my gaze and smiled. "I suppose so."

I tried to look shocked but didn't succeed, because his smile took my breath away.

I dropped my chin and pressed a hand to my heart, blinking rapidly. "Me, Vincent? You can imagine me being a pain in the ass?"

He snorted a laugh, then nodded emphatically. When I figured out what he meant, I laughed so loudly that a nurse looked over and frowned.

"Oh shit," I said, looking down. "Can you pretend to be in pain? She probably thinks we're having a ball over here."

"I *am* in pain," Vincent said.

"You need to moan or something. Be dramatic about it. Otherwise, we'll be here until tonight."

He made a pitiful little mewl that only I heard and looked about frantically. My poor Vincent didn't like to attract attention.

"Never mind," I said. "I'm sure you're on the list."

It was two hours before Vincent was seen, and another hour waiting for the doctor to stitch his hand. I introduced myself as his boyfriend and was allowed to stay and provide moral support while Vincent received the care he needed. It didn't take long, and the young doctor gave us instructions about caring for the wound.

"Thank you," Vincent said, obviously relieved to be in one piece.

"You're welcome. Now, be careful using that hand until it heals completely." He turned to me with a smile. "You'll have to do the cooking for a while."

Until he'd mentioned it, I hadn't thought of that. It wasn't really a problem, although I'd gotten used to Vincent doing so much around the house and he was a better cook than me.

But Vincent did a *lot* around the house. I wasn't sure I'd be able to keep the place up like he did.

"I'm so sorry, Nic," Vincent said, so apologetic that the doctor seemed confused.

"Vincent, it's fine," I said, directly to him. "I can cook. I can clean. You're more to me than a housekeeper, you know." I squeezed his uninjured hand. "Much more."

"I won't be able to play the piano," Vincent said sadly.

The doctor nodded. "Not for a couple of weeks. But after that, the motion will be helpful for healing the muscle. It will regenerate pretty quickly. But please take it easy for two weeks. The wound needs to heal." He eyed me meaningfully and I nodded.

When we got into my car to head home, Vincent rested his head on the back of his seat. "I'm sorry to be so much trouble."

I stared at him. "Vincent, you're my boyfriend. I'm *supposed* to look after you when you hurt yourself."

"But I'm supposed to look after *you*. I won't be able to do anything for two weeks!"

"Well, we'll just have to make up for that with lots and lots of sex," I said, giving him a cheeky grin. "There's nothing wrong with your ass or your dick. And I'm usually the one using my hands for that."

The hint of a smile emerged on his pretty face. "Fine. Okay. Maybe Taylor can help around the house."

"That's a great idea. There's no reason he can't contribute while he's enjoying the free lodging."

A strange idea occurred to me. "Maybe I can enlist the aid of some of Daphne's subs as well."

Vincent laughed. "Now you're talking. Let's get some payback for letting her use the basement."

"Exactly," I said, feeling better about everything now we had come up with some options.

* * * *

I'd texted Daphne about Vincent's injury while we were at Emergency. Once we got home, I let her know that Vincent was fine but that we might need to call on one or two of her subs for some housekeeping assistance in the next couple of weeks.

Oh my God. Nic, that's perfect. I have just the guy for you.

Brian?

Brian's a pain slut. But Matteo would be perfect and he's free most evenings and weekends. I might be able to get him to help you out tomorrow. Let me work my magic. Do you and Vincent like Italian food?

shocked face emoji. Uh, yeah. We can manage til Monday, but I guess if he's free… How's Taylor?

He's adorable. We're having a great time! I'll let him know he might be called upon for some assistance at your place too.

Thanks, Daphne. You're the best.

Look after your boy.

I cleaned the kitchen while Vincent relaxed on the sofa and watched TV. He'd taken ibuprofen for the pain and seemed comfortable now that he was stitched and bandaged. But he was wiped out from the emotional toll of his sudden injury.

As it neared five-thirty, I slipped in beside my sweet boy on the couch and squeezed his thigh under the blanket.

"How are you feeling?"

He gazed at me out of those beautiful eyes that now looked calm and focused. "So much better. Thank you for looking after me today."

"Ah, Vincent, sweetie. You look after me every day. I can look after you once in a while," I said, smiling and kissing him on the cheek.

"I'm not going to be much help with a gimpy hand."

"I already spoke to Daphne. She has someone named Matteo she thinks can help out. And the great thing is he'll love every minute of it, so we won't have to pay him."

"Bonus. And, like I said, Taylor can help."

"Yeah, Daphne said she'd let him know he'd be expected to pitch in."

Vincent smiled. "I wonder how that little playdate is going?"

"Well. At least, that's what Daphne said. I'm sure Taylor will let us know all the details when he gets home tomorrow. He doesn't hold back."

Vincent laughed. "No. He's pretty out there. I'm not sure how he's been able to stay with his parents for as long as he did, honestly. He must have really had to bottle things up to get by."

"I don't know how people manage with restrictive families like that."

"Some don't. They either get thrown out at a young age or decide to end things."

"Why do people have children if they don't plan to support them unconditionally? I don't mean financial support, although that's valid too. I'm talking about emotional support. Aren't you supposed to give them wings so they can fly? Not tramp them down under the weight of your own expectations." I shrugged. "Then again, what do I know? I don't have kids and don't plan to ever have them."

Vincent stared at me, blinking slowly.

"What?" I asked.

"Never? You *never* want to have kids?"

We stared at each other as the knowledge of our first incompatibility became clear.

"Well, I...I mean, I don't think so? I've never seriously considered it, to be honest."

"Hmm."

"What does that mean, Vincent? Do you want to have kids someday?"

"I don't know. Maybe? I think it might be kind of nice to be able to nurture and guide a little human."

Wow. Okay. That was unexpected.

"Hmm," I said.

"What does *that* mean?"

"Vincent, I know, I mean deep, down, *know*...I don't want to be pregnant. *Ever.*"

"Okay," he said, nodding. "And it would be impossible for me. But there *are* other options."

"True. There are." I sighed and gave an exhausted laugh. "Wow. This day started with a flesh wound and now I'm re-evaluating my entire future. You've really got me spinning today."

He covered my hand with his. "Don't do that. Don't re-evaluate your future. It isn't a deal breaker for me. It's something I might want to think about at some point. But it's not so important to me that my life would be meaningless without it."

"Good to know. I'll keep that in mind." I thought about it for a second. "How would we be able to be kinky and stuff? With a kid around?" *Or kids.*

Vincent shrugged. "I'm sure there are kinky married people with kids. Probably it's tricky, but they make it work. And the kids aren't at home forever."

Jesus, this subject was making me uncomfortable. I wasn't ready for this conversation…*at all.*

"Um, okay. Can we table this for another day? I'm open to discussing it in the future—just not right now."

"Sure. Yeah, of course," Vincent said softly. "I mean, we don't even know if we're going to…"

"If we're going to what?"

"If we're going to be together…for the long term. I mean, I hope you— I mean, I want to be." He glanced up at me with nervous eyes.

"Vincent, I want to be with you long term. Our relationship is really strong, and I can't imagine feeling this with anyone else."

"Okay. Good."

"We can absolutely have that discussion someday soon. Just give me time to think it over."

"Okay."

"Okay." I clapped my hands together, feeling an inordinate amount of relief. And hunger. "Let's order a pizza."

Chapter Nine

On Sunday morning, Daphne phoned me.

"How's Vincent?"

"He's fine—only frustrated he can't use his left hand."

"Poor little soldier. Matteo will be at your place around two this afternoon."

"He'd better be wearing clothes, Daphne," I said.

She laughed. "Yes, Nic, he'll be dressed. He knows it's not a typical session. He's excited to help you out."

"Fantastic. I don't have to treat him any particular way, do I? I'm not really his Dom."

"No, but I think it would be reasonable for him to address you as 'Sir' while he's there, don't you? It will keep him in the appropriate, subservient frame of mind. And he'll enjoy it."

That made sense. "Sure. Yeah, okay."

"And, like most submissives, he likes to have direction. So, tell him what to do and he'll do it. You'll like Matteo. He's a sweetheart."

"Thanks, Daphne. When are you bringing Taylor back?" I asked, wondering how things had gone over there.

She laughed. "I don't know. I might just keep him. He's made me piss myself twice."

"What?"

She clicked her tongue. "With laughter, Nic. He's hilarious."

"Okay," I said, kind of weirded out. It was strange for Daphne to be in such a giddy mood.

"I'll bring him back after supper and take Matteo home."

"Sounds good."

* * * *

Right on time, at two in the afternoon, the doorbell rang.

I opened it to a medium-tall man with short, curly black hair, lovely green eyes and a hesitant smile. "Hello. Nic Walker?"

"Come in, Matteo," I said, glancing at Vincent, who had just descended the stairs. "I'm Nic, and this is Vincent."

"I'm pleased to meet you. Sorry about your accident," Matteo said to Vincent as he toed off his shoes. "How is your hand?"

Vincent lifted his bandaged appendage. "Feeling better but not very useful." He stepped forward and shook Matteo's hand after I let it go. "Nice to meet you. Thanks for helping us out."

"You're very welcome." He walked into the room and looked about, taking the measure of my home. "What a lovely place you have, Nic."

114

"Thank you," I said.

Matteo was attractive, elegant and at least thirty. He had the body of a laborer—built and sturdy. He wore khakis and a soft blue button-down shirt under a gray wool coat, which he took off and hung on the hook by the door.

"Where would you like me to start, Sir?"

"Uh," I said, glancing at Vincent, "why don't you show Matteo the washer and dryer and have him finish the laundry? I think there are a couple of baskets of clean clothes to fold and put away."

"Sure," Vincent said with a shy smile at the older man. "Follow me."

Matteo turned and bowed to me. "Thank you, Sir."

He followed Vincent as I stared after them and wondered whether we would regret having Matteo here or come to value him as a trusted friend.

When Vincent returned to the living room several minutes later, his forehead was creased with concern. "He insisted on calling me 'Sir'. It felt weird."

I laughed. "That's because you're not used to it. And you're generally a bottom. But don't knock it. You might come to like it."

Vincent leaned against the piano and crossed his arms over his chest. "He's handsome."

Since he'd been a client of Daphne's, I'd suspected he would be. "Yes, he is."

Vincent raised an eyebrow.

"What?"

He shook his head, blushing. "Nothing. Never mind. It doesn't matter."

I walked over to him and took his dear face between my hands. "So he's handsome. So what?"

"I kind of wish he wasn't."

I laughed softly. "Sorry. I should have asked Daphne for one of her ugly clients."

Vincent, realizing how ridiculous his comment had been, laughed too. "Yeah, maybe." He smiled. "Well, I guess you can enjoy the eye candy."

"Hey, I wasn't the one pointing out how handsome Matteo is," I said, pulling Vincent close. "Besides, you're all the eye candy I need."

Matteo finished the laundry, vacuumed the upstairs and made supper. He used the chicken breasts Vincent had purchased on Saturday morning and cooked them in a spicy tomato sauce with melted cheese on top — a healthier chicken parmigiana — that turned out to be delicious.

I made sure Matteo would include himself as a dinner guest because it would feel weird to have him cook for us and not eat, especially since he wasn't being paid for his efforts. Plus, Daphne was bringing Taylor by in an hour and taking Matteo home. Although initially declining out of a polite deference, when I insisted, Matteo agreed to sit with us and enjoy the food he'd prepared.

"How long have you known Daphne?" I asked Matteo. I wanted a little more info on our resident house-helper, since he would be sharing space with us for a couple of weeks.

He smiled. "Oh, it's been a few years at least. She's very good at what she does."

I grinned. "Yes. She is."

"Exactly *what* does she do?" Vincent asked as he sliced a piece of chicken and lifted it to his lips.

We gazed at him, confused. Vincent knew very well what Daphne did with the men she dominated. He'd written an entire essay about it.

"For you specifically, I mean," Vincent clarified.

I nudged his knee with mine and raised a questioning brow.

Vincent glanced at me, then qualified his question. "If you don't mind my asking?"

Matteo cleared his throat as he blushed a pretty pink.

"Well, I enjoy many different...things. Mainly, um, a little humiliation...and bondage...and orgasm denial...that sort of thing."

"Hmm," Vincent said. "Me too."

Matteo followed Vincent's gaze to me.

"Nic is very skilled at all those things."

Matteo swallowed thickly. "Is he?"

Matteo's face had turned completely red, and I wondered where Vincent was planning to take this conversation. I decided to be quiet and find out.

Vincent looked at the table, rubbing the edge of his plate with the finger of his good hand. "Are you straight?" he asked, without looking up.

This time I stomped on Vincent's foot. *What the hell is wrong with him?*

"Ow!" Vincent exclaimed. "Hmm, sorry. That's none of my business," he mumbled, frowning at me. I put it up to the stressful day he'd had. Vincent was unerringly polite in most circumstances.

Matteo cleared his throat and blushed, but he answered Vincent's question. "Most of the people I meet presume that to be the case, yes."

Which was the most non-answer answer I'd ever heard to that question.

"Pardon?" Vincent said.

I felt I had to intervene at this point. "Matteo doesn't have to define his orientation if he doesn't want to."

"No, I'm sorry. You don't. I'm just curious," Vincent said.

And I decided, Vincent's injury notwithstanding, that he would get a fucking spanking at some point this evening. Although I might have to drag him into the basement so Taylor didn't hear it.

Matteo didn't seem offended. He ate a few more bites of chicken, then looked at us. "My orientation is very fluid, as a matter of fact. I had a male Dom before Daphne."

"So, you're bisexual?" Vincent asked, with a smile this time so Matteo wouldn't take it as anything but an innocent query.

Matteo shrugged. "I think the term nowadays is pansexual. I don't generally pay any attention to gender. For me, it's all about the person." His gaze went back and forth between Vincent and me. "Or *people*."

Vincent nodded. "I feel the same way. Thank you for sharing that with me."

I gave him points for a graceful recovery.

Matteo threw Vincent a sweet smile and I wondered what was happening there. "You're very welcome, Vincent."

We ate the rest of the meal in silence, mostly because I was puzzling out Vincent's sudden interest in Matteo's sexual orientation. He had said he found Matteo handsome. I'd thought that was due to his jealousy of me looking at another man. Now I wasn't so sure.

After supper was done, Matteo put on a pot of tea, and we moved into the living room. While he was in the kitchen, I glanced at Vincent.

"What the hell was all that about?"

"What?"

"You quizzing Matteo about his orientation. Are you into him?"

Vincent looked alarmed. "No!"

I narrowed my eyes. "Hmm." I scratched my chin. "You did point out he's very handsome."

Vincent opened his mouth to say something, but I held up a finger.

"Do you think Matteo is handsome, Vincent?"

"I mean, we agreed he was. Right?" He was deflecting.

"Do you think Matteo is sexy?"

Vincent had noticed a thread on his pants that was unravelling and was concentrating on it very hard. "I...um. I don't know."

"Sure you do. You can admit it, if it's true."

"But I'm in a relationship with you. I'm not supposed to find other people sexy."

"That's ridiculous. Of course you're going to find other people sexy." I sat down beside him and stilled his fingers. "What I want to know is, is Matteo someone you find sexy? He seems very nice, and I have to admit he's hot."

Vincent nodded.

"When you were asking him about his orientation, were you trying to figure out if Matteo might be attracted to you?"

Vincent put his head in his uninjured hand. "I don't know. Maybe. I'm so confused."

I sat there thinking about this for a moment, while I heard the kettle whistle. The tea would be coming out soon.

"Well, there are two ways we can approach this, Vincent. We can ignore your obvious attraction to the man who will be providing service in your place for the next two weeks, or we can face it head on and ask if he might want to provide a different kind of service for us."

Vincent's head shot up and he gaped at me. "What are you suggesting?" He licked his lips. "Sir?"

I smiled slowly. The fact he tagged on the "Sir," at the end told me he had a good idea what I was suggesting but wanted me to confirm it.

"I'm suggesting we ask Matteo if he wants to come upstairs with us. Although, when I talked to Daphne, I didn't ask for a sub for sexual games — just domestic service. Maybe I should check with her before we broach this with Matteo." I tapped my jaw. "I'm not sure how it would work. Would I Dom you both? Or would you and I Dom Matteo?"

Vincent shook his head. "I don't know. But I'm going to need something to take my mind off this." He lifted his injured hand. "And the thought of watching you Dom someone else…is seriously hot to me."

"I never thought you'd consider inviting anyone else into our sexual bubble. But now that you've absolved me of my preconceptions, I must admit I'm considering this…unusual development…very seriously."

The doorbell rang. That would be Daphne and Taylor…to further complicate my evening.

My brain spun with images and ideas as I answered the door. I'm not sure how much of that showed on my face, but Daphne's eyes narrowed when she saw me.

"Jesus, Nic, you look upset. Is Matteo not working out?"

"Hey, Nic," Taylor said. "I beat Daphne at three different games! She thinks she's so scary, but she can't play Super Smash Bros for shit."

Daphne looked to the ceiling as if searching for patience she didn't know where to find. "Are you sure you can't let me paddle his ass just a teeny, tiny bit? I'm sure it would do him some good."

Taylor dissolved into laughter while kicking off his shoes and moving into the living room. "Good one, Daf."

"I'm not even joking," Daphne muttered, but Taylor was oblivious, already plopping down on the sofa beside Vincent.

I answered Daphne as Matteo came in with the tea. "No, and Matteo is working out just fine. He's lovely."

"Thank you, Nic," Matteo said, placing the teapot on the coffee table and returning to us. He sank to his knees at Daphne's feet. "I hope I have pleased you, Mistress."

Daphne smiled and petted his hair. "Yes, Matteo, you have. Now get your things and I'll drive you home."

"Hold on a second, Daphne," I said. "Can Vincent and I have a word with you? In the kitchen?"

"Of course. Matteo, you stay right there."

"Yes, Mistress."

"Can I have some of this tea?" Taylor asked as he poured a cup for himself.

"Yes, Taylor. We'll be back in a second. Just watch TV and drink your tea like a good boy," Daphne muttered, rolling her eyes. "Perhaps an entire weekend was ambitious."

"*Like a good boy*. You're hilarious, Daf."

"Yep, that's me. A big pile of laughs until the handcuffs come out." She grinned a little too devilishly for my liking.

I crossed my arms across my chest. "Daphne. He's seventeen. He's too young for that."

"That's bullshit and you know it, Nic. He is ripe for the taking."

Vincent and I yelled, "*Daphne!*" while Taylor did a spit-take and dissolved into hilarity.

"You are *not* corrupting Vincent's cousin," I said sternly, while fighting a smile, because I knew Daphne was deliberately provoking us and making Taylor laugh.

"Fine. But you're no fun."

We moved into the kitchen, where she turned and stabbed me with a glance. "So. What did you want to ask me?"

The irony of broaching this subject to Daphne after forbidding her to make innuendos about Taylor hit me like a steam roller. "Um, I, uh… Vincent, why don't you ask her?"

"Me?" he said, surprised to be thrown under the bus — or steam roller.

"It was *your* idea. Right?" I said.

"I only said he was attractive!"

"And quizzed him about his sexual orientation at the dinner table."

Daphne grinned and looked at Vincent. "You dog. You hot for Matteo?"

Vincent gave Daphne one of his sweetest smiles. "We were wondering if you'd let us ask Matteo to, uh, perform some other services…for us."

I had to give it to Vincent. He could sweet-talk a horse out of an apple.

But Daphne only raised her eyes and placed her hands on her hips. "Vincent Blake, did you just ask if you could use my submissive for your own personal pleasure? And *his*?" She gestured offhandedly at me.

I didn't know whether to be offended or relieved that I wasn't the precise target of her ire.

Vincent widened his smile that much more and cradled his injured hand in his healthy one, causing Daphne's eyes to track to it. "Oh, sweetie, I didn't even ask how you were doing! Is your hand very sore? Did you take something? You poor thing!"

And just like that, Vincent had her. I wondered if he'd used those skills on me without me realizing. I suspected he had.

I cleared my throat. "Daphne, let me explain. While we were eating supper, Vincent engaged Matteo in a discussion of his sexual proclivities. It seems he and Vincent have similar...tastes...shall we say?"

Daphne gathered Vincent to her and stroked his forearm in a very maternal and comforting way. "Yes. And?"

"And, after supper, Vincent and I decided that we might be interested in having Matteo help us out with—some things—that I didn't discuss with you previously. We haven't mentioned anything to Matteo, in case you were wondering. We don't know if he'd be on board."

Daphne squinted at me, looked at Vincent, who blushed on cue, then turned toward the door.

"Matteo! Come into the kitchen, please. Nic and Vincent have something to ask you."

"Not now, Daphne!" I protested. "We don't want to ask him *now*!"

Vincent's face lost its color and he glanced in alarm at Matteo, who entered the kitchen and knelt at

Daphne's feet. "Yes, Mistress?" he asked, staring at the floor.

"Then I'll ask him. Matteo, would you enjoy fulfilling duties beyond the usual domestic ones I'd indicated when I told you what Nic and Vincent needed for the next couple of weeks? You may look at me."

Matteo peered at Daphne with a rosy hue to his cheeks. He had the kind of face one would find on the cover of a men's fashion magazine—chiseled features and a rugged attractiveness I found more interesting the longer I spent with him. But he lacked the customary narcissism a man of his good looks generally possessed.

"What kind of duties, Mistress?"

"Sexual services, Matteo, to be explicit—which I must be in order for you to understand the question properly."

Matteo's mouth opened in surprise. He swallowed thickly, then regarded me and Vincent. "I...uh..."

He seemed unable to speak.

"Hmm. He gets like this when I offer him an unforeseen reward," Daphne said, examining him. "Yes or no, Matteo? Is that something that might interest you?"

Matteo swallowed again and closed his mouth, nodding. "Yes, Mistress."

And *bingo*. He definitely seemed into it.

But I began to wonder if this was a good idea after all.

Daphne shrugged. "There, you have your answer. How do you want to do this?"

"Uh, we'll handle it. Maybe the three of us can discuss it tomorrow, after Vincent and I decide how best to approach it."

Daphne nodded and bowed with a flourish. "As ever, I am at your service. Let me know if there is anything else you need."

"No, that—that's quite enough. Thank you."

"Very well. Matteo and I will be going. He'll be back at four o'clock tomorrow, in time to make supper and...assist you during the evening."

"Fine. That's great," I said, nervous all of a sudden.

What the hell are we doing? All I'd wanted was a domestic servant to ease the burden, and now we had a sex slave.

Kind of.

Chapter Ten

When I got home from work on Monday, Matteo was already in the kitchen preparing dinner. Taylor was wearing my 'Kiss the Cook' apron, while Matteo appeared to have brought his own striped one. Matteo and Taylor sliced vegetables next to a big pot on the stove, while Vincent sat primly at the kitchen table.

He seemed relieved to see me and got up to give me a welcome-home kiss.

"Hi."

"Hi. Well, I'll be darned."

"Hey, Nic," Taylor said, turning toward me and waving with his knife. "I'm helping Matteo with supper."

"I can see that. Just watch yourself. I don't want to deal with another knife injury."

"Good evening, Sir," Matteo said. "We're making spaghetti Bolognese. I hope that is acceptable?"

"Sounds delicious," I said, returning his smile. Matteo had dressed in jeans and a polo shirt today. I noticed a pair of leather moccasins on his feet. He registered my gaze.

"I hope you don't mind. I bought them to wear inside your home, Sir."

"Not at all, Matteo. Whatever makes you comfortable."

"Perhaps I can leave them here for the duration of my—assignment?" he said, searching for an appropriate word.

"Of course. Feel free to find a spot in the front hall."

"Thank you, Sir."

"I'm going to get changed. Vincent, why don't you come along? It looks like these two have everything under control."

A loud smack came from the basement, accompanied by frantic words of apology and Daphne's no-nonsense reply.

I closed my eyes and shook my head. "I'm not going to get used to having someone else's play-space in my basement, am I?" I asked of no one in particular.

Matteo chuckled.

"At least they're having fun," Taylor commented with a grin.

"I suppose so," I said. "Come on, Vincent. You can tell me about your day."

As we made our way to the stairs, we heard a louder smack and groveling, but I tried to ignore it and concentrate on Vincent.

"How's your hand?" I asked as Vincent followed me to the second level.

"Fine," he said, "except for the fact I can't use it. It's frustrating not to have two working hands, you know."

"I'm sure it is."

"I can't play video games, or type, or play the piano…"

"You can read and watch TV," I said, heading into the bedroom and dropping my leather messenger bag in the corner. I took Vincent's arms, giving him a stern look. "You are supposed to be taking it easy."

He sighed. "It's hard. I like to be busy."

"Mmm, I know. Why don't you run a bath while I get changed into some comfortable clothes. I'll come in and sit with you and we'll talk about what we're going to do with Matteo tonight."

"I'm kind of nervous about that, actually."

"Have you changed your mind?"

"No. I haven't. I'm about equal parts excited and anxious."

"Uh-huh. Well, that's why we need to have this discussion."

When I'd finished changing into some sweats and a T-shirt, I went into the en suite. Hot water cascaded from the tap into the soaker tub as bubbles formed and the scent of lilacs filled the space. Vincent stood from adjusting the taps and gazed at me, a question in his eyes.

"Get naked," I said with a smile.

Vincent smiled slowly. "I'll need some help, Sir. To undress."

I grinned. "Oh. Well then." I stepped forward and took the hem of his Henley between my fingers. "Arms up."

The look on his face as he slowly lifted his arms made me want to kiss him all over. I peeled it off and threw it into the hamper. "You won't need this anymore today. I'm dressing you for dinner."

"Oh," he said, pink lips forming a sweet oval as he blinked naively.

"Alas, in deference to Taylor, I'll have to choose something fairly PG," I said, popping the button of Vincent's jeans and unzipping them with a zing. "How is your hand, anyway?"

"Feels fine. Not so sore, except if I forget and move my fingers too much."

"That's good. Try to keep it still or we'll have to wrap your whole hand."

"Yes, Sir."

"You're a good boy, Vincent. You're a very good patient. I, in the same situation, would have ripped my stitches and made everyone's life miserable."

Vincent smiled but didn't argue.

I licked my lips at the sight of the baby-blue silk panties I had helped him put on that morning. "We'll save these. We can put them back on when you get dressed," I said, peeling them down his legs and getting him to step out of them. I hung the dainty panties on the knob of the vanity drawer. "Okay, get into the tub, beautiful."

I helped Vincent get in and sit down, keeping his injured hand on the tub's edge so the bandages would stay dry. He closed his eyes as the hot water enveloped him. "That feels so good."

I pulled the metal chair from its position beside the vanity and set it beside the tub with its back facing Vincent, then straddled it and rested my crossed arms on it, gazing at my lovely naked boy surrounded by lilac-scented bubbles.

"We need to figure out what we're going to do with Matteo," I said.

Vincent's eyes flew open, and he regarded me curiously. "What do you *want* to do with Matteo?"

I raised my eyebrows. "This was largely your idea, Vincent. I'm on board but I need to know what you had in mind."

He blushed and nodded slowly. "I'm not sure. I know I want him in the room, but I don't know if I want him involved right now, you know? I mean, not yet, but possibly in the future. Does that make sense?"

"You want to start slowly, you mean?"

"Yeah." He watched me closely. "And if any of us feel weird or it's not working at any point, we can stop."

"Sure. That makes sense."

"I've never... I've never gotten up close and personal with anyone's penis but my own, y'know? I'm a little nervous about that. But I'm kind of into it, too."

I nodded. "Would you prefer if Matteo watched us for now?" I grinned. "Or only listened, even?"

"You mean blindfold him? So he can't see us but he can hear us? I like the idea of that."

I could picture it.

"Mm-m. What if I blindfold him and bind his wrists to his ankles while he kneels on the carpet, by the dresser. He won't be able to see what we're doing, but he'll be able to hear it and smell it. And he won't be able to touch himself either."

"That's perfect."

"I'll send Daphne a quick text to see if that's a scenario that might appeal to Matteo."

"You could just ask him."

I nodded. "But he might be too eager to say yes because he doesn't want to miss out on this opportunity. Whereas Daphne would know, and we can keep the anticipation and suspense at a nice level for him."

"Sure. If it were me, I'd love it," Vincent confessed.

"Noted," I said, with a wink. "I'm sure Matteo will look delicious trussed up for our visual enjoyment while we make lots of noise and get him going."

"Exactly."

I laughed. "I like this adventurous side of you, Vincent."

"I'm glad I feel safe enough with you to explore it."

"Me too."

After Vincent's soak, I washed him and helped him dress in a pair of tight black jeans and a soft blue turtleneck sweater that set off his eyes. When we came downstairs, Taylor, who was placing glasses and cutlery out on the dining room table, whistled.

"Wow, you look hot, Vincent."

"Thanks," Vincent said, blushing furiously.

"But...why is he dressed up and you're in sweatpants?" Taylor asked me, his forehead creasing. "Is this some kind of kinky fashion dynamic you've got going?"

"You could say that." I winked at Taylor. "How is supper coming along?"

"Great. Almost ready. By the way, Matteo is amazing. Can we keep him? Wait till you taste his sauce!"

Vincent and I glanced at each other and tried not to laugh while Taylor groaned. "Jesus, *I'm* supposed to be the immature one here."

"Sorry," I said. "So, his sauce tastes good, does it?" I kept my face straight for once.

"Yes, it's delicious." Taylor raised his voice and called into the kitchen. "Matteo, they're making your spaghetti sauce sound dirty."

Matteo came out of the kitchen on cue and placed a serving bowl full of meat-sauce-covered spaghetti on the trivet, smiling benignly. "My sauce is a refined vintage," he said.

Taylor snorted a laugh and I finger-gunned Matteo.

"Good comeback." I swiveled to point at Taylor, who had opened his mouth. "Don't. I don't want to hear it."

"Oh, I see. You and Vincent can make lewd suggestions, but I have to shut my mouth?"

I held up my hands. "We didn't *say* anything."

"No, but you…I mean, you laughed. It was obvious," Taylor protested.

"You know what's obvious to me right now, Taylor?" I asked in my Dom voice, folding my arms.

"Oh, God. What, Nic?"

"The fact that we're all standing here not eating." I gestured at the table. "Why don't you sit down, unless you're helping Matteo to serve this wonderful meal?"

"God, when you talk to me like that…" Taylor said, shaking his head and pulling out a chair. "I get why Vincent likes you."

I barked a laugh. "Only then?"

Taylor laughed.

At least there weren't any sounds coming from the basement dungeon, so I assumed Daphne had taken her leave and taken her client with her.

I sat down beside Vincent while Taylor and Matteo took their seats.

"Wow! Smells amazing. We're so grateful for your help, Matteo. And yours, Taylor."

"It's my pleasure," Matteo commented, holding his hand out for my plate, which I gave him. "Taylor is a big help."

"Ha-ha," Taylor said. "It's *literally* your pleasure. Right?"

Matteo squirmed but didn't seem to know what to say.

"I don't think Matteo gets hard from making dinner for us," I said, then realized I shouldn't make assumptions. I glanced his way. "Do you?"

Matteo cleared his throat and passed my plate back with a heap of steaming spaghetti Bolognese on it. "Not always. It...depends on the circumstance."

"Like...how?" Taylor asked.

"Taylor. You're being rude," I said.

"I'm just curious about this whole service fetish thing."

Matteo piled spaghetti onto Vincent's plate. "It's entirely all right. I don't mind sincere curiosity." He gave Vincent's plate back to him and held his hand out for Taylor's. "Although I get a lot of enjoyment out of being useful and helpful to people, it's not always a sexual thing. It's more a feeling of happiness and fulfillment."

"Oh," Taylor said.

As Matteo ladled spaghetti onto Taylor's plate, he said, "Now, if Miss Daphne was standing behind me with a paddle or a switch, and I wasn't wearing anything except a short apron..."

Taylor's eyes widened as he took his plate back.

"...then it would be a sexual thing. And I would be hard. Very hard, indeed," Matteo said quietly, his eyes calm and steadfast as he gazed at us.

"Well," I said, picking up my fork as Matteo sat down. "Thank you for your honesty, Matteo."

"*Jesus Christ*," Taylor said. "Daphne is *the* coolest person in the fucking world."

I stared at Taylor with my eyebrows raised.

"Except for you and Vincent. But you haven't told me much about what you do together."

I shook my head and forked some spaghetti into my mouth, chewing slowly as I stared at Taylor. Then my gaze shifted to Matteo and I spoke with my mouth full. "Oh my God, this is so good!"

The others sampled the spaghetti while Matteo smiled and nodded to me in thanks. Vincent and Taylor offered similar praise.

I swallowed my second forkful. "Matteo, seriously, what the *fuck*? Did you go to culinary school?"

Matteo wiped sauce off his chin with a napkin. "My mother was a wonderful cook. She taught me."

"This is the best spaghetti Bolognese I've ever eaten. Thank you for making it for us."

"You're very welcome, Sir. I'm so glad you like it."

Silence reigned as we ate the delicious meal that Matteo had prepared. To my great surprise, Taylor offered to clean up the kitchen. Matteo had placed items in the dishwasher as he cooked, so the amount of clean-up required was minimal.

"Go on," Taylor said, gesturing to the three of us. "I know you want to go upstairs."

"Thanks, Taylor, I appreciate it," I said.

I turned to Vincent. "Take Matteo upstairs, please, and wait for me, both of you. I need to call Daphne before we begin."

"Yes, Sir," they said. Vincent smiled at Matteo and beckoned as he headed for the stairs.

"Let me grab my bag," Matteo said. "I'd like to brush my teeth and freshen up."

"Sure," Vincent said as I gave him the thumbs up and took my phone from my pocket.

I stepped outside the kitchen and called Daphne.

"Hey, Nic. What's up?"

"Well, we just had the most incredible dinner that Matteo prepared. Thank you so much for setting this up."

"You're very welcome, Nic. It's the least I could do, honestly."

"It was a brilliant idea. But I need to ask you something."

"Ask away."

I peeked around the doorway to the kitchen and saw Taylor eating the leftover spaghetti off my plate. *Teenagers.*

"We're thinking of having Matteo present for a scene but blindfolded and bound so he can't do anything but listen and get hard."

Daphne laughed. "Sounds wonderful."

"Do you think that's something he's likely to enjoy?"

"I think that's perfect. Matteo enjoys waiting for his pleasure. He's very patient and he will get off on not being able to touch himself."

"Okay, great," I said, starting to look forward to the evening. "That's what I thought."

"Do you plan to get him off at the end?" she asked.

"I hadn't thought that far ahead. I could force him to get himself off while we watch? Or would he enjoy being left frustrated?"

Daphne chuckled. "Why don't you have him there for a scene every evening this week and only let him get off on Friday? The waiting would just about kill him. In a good way, I mean."

I examined a crack in the paint on the wall. "Would he prefer that?"

"Oh, indubitably. Matteo likes to suffer while anticipating an eventual reward. He's not into pain so much, but denial? *Big time.*"

"Okay. Good to know. Thanks, Daf."

"How's my little teenager? Is he helping out more?"

Something in my brain clicked. "Uh, yeah, now that you mention it," I said, suddenly suspicious. "What did you do?"

Daphne laughed again. "Oh, I might have mentioned an incentive if I heard good things."

Dear God. "What kind of incentive, Daphne?"

"You should ask him," she said, mysteriously. "Gotta go. Bye. Have fun tonight."

She disconnected and I was left holding my phone, staring at the entryway and wondering what the hell Daphne had said to Taylor to motivate him to help out around the house.

"Taylor," I said, walking into the kitchen.

"I heard that entire conversation," Taylor said, leaning up against the counter, holding a wet dishrag.

"What did Daphne say to you? Why are you so eager to help out now?"

He cleared his throat and looked at the floor, then glanced up from beneath his eyelashes. "Uh, she said she might let me watch her do a scene with Cameron."

I processed this slowly, remembering Cameron was the good-looking man who'd drunk water out of a bowl on my kitchen floor when Taylor had first come over.

Of course.

"I see. You want to watch that hot guy get spanked and treated like a dog?"

Taylor shuddered and closed his eyes, nodding. He opened them again, looking so young and innocent that it made my heart ache. "Yeah. Is that bad? I kind of want to see Daphne in action, too…if you say it's okay."

I watched Taylor, noticing the tell-tale flush to his skin and sudden awkwardness. And also a spot of Bolognese sauce on his chin. He reminded me of Vincent. "Well, luckily, you're older than sixteen, which is the age of consent in Canada. And I'm not your legal guardian. So, I guess it's entirely your choice," I said, taking the cloth from his hand and wiping the sauce from his chin.

His eyes widened but he nodded. "Oh. Good." He swiped his hand across his chin as I gave him back the cloth.

"I just don't want to be sued by your religious parents for corrupting their son."

"We're not actually on speaking terms, so that won't be a problem."

"You should thank Daphne. She seems to have taken you under her wing as an apprentice or something."

Taylor's face broke into pure pleasure. "You think? Really? I'd fucking love to be like Daphne someday."

I rolled my eyes. "Please promise me you'll set your sights a little higher, Taylor? I love Daphne, but I'd feel a lot better knowing you're planning to go to college and not set yourself up as a professional Dom at the tender age of nineteen or twenty."

Taylor laughed. "Nah, I see it as more of a sideline. Like, a hobby."

"Well, in that case, fill your boots. Good night, Taylor."

"Good night, Nic. Have fun with Matteo."

I gave him a little salute and a smile as I turned.

"Have fun fucking my cousin."

Jesus Christ. Is this actually my life right now?

I flipped him the bird without looking and headed upstairs to the sound of his hysterical laughter.

Chapter Eleven

When I opened the door to the bedroom, Vincent looked up from where he stood beside the dresser with his underwear drawer open, Matteo gazing down on the piles of silk and satin panties with an indulgent smile.

"Matteo's helping me pick a pair to wear for our scene," Vincent said with a sly smile.

I sat on the edge of the bed. "How lovely. Shame he won't be able to see you in them."

Vincent's gaze shifted between the two of us. "Why don't we let him see me in them before we blindfold him? So he knows what he's missing."

Matteo smiled at Vincent's deviousness. "I would like that very much."

I leaned back on my hands, watching the two attractive men, one slight and fair, the other sturdy and dark. "Perhaps I'll let Matteo undress you and put you in them."

Vincent blinked quickly and gazed at Matteo. "Okay. If Matteo's okay with that."

Matteo nodded. "That would be fine. Thank you, Vincent, Nic."

"You'll need a safeword, Matteo. Not that we're planning to do anything directly to you tonight, but you should have one anyway. In case it gets to be too much, or you get bored, or whatever."

Matteo smiled. "Of course. Would you choose one for me, Sir?"

"Certainly. But it has to be something you'll remember. How about 'spaghetti'?"

"That sounds fine, Sir."

"'Spaghetti' it is then. Now take your clothes off, please. Vincent and I are dying to see what you look like underneath all that fabric."

"Of course, Sir. I'd be happy to satisfy your curiosity." He blushed but proceeded to lift the golf shirt over his head and fold it carefully, placing it on top of the dresser. "By the way, the painting above the bed is extraordinary."

"Thanks. A friend of ours painted it from a photo of Vincent and me."

"It's lovely." He smiled. "It has your energy."

As he unbuttoned and unzipped his jeans, I examined his exquisitely toned torso. His body was so unlike Vincent's, but attractive in a different way. He had darker hair on his chest and in his armpits, and there was even a small tattoo on his shoulder of an owl sitting calmly on a branch, its large eyes watching everything.

"Nice ink," I said.

Matteo glanced at his own shoulder and smiled. "Thank you."

Vincent stepped closer. "Wow. Yeah, that's beautiful."

"Thank you."

"Why an owl?" I asked as Matteo shucked his jeans and folded them, standing there in a pair of black boxer briefs that hugged his ass and thighs alluringly.

He shrugged. "Wisdom. Serenity. Cunning. Power."

I nodded. "Nice."

He held my gaze as he pushed his boxer briefs down and off, revealing an average, circumcised erection jutting from a dark patch of neatly trimmed pubic hair.

I grinned. "I hope you haven't been hard all evening."

Matteo smiled, the dimples in his cheeks showing. "No, Sir. Only since Vincent showed me his panties," he said, gesturing at the drawer.

"I see. Well, you can undress him now, and put him in the chosen pair."

"Yes, Sir," Matteo breathed, glancing shyly at Vincent as he reached out to grasp the hem of Vincent's blue turtleneck with hesitant fingers. "May I?" he asked as Vincent nodded and tried to avoid looking at Matteo's penis.

"Vincent's never been intimate with another cis-male before," I said.

Vincent involuntarily focused on Matteo's erection then admitted, "I may be a little more bisexual, or pansexual, than I realized."

Matteo smiled and folded Vincent's shirt. "May I just say that I find you very attractive, Vincent. And sweet. And quite adorable."

"Oh, stop," Vincent said softly, blushing and glancing my way. "Now I'm feeling self-conscious."

"But I'm the only one who's naked," Matteo pointed out.

"Not for long," I grinned. "I want to see Vincent in those panties." I pointed to the pair of black-and-white polka-dot panties Matteo had selected from Vincent's stash.

Matteo unbuttoned and unzipped Vincent's black jeans and tried to pull them down. He got them to mid-thigh before gazing at me in defeat and laughing. "They're very tight."

"Yeah, I know. Vincent, you'll have to lie down and help him."

After some clever maneuvering, Matteo got Vincent's jeans off him. He straightened and stared down at my pretty angel. Vincent looked delicious in nothing but a skimpy pair of black panties that did little to contain his prodigious erection.

"My goodness," Matteo said.

"Good boy," I said to Vincent. "Now let Matteo take those pretty panties off you so he can help you into the polka-dot ones."

"Yes, Sir," Vincent panted, giving me a wide-eyed look.

Matteo cleared his throat. "Yes, Sir."

He leaned over Vincent, who was splayed on the bed beside me, and slid his finger under the waistband of the black panties, his gaze meeting Vincent's as he hesitated and swallowed. Their eyes locked and my own arousal level ramped up at the sight of their connection. They held each other's gazes as Matteo slid the black panties down Vincent's thighs, releasing Vincent's erection to bob like a metronome while Matteo drew the panties over Vincent's feet.

"This is beautiful," Matteo said, touching Vincent's steel anklet with his finger. Then Matteo scrunched the panties in his hand and lifted them to his nose, inhaling the scent of Vincent's pre-cum, before opening his eyes and shooting me a guilty look.

"I'm sorry, Sir. I didn't mean to—" he said as Vincent's mouth dropped open and his eyes flew wide.

"That's entirely all right, Matteo. I completely understand." I had done the same thing on numerous occasions.

"Thank you, Sir." He straightened out the crumpled panties and placed them on the dresser before taking up the polka-dot pair and guiding them over Vincent's feet. Vincent wriggled to help and lifted his ass as Matteo put a knee on the bed and arranged the panties as best he could over Vincent's hard cock.

"There. Oh, these are perfect." He hovered his hand over them as if he wanted to smooth his fingers over the curved bulge, but he stopped himself and moved off the bed, placing his hands behind him and awaiting further instruction.

The expression on Vincent's face was a hilarious mix of astonishment and desire as he gazed at Matteo, then shot me a guilty glance of helplessness.

I smiled to show him I had no issue with him being so turned on by our talented chef and play partner, but I needed to get things under control or we'd alter our plans in a way that might undermine how I wanted to manage Matteo's involvement. It was important that he be passive for our first few sessions, or Vincent and I, or Matteo, might become overwhelmed and uncomfortable.

I straightened from the reclining position I'd relaxed into. "All right, Matteo. I'd like you to kneel by the dresser there with your hands behind your back while I gather a few things."

"Yes, Sir. Of course," he said as he gracefully got into position.

I restrained Matteo the way I wanted him — kneeling with his wrists and ankles cuffed and clipped together so he sat on his calves while I affixed the blindfold over his eyes. By the time I'd finished, his erection had grown and seemed interested in what was about to go down, although Matteo was prevented from being involved.

"Are you comfortable?" I asked, stepping back.

"Yes, Sir," he said, swallowing thickly and licking his lips.

"You look lovely."

"Thank you, Sir."

I turned to Vincent, who was reclined on the bed, teasing his dick through the satin of his polka-dot panties, his gaze swinging back and forth between Matteo and me.

"All right. Let's get this show on the road." I clapped my hands together.

Vincent smiled as I grabbed two more pairs of cuffs from my stash.

"Spread-eagled, baby. I'm locking you down, too."

"Yes, Sir," he said, then stretched out on his back with arms and legs spread wide.

But I shook my head. "Oh no, darling. On your front, please."

Vincent inhaled a breath and scrambled onto his belly, spreading his legs and arms again. I took my time attaching him to the four corners of our bed, giving him teasing strokes and pinches as I went. I tried not to get distracted by his pale skin and the fact that he was already rubbing himself off on the bedspread.

"Vincent. Stay still. If you come before you're allowed, you will be soundly punished."

"Yes, Sir," he said. "Sorry, Sir."

I glanced at Matteo. He sat still with his chin raised and head angled toward us, his body as stiff as his standing cock.

"I wish you could see this, Matteo. Vincent has a spectacular ass and I'm just about to peel those polka dot panties down and spank it."

Matteo cleared his throat but remained obediently silent.

I hooked the waistband of the panties with my finger and slid them slowly down over the globes of Vincent's ass until they rested just beneath the swell of his glutes. Then I spread my fingers out, squeezing and stroking the tempting flesh as Vincent moaned.

"Oh fuck, yes. Your ass is so gorgeous," I crooned. I hauled a hand back and slapped him hard across both cheeks, delighted with his sudden gasp and an echoing exhale from Matteo.

"Ooh, Matteo likes that sound, Vincent. Let's give him another."

Before Vincent could reply, I spanked him again. This time he groaned and pulled on the straps that bound his wrists to the bed. He whimpered as his ass turned pink.

"More?"

"Yes-s-s," Vincent said, prolonging the 's' and trying not to rut against the mattress. "Spank me, Sir."

Matteo made a noise. I turned my head to look at him, where he knelt, his wrists pinioned behind him, his cock waving in the air. A bubble of fluid at the top of his glans expanded as I watched.

So far so good. Everything was going to plan.

I smoothed my hand over Vincent's ass, then began to spank him in a slow rhythm, enjoying the jiggle of his buttock each time my hand connected and the way the pink flush spread out until it reached up his back and down his thighs. I alternated from one side to the other, watching Vincent's responses and listening to the tortured sounds from Matteo behind me.

It was too bad he couldn't see what was happening. It was obviously driving him to distraction.

Once Vincent's lower half was a nice shade of pink, I soothed my hands over him, feeling the heat emanating off his skin and enjoying his desperation. He panted and rocked himself into the mattress.

"You'd better not come. We've only just started."

He froze, trying to keep from thrusting his dick against the sheets.

"Shall I describe how your ass looks for Matteo, Vincent?"

Vincent moaned softly, then murmured, "Yes, Sir," very quietly.

"Hmm? Speak up. What should I do?"

I waited patiently while he gathered his courage.

"You should describe...the way my ass looks...for Matteo. Sir."

"I think so, too." I tilted my head and regarded Vincent's ass objectively. "Well, Matteo, it is presently the color of an almost-ripe strawberry—not quite red but close, a very dark pink. I feel warmth when I hold my hand near the surface of his skin. Perhaps Vincent can describe how it feels."

Vincent made a noise of protest, but I smacked his ass again, causing a groan and a quiet curse.

"What was that, Vincent?"

"I mean, yes, I'll tell him."

"Good boy."

"It's on fire, Sir. Like the fire is under my skin and warming me all over."

"Thank you, Vincent. That's perfect. And very evocative," I said. "What do you think, Matteo?"

"I think," Matteo began, voice vibrating with arousal. "I think I'm very lucky to be here."

"Even though you can't see what's going on?" I asked.

"I *can* see it. In my head, as I listen to the sounds and movements."

"That's wonderful, Matteo. I can tell you're enjoying it."

He nodded with a small smile. "I can assure you I am."

"All right, then. Let's keep going," I said with a slap to Vincent's behind that elicited a tortured groan.

I got up and pulled open the drawer in the nightstand that held Vincent's favorite toys. "Hmm, what shall I pull out of the treasure chest today?"

Silence.

"What would you like in your ass, Vincent? The plug? Or the vibe? Or maybe the beads?"

Vincent moaned and blinked in confusion.

"I'm giving you the choice," I explained.

He licked his lips. "The…beads, Sir." He shuddered with clear anticipation.

I smiled. "Good choice."

Vincent rubbed his face against the bedspread and moaned again.

I drew out the black string of anal beads that graduated in size from very small to medium sized. Vincent had a few strings of beads, and this one was the least intimidating. It was more of a tease than anything, but he enjoyed having it inside him during a spanking, so that he felt the little rubber balls everywhere.

Before approaching Vincent, I walked to Matteo. "I thought you might like to know what I'll be inserting into Vincent."

Matteo twitched as I trailed the rubber beads over his belly and chest, over one shoulder then the other, and along his cheek, so he got a good idea of the size of the balls and the length of the cord. He gasped, tilting his head to follow the toy, but the blindfold stayed in place.

"Hmm? Do you think Vincent will like to have this stuck up his bum?"

Matteo made a sound deep in his throat before licking his lips and whispering, "Yes, Sir."

I chuckled. "Oh, I know he will. And I'll have him describe how it feels, so you don't feel left out."

"Yes, Sir. Thank you." Matteo's cock twitched and leaked as he contemplated the torture ahead of him.

It felt exhilarating to dominate two beautiful men. They were at my mercy and completely transfixed by my actions. Never in my wildest dreams had I imagined this, but now that it was occurring, there was no turning back. I'd thought dominating women was my place, until I'd been lucky enough to have Vincent bend to my will. Now I flourished in the heady sensation of having men submissive to me, having never imagined it until Vincent had come into my life.

I laid the string of beads across Vincent's back while I got the lube from the drawer and placed it beside him. When I opened it, his adorable hole clenched and unclenched in anticipation, the satin panties bunching below where I had placed them.

"Ooh, you are so, so pretty, Vincent," I murmured. "How's your hand?"

"F-fine, Sir."

"Let me know if it starts to hurt and I can uncuff that one, all right?"

"Yes, Sir. But it's fine. I'm trying not to move my fingers."

"Good boy," I said, smoothing lube along his crack. He groaned, shifting on the bed.

"Are you hard?"

"So hard, Sir."

"Excellent," I said. "Matteo looks ready to bust, but he's in the same predicament. No hands free. Can you see?"

Vincent focused on Matteo where he knelt. I'd made a point to place him in Vincent's line of sight. "Yes, Sir."

"I think he's enjoying himself, don't you?"

"I think so, Sir. His cock is leaking, and he keeps licking his lips."

"I know. He looks so lovely in his distress, doesn't he?"

"Oh yes, Sir."

Matteo made a sound—a low groan of frustration that stroked through me, whetting my appetite. But I had work to do.

I ran a finger down Vincent's crack and rubbed it slowly against his hole until he begged me to breach him.

"Please, please, Sir. Oh, please!"

"I love it when you beg."

Vincent whimpered as I quickly inserted my finger up to the first knuckle. He panted as I left it there. I didn't move.

"Please...more...please... Oh, God, please..."

"What's the matter?"

He made a high-pitched, frustrated sound and pushed his ass against my finger to get what he wanted, but it didn't work.

"You want me to go deeper?" I ask ingenuously.

"Yes!" he moaned. Then, quietly, "Yes, please…oh, please…please…"

When I pushed my finger in all the way, Vincent groaned and shuddered.

"Like that?" I asked with a smile.

"Ah, yes…yes!"

As Matteo whimpered, a knock sounded on the bedroom door.

Are you fucking kidding me?

I ignored it and continued fingering Vincent's ass and concentrating on his moans and whimpers.

Then Taylor's voice interrupted the scene.

"Nic? Sorry to bother you, but the Wi-Fi's down or something. I can't get my laptop to connect."

I cleared my throat. "Uh, Taylor? We're kind of in the middle of something," I said.

"Shit, I know, but I'm not sure what to do…"

I grasped at the easiest solution to this problem. "The modem's beside the TV in the living room. Try unplugging it for a few minutes and plugging it in again. It'll reset."

"Okay, thanks, I'll try that. Sorry to interrupt." There was a pause. "How is it going?"

"Taylor! Go reset the modem. If it still doesn't work after that, read a fucking book!"

"Geeze, so testy. Okay. Sorry to bother you."

I was tempted to tell him I had a finger up his cousin's ass and a man about to orgasm on my rug because I hadn't thought to put a towel down, but I decided Taylor didn't deserve to enjoy that image — or be traumatized by it — so I didn't say anything.

"Now, where were we?" I said, trying to minimize the damage of Taylor's interruption. "Ah, yes." I withdrew my finger from Vincent's ass and grabbed the beads off his back. "Anal beads. That's next on the agenda." I slapped them on Vincent's ass a few times before slathering them with lube and slipping the first couple into him without ceremony. We needed to get moving.

Vincent yelped, welcoming the intrusion, although seemingly not mentally prepared for the pleasure of it.

"Ah, fuck...oh, God..." His voice was high-pitched and needy.

"Feel good, Vincent?"

"Ah, yes..." he said, groaning as I pushed two more in. "Oh...my...God."

"Hmm, looks nice sticking out of you this way. Like a bubbly little tail."

I smacked him hard, making him groan. "Oh, God!"

"Feels good, huh? Like being spanked on the inside, too?"

"Oh, God, Sir."

"More?"

"Yes, please. Please!"

I jiggled them and pushed them deeper, seeing Vincent's hole open and close on the larger ones. He squealed and squirmed as they went in.

"Oh, God, Matteo, it's too bad you can't see this. It's so hot."

Matteo whimpered. When I looked over, he visibly quivered with arousal, his dick waving in front of him, hips thrusting into empty air.

"Shit, I'd better get a towel."

Matteo made a pitiful sound. I left the beads where they were—almost all the way in—and quickly retrieved a bath towel, placing it on the carpet in front of Matteo.

I glanced at Vincent. Seeing the beads almost completely buried in his ass, the way he moved against the mattress, his ass clenching, made my desire surge.

"All right. Let's get back to business." I got onto the bed and, without waiting, pushed the two remaining beads into Vincent so all that was visible was the round handle.

Vincent made the most delicious noises as he accommodated this invasion, his ass shaking, his breaths quick and excited.

"Are you close, Vincent?"

"Yes, Sir."

"I thought so. I want you to come on the fifth spank. Got it?"

"Yes, Sir. I'll try. I'll try."

"I know. See if you can do that for me."

Desperate sounds from behind caused me to check on Matteo. I'd hoped he'd enjoy the scene and I was pleased with how he'd responded so far. He looked more distressed than ever.

I couldn't help grinning as I turned back to Vincent.

"One," I said, spanking him hard on the right cheek. "Two." The left this time.

Vincent rutted against the mattress and moaned. Would he be able to hold off until five? There was only one way to find out.

"Three," I said, slapping him again.

"Four."

His breaths came quicker. He thrust against the sheets.

"Five," I said, slapping him across both cheeks as he cried out and came hard. The headboard of the bed creaked as he pulled against his bindings.

I turned to see Matteo, his muscles tight and body stiff, grimace as his cock spat thick white ropes into the air and his mouth opened in a silent scream.

Chapter Twelve

"Oh, fuck yes," I said, so pleased with both my subs. "A double header if I ever saw one."

Gosh, look at me, using a sports analogy!

I unbound Matteo first, since he was in the most uncomfortable position by far. His breathing calmed while I unclasped the cuffs from his wrists and ankles and helped him to stand.

"That was impressive, Matteo," I said with a smile. "I didn't expect you to come from listening to a scene."

"I apologize, Sir. I couldn't help it. Sorry about your carpet."

"I didn't forbid you, so it's all good. In fact, I'm pleased. And a little soap and water will fix the rug."

When I took the blindfold off, Matteo blinked in the dim light from the lamps, his gaze finding Vincent.

"He still has the...beads in?" Matteo said, with a remnant shudder.

"Yes. I would offer to let you watch me pull them out, but I'm leaving them in and flipping him over. I'm going to send you home, Matteo."

Matteo nodded, smiling. "Yes, Sir. Thank you so much for letting me be a part of this scene."

"You're welcome. We'll see you tomorrow at four?"

"Yes, Sir. I'm planning to make chicken cacciatore, if that's suitable."

"That's lovely, Matteo. I'll walk you downstairs once you're dressed."

* * * *

Tuesday evening went much the same way as Monday. Matteo and Taylor cooked supper, we sat down to eat with Daphne's clients providing an unconventional background medley of cries, moans and pleas, and the three of us retired upstairs for a scene while Taylor set up his video games in the living room. Vincent had connected his PlayStation 4 to the TV in there when he'd moved in, and Taylor seemed to have commandeered it.

I'd never gotten into gaming, preferring to lose myself in a good book or a relaxing piece of music, but if they enjoyed it, who was I to judge?

This time I dispensed with the eye covering and Matteo watched the scene unfold. When I finished playing with Vincent, I let him up and had him jerk Matteo off.

The look on Matteo's face as he observed us was so sweet that I couldn't look away. It was a combination of gratitude, awe and fondness that made my gut clench with anxiety. Was Matteo falling for Vincent? But who wouldn't fall for Vincent? *I'd* fallen for Vincent. I was still head over heels for Vincent and hadn't hit the ground yet. What if Matteo was getting into this a little deeper than we'd intended?

On Wednesday, Vincent texted me at work that he thought we should watch a movie with Taylor and Matteo instead of going upstairs for a scene. I asked if he felt Matteo's sexual involvement was too much, too soon, but he said he didn't feel that way at all. He didn't want to neglect Taylor, who had been left alone for two evenings and might be suppressing some lingering trauma from leaving his parents' home.

After supper, we told Matteo and Taylor of our plans.

"A movie? You want to watch a movie with me instead of going up to the 'Tower of Song' with your acolytes?"

I smiled at him. "Yes, Taylor. You know, Vincent and I are able to do things together that don't involve sex."

"Well, I figured that. But why would you want to spend the evening with me when you could be upstairs getting wild? I mean, seriously?"

Vincent put a hand on Taylor's shoulder. "Why wouldn't we want to spend the evening with you, Taylor?"

"Uh, because you can't have sex with me? So...boring?"

"Okay, well, I'm insulted," I said, walking into the living room and sitting on the sofa, folding my arms.

"Why would you think your company is boring because we can't have sex with you? And, by the way...*ew*. I'm your cousin. So of course I don't want to go there."

"Well, duh. But watching a movie with a freeloading seventeen-year-old seems like a pretty lame way to spend the evening when you could be up to something more exciting."

"Well," Matteo said, rescuing us, "I for one have found the last two evenings to be exciting and lovely but incredibly exhausting. I can think of nothing better than relaxing with a movie in such pleasant company, Taylor."

"Aw, Matteo, you old softy," Taylor muttered.

Vincent whistled. "Yeah, *softy* isn't exactly a nickname I would have thought of for Matteo."

I laughed loudly. "Yeah, no. Definitely not that."

"Okay, too much information," Taylor said. "What are we gonna watch? Nothing sexy, please. I don't think I can handle self-consciously sitting through a detailed sex scene with you all here critiquing it."

"I'm sure we can find a movie with no sex in it."

We settled on *Parasite* after convincing Taylor he'd get used to the subtitles and that it must be a good movie since it had won so many awards.

I hauled out my air popper and made two big bowls of popcorn, loaded with salt and butter. Because, hey, why not? It wasn't every day a person sat down to watch a movie with their boyfriend-slash-submissive, his gay cousin and the borrowed pansexual service slave.

The Korean-made film transfixed us all for two hours. There was only one minor sex scene that Taylor blushed through, and when the movie ended, we argued over its meaning. Was the ending a dream or did the protagonist buy the luxury property?

Matteo and I said it was a fantasy, but Vincent and Taylor rallied behind the more optimistic idea that the central character had bettered his circumstances and ended up escaping from poverty and avoided repeating his father's mistakes.

While Vincent and Matteo hashed it out, Taylor turned to me. "Nic, can I ask you something?"

"Sure. Of course."

"There are a few things I need to get from my parents' place. They're things that belong to me that I left behind because I was in such a hurry to get away. But they're mine and I want them."

"That sounds tricky. Are you going to be able to get into the house?"

"I still have my key. I doubt they would have changed the locks."

"And you just want to go back and get some of your things that you left behind? Like what, for instance?"

"Well, like my guitar...and my video games. I basically packed what I could into my backpack when I left, so I have my laptop, my phone and some books. I wouldn't mind grabbing some of that other stuff." He shrugged, unsure. "If they haven't just thrown it all out."

"Do you think they would have done something like that?"

"I don't think so. Not yet, anyway. They don't know for sure I'm not coming back."

I narrowed my eyes. "Taylor, have you run away before?"

"Once, when I was fifteen. And the police made me go back because I wasn't of legal age."

"Oh wow, I'm sorry."

He shrugged. "Not a big deal. I wouldn't have made it very well anyway. I was surviving on the streets and pretty close to getting fucking desperate. So, I sucked it up and put up with them for a little longer. They didn't beat me or anything. Just a lot of emotional bullshit and abuse like that."

"Vincent and I can drive you to your parents' place and wait outside. I don't want to get involved, but I don't mind helping you get there and back." I took a handful of popcorn. "It's in Gatineau, right?"

Taylor nodded. "Yeah. Just about ten minutes from the bridge."

"Okay. When do you want to go? Tomorrow?"

"No. Probably Sunday morning? They'll be at church, so I won't have to worry about any drama."

My eyes narrowed. "Ah. They go to church every Sunday?"

He looked at me like I had two heads. "Uh, yeah. They're a little extreme."

I laughed. "Well, I'm glad you turned out okay."

He smiled. "Me too. Although maybe I've swung way far the other way."

"What do you mean?"

He raised his eyebrows. "Innocently asks the kinky, non-binary Dom who has a kitchen slave *and* a devoted submissive to warm his bed every night, plus a Domme in his basement."

I held up a finger. "One, the kitchen slave doesn't share my bed. He kneels at the foot of it."

Taylor opened his mouth to say something, but I held up another finger beside the first.

"And, two, the Domme isn't staying. She's supposed to be out by the weekend."

Taylor smiled.

"And, three, what exactly is your point?" I smiled.

"My point is that your house is like the farthest thing from the environment I grew up in that I can imagine — and thank fucking God."

I smiled. "How ironic for you to say that."

Taylor laughed, running a hand through his mop of hair. "I believe in God, just not the way my parents do."

"Yeah?"

"Yeah. The God I believe in doesn't care that I'm gay or you're kinky and simply wants us to be happy and lead fulfilling lives."

I nodded, smiling. "I'm glad to hear that, Taylor. That's what I believe, too."

Chapter Thirteen

Thursday and Friday, we used Matteo as a bound spectator again, a position in which he seemed quite comfortable. By the time he left to go home on Friday evening, we were considering involving him more closely in our escapades.

"What do you think? Do you want to bring Matteo in as an active participant?" I asked Vincent on Friday as we cuddled under the blankets before going to sleep. "I know you were nervous at first, but you seem to not care about Matteo being biologically male anymore."

Vincent looked at me. "Okay, I admit I'm thinking of testing those boundaries. I'm attracted to Matteo and I'm curious about what that means — and what it would mean to actually…get physical with him."

I grinned. "I knew it."

"Fine. I'm totally bisexual, just like you. I admit it."

His blush was beautiful to see. And I couldn't deny the excitement that rose in me at Vincent's words.

"I'd love to watch you and Matteo together," I confessed, running my finger down his chest and flicking over a nipple. "Do you think if I was ordering you to do things to Matteo, or vice versa, it would make things easier for you or more difficult?"

He blinked and his eyes sparkled in the darkness. "Easier. Definitely."

"That's what I thought."

"We need to ask Matteo what he thinks of the idea," Vincent said.

"Yes, we do. But I have a feeling he's been waiting for an invitation. I've seen the way he looks at you."

Vincent giggled. "Really? How does he look at me?"

"Like he can't believe how beautiful you are, or how much he wants to touch you and do other things to you," I said, slipping my hand lower and playing with the soft hairs on Vincent's belly.

He covered my hand with his and stroked it. "I think you're projecting."

"I think I'm right. Anyway, we can talk to him on Sunday while he's making supper. I gave him tomorrow off. We'll order in."

* * * *

On Sunday morning, Taylor was a mess of anxiety and irritation.

"I don't know why I'm so nervous. They'll be at church. I know they'll be at church. It's the perfect time for me to get my stuff."

"Seems convenient, yeah," I said.

"Do you want me to go inside the house with you?" Vincent asked. "Nic can wait in the car, but I'll come with you. I'm family, anyway. I've met your parents enough to know how involved they are in their religion—how narrow-minded their views are. I don't know how you stuck it out for so long."

Taylor sighed. "Yeah, me neither. Feels so good to be away from there, like this dark cloud over my head has vanished and the whole world has opened up. I mean, it's scary too, because your parents are supposed to be there for you, financially as well as emotionally. But the emotional support has been gone for a long time and the financial support was contingent on me hiding who I really was—and I can't do that anymore."

I put my arm around Taylor's shoulders. "I know. I think you made the right choice to get out of there, and Vincent and I will help you as much as we can."

Taylor blinked back sudden emotion. The smart-ass kid making jokes all the time was gone, and the fragile, abandoned child regarded me with unbounded gratitude. "Thank you. I don't know what I'd do if you weren't letting me stay at your home, Nic."

"You're welcome. As Vincent's cousin, I feel like you're my family, too."

He threw his arms around me and hugged me tight. "I think you both are fucking awesome."

"Hey, hey. We think you're pretty awesome, too," I said, as Vincent offered himself for an embrace.

Taylor moved from me to Vincent, holding him close for a few moments, then pulling away and blinking rapidly. "Okay. Um, sure, make me cry, you assholes," he said, flashing a smile. He'd probably needed those hugs for a while.

"Let's go, then," I said, resolved to get this underway and over with so we could come home and look forward to a relaxing Sunday afternoon and Matteo's return.

We piled into the car and headed out. The journey through the downtown core and over the Pretoria bridge was a pleasant one, since traffic was at a slower pace on a Sunday.

The suburban neighborhood in Gatineau where Taylor's parents lived looked like most middle-class suburban neighborhoods in Canada — peaceful, well-maintained and orderly.

The two-story craftsman home on the corner seemed idyllic to anyone looking at it, except for Taylor, who had experienced the bigotry and homophobia that was present inside it, and Vincent and me, who knew it had driven Taylor to leave. The driveway was empty, so it looked like Taylor's supposition had been correct and his parents were at church.

I parked the car by the curb a couple of houses down so we wouldn't look suspicious.

"Ready?" Vincent asked, raising his brows at Taylor.

"Yeah. Let's go. It won't take long."

I kept the car idling so I could listen to the radio without draining the battery, even though I felt guilty about polluting the atmosphere. I needed to distract myself from worrying about Vincent and Taylor invading enemy ground.

What if one or both of Taylor's parents were home instead of at church? What if they came home while the two of them were in there? What if they had changed the locks and Taylor's key didn't work?

I tried to think positively and hope for the best, ready to pick up the pieces if I needed to. I wasn't exactly practiced in emotional first-aid, but I'd do my best.

Vincent's ringtone — *Sex and Candy* by Marcy Playground — sounded from my phone and I closed my eyes, almost dreading to answer. Was there a problem already?

I fished it from my pocket and hit answer. "Hi. What's up?"

"They must have changed the lock. His key doesn't work."

I closed my eyes. "Are you kidding me? What the fuck kind of parents — ?" I didn't finish.

"He's going to see if he can get in through a first-floor window. He says the latch has been broken for years and he's done it before."

"Great. Now we're accomplices to break and enter."

"But this is his *home*."

"It's not his home anymore if he left, Vincent. He's seventeen," I said.

"But his stuff is inside."

"Yeah, I know." I sighed. "Just, be careful. I don't want *you* to go inside. Because you could totally be charged with breaking and entering and I don't think you'd enjoy prison, honestly."

"Har-har. Maybe it would be right up my alley," he joked.

"Very funny. I can tell you what would be up your alley." I tapped my fingers on the dash.

"Gotta go. He's inside. Hopefully this won't take long."

"Ten-four. Stay safe."

I disconnected the call and squinted into the distance. It looked like the coast was still clear, so I settled in to wait.

I hated to wait...for anything or anyone. I couldn't sit still and was cursing at the misguided choices the DJ of my favorite radio station kept making when I saw Taylor and Vincent approaching. I'd expected Taylor to have a bag over his shoulder and a few things in his hands, but he wasn't carrying anything. Vincent was talking to him, but Taylor was scowling at the ground and walking briskly.

I sat up straight, prepared for anything.

Taylor wrenched the car door open and flung himself into the back seat while Vincent opened the passenger door more gently and slid inside, shooting me a warning look.

"Let's go," Taylor said harshly.

Vincent shook his head when he met my gaze, so I started the car without a word and drove down the street.

"What happened?" I asked, when we were on the bridge back to Ottawa.

"They threw out all my shit," Taylor said quickly. "Fuck them."

I understood his animosity. "Yes, I agree." I couldn't believe they'd changed the locks.

We were silent the rest of the way home.

After Taylor thanked me for driving him and disappeared upstairs, Vincent told me about the note.

"What?"

"His parents left a note, in case he came to get his stuff," Vincent said, frowning.

"The stuff they had gotten rid of?"

"Yeah."

"What did the note say?" I asked.

Vincent shook his head. "He wouldn't tell me. But after he read it, he stopped looking for his things."

I moved close and embraced him. "You're a good cousin. Taylor is lucky to have you."

"What the fuck is wrong with people, Nic?" he said.

I kissed him on the cheek and rested my forehead against his. "Damned if I know."

* * * *

It seemed so normal when Matteo showed up at four o'clock with a smile and plan for supper. He'd given us a list of groceries, which we'd purchased on Saturday.

"How are you, Nic?" he asked as he removed his boots and got his moccasins down from the shelf.

I suddenly realized I'd missed him yesterday.

"I'm fine. It's good to see you, Matteo — and not just because you're making us dinner." I winked, leaning against the kitchen counter.

He blushed beautifully. "Are we...are we going upstairs after dinner?" He sounded hopeful.

I nodded, glancing at Vincent, who had wandered in. "Sure. But we need to sit down and discuss some things first."

"All right. That sounds perfect." He fished something out of his bag and held it up. "I brought this for Taylor. We were talking about science fiction books, and he mentioned he had to leave this behind."

It was a dog-eared copy of *Dune* by Frank Herbert, obviously well-loved but still fairly intact.

"Matteo, that's so kind of you," Vincent said. "I'm sure he'll appreciate it."

"Yes, especially since we took him to get his stuff and it was all gone," I muttered.

Matteo cocked his head. "Pardon?"

Vincent explained. "We drove Taylor to his parents' place to get the things he'd left behind, and they'd gotten rid of everything. All they'd left was a note that he won't divulge the contents of."

Matteo's face paled. "How awful. Is he all right?"

Vincent and I exchanged a look.

"I don't know," Vincent said. "He's been upstairs all day."

"I'll check on him," I said.

When I rapped on the guest room door, I expected an immediate response. Taylor had been a polite and fun house guest so far, but I knew he'd been disappointed, to say the least, by what he had discovered in Gatineau.

"Yeah?" he said, when I was about to knock again.

"Matteo's here, Taylor."

There was no response. After a moment, the door slowly opened. Taylor's expression was the bleakest I'd ever seen it.

"Is it okay if I don't help with supper today?" he asked without any emotion.

I stared at him, concerned. But I didn't really know what to do. "Sure. Are you going to come down to eat, at least?" I asked softly.

He made a small movement of his head. "I don't think so. I'm not hungry."

"Are you sure?"

"Yeah. Thanks, Nic," he said, closing the door.

I stood there for a long moment, shocked and confused by Taylor's sudden shift in behavior. I supposed it was a natural reaction to what had happened. But I hated seeing the normally upbeat and energetic kid like this.

When I arrived back downstairs, Matteo looked over. "Is Taylor coming to help with supper?"

I shook my head. "Not tonight. He's feeling pretty down. I said it was okay." I grabbed an apron and joined Matteo at the counter. "I know I'm not as cute and funny as Taylor, but I can help," I said with a smile, determined to make the best of things. I wasn't used to worrying about people the way I was starting to worry about Taylor.

"I'll go talk to him," Vincent said. "I'm sure he's feeling pretty rotten."

"He might just want to be alone right now," I said, raising my eyebrows. "Why don't you wait until after supper?"

"He's not coming down at all? I don't think he had any lunch." Vincent stood up but I shrugged and waved him down.

"He says he isn't hungry. Why don't you take a tray up after supper?"

Vincent's forehead creased. "This isn't like him."

"I know. I'm worried, too. But I suppose it's an understandable reaction to finding out your parents don't give a fucking shit about you," I said, slicing the carrot I was holding.

"I guess. The tray is a good idea."

"You can take him the book, too," Matteo said.

We sat down to supper, and I was determined to raise everyone's spirits by bringing up what Vincent and I had discussed last night.

"On another subject, Matteo, Vincent and I were talking about expanding your involvement in our bedroom activities," I said, sipping my wine.

Matteo looked at his plate, then peeked at us. "What was the verdict?"

"If you're on board, we'd love to bring you in for actual physical involvement in the scenes," I said, smiling. "We feel like that's the next logical step."

Vincent rolled his eyes.

"What?" I said.

"Sometimes you're overly formal," he said, grinning. He turned to Matteo. "Nic wants to know if you want to get down and dirty with us, rather than being tied up in the corner."

Matteo gazed at each of us, then cleared his throat and nodded. "The answer to that question, Vincent, is yes. Nic is a tremendously talented Dom. And" — he gazed at Vincent with an intensity that I noted — "I've never met anyone like you."

"Meaning?" I asked, because I was curious.

Matteo smiled, raising his glass and sipping some wine. He put it back down. "A man who enjoys wearing lacy, frilly things and looks so good doing so."

"Yes, that's kind of Vincent's thing."

"I like it," Matteo said softly.

"Yes, so do I. Very much," I said, wondering if Matteo was already falling for Vincent, just like I had. The thought gave me pause, but didn't alarm me for some reason. It felt…natural and expected.

Vincent squirmed under our attention. "Oh, come on. It's just a bit of lace."

"Blasphemy," Matteo said. "On you, it's more than that. It's a transformation." He splayed his hands on the table beside his plate. "At any rate, after the tremendous tease this past week has been, I would love to take the 'next logical step'."

"Excellent," I said, raising my glass. "Let's toast to that."

After we'd finished eating, Matteo filled a tray with some supper for Taylor and placed the copy of *Dune* on it. Vincent took it upstairs.

After about ten minutes he came down again, carrying the tray with everything still on it and looking worried.

"He won't open the door."

"Give it to me."

I took the tray from Vincent and climbed the stairs. When I got to Taylor's room I knocked sharply. "Taylor, it's Nic. Open this door unless you want to be hauled over my knee for a very non-sexual spanking."

After a moment or two, I heard shuffling and the door opened. Taylor stood there, his hair messed as if he'd been asleep, squinting at me with an exhausted expression.

"I told Vincent I didn't want it."

I raised my eyebrows. "The tray of food Matteo prepared for you or the paperback he brought over today?"

Taylor's eyes scanned the tray and he nodded. "Fine. I'll take it. But I don't know if I can eat anything. I'm just not hungry."

This was so unlike Taylor that I was beginning to become alarmed.

"Can I come in?"

He shrugged and turned, walking to the bed and sitting on it. "It's your house."

I carried the tray in and placed it on the dresser, then handed Taylor the book. "Matteo brought this specifically for you. Pretty thoughtful of him, don't you think?"

Taylor nodded.

"Look," I said, sitting on the bed next to him. "I know you're upset about what happened earlier. I don't blame you. It must be horrible to find out your parents threw away your things."

Taylor didn't say anything. He looked at the cover of the book in his hands and sighed. Then he reached with his left hand and took a paper off the dresser, passing it to me.

I took it from him.

If you have found this note, then you tried to come back and get your things. However, we decided to donate everything to the church, so they can sell it and use the money. That way, another family might not have to go through the same upset we did. We don't hate you, Taylor, because God teaches us to forgive, but we can't be involved in your life anymore. Your sinful ways aside, when you chose to leave our home, where we have done nothing but cherish you, teach you right from wrong and how to love the Lord, you gave up any right you had to anything in this house.

We will pray for you, but that is all we can offer.

Hopefully, you will find your way back to the Lord, but it will not be through us.

Barbara and John Carpenter

I stared at the note for a long time, trying to process what it would feel like to read it as Taylor had done. *What a piece of work his parents are.*

"Wow. This is really shitty," was all I could think to say.

Taylor snorted. "No kidding. I don't know why I thought my stuff would be waiting there for me to take. I'm so stupid."

"No, you're not," I said. "*They* are stupid."

He rubbed his face with the side of his hand. "Anyway, I don't think I can eat anything. My stomach feels like there's a rock in it."

"Okay."

"I'm sorry."

"It's all right. I'm going to leave the tray, in case you feel better in a little bit. If you don't eat anything, can you bring the tray down and leave it on the counter, please?"

"Sure."

We sat beside each other silently for several moments. "I'm so sorry, Taylor. But I want you to know you're welcome to stay here as long as you need to."

He blinked quickly and nodded, turning away from me.

I stood and left him to his misery, but it broke my fucking heart.

Chapter Fourteen

I was worried about Taylor. Ever since he'd gone to his parents' place and found the note, he'd been different. He was going through the motions of living, but without the wisecracks and irreverence I'd gotten used to and enjoyed, even though I'd pretended to find it annoying.

"What's wrong with Taylor? He seems glum. I make dirty jokes and he just looks at me. It's weird," Daphne said on Monday.

I told her what had happened and about the note.

"Oh boy. That's rough. Poor kid."

"I guess his reaction is normal? It's got to take some time to get over something like that. He really expected his things to be there waiting for him. They should have been."

"Keep an eye on him, but maybe waiting it out is the best idea. He'll come around."

I hoped Daphne was right.

Meanwhile, Vincent and I carried on with our plan to involve Matteo in the bedroom.

"I'm going to need to ask both of you these questions," I told Matteo as we sat with Vincent in the living room. "Because Vincent and I have never discussed any of this either. It's always just been me and him. I need to know what his limits are in this regard, and what he might be interested in."

Matteo nodded and scratched his chin nervously. "That seems like a good idea."

"Well, it's a good idea that everyone knows what's going on or what might go on," I grinned. "It's also fairly arousing to discuss plans in advance when it comes to kinky scenes — right, Vincent?"

Vincent shifted in his spot and nodded, already flushed and aroused. "Oh, yes."

I winked at him.

"Okay. Let's start with basic stuff. I'm going to pose a scenario and I want you each to give me a thumbs-up or a thumbs-down, and I'll take notes. Sound good?"

They nodded.

"Okay. Scenario one. Matteo, I get you to suck Vincent's dick."

Two thumbs-up, as I'd expected. The side of my mouth quirked. "Scenario two. Vincent, I get you to suck *Matteo's* dick."

Matteo's thumb went up and Vincent's followed more slowly. Two thumbs-up again, although I realized it would be an entirely new experience for Vincent. I was pleased that he seemed on board, and if the expression on Matteo's face was anything to go by, he seemed pleased too.

"Okay, scenario number three. I spank you both, one after the other, and have you stand in the corner together, not permitted to touch."

"Fuck," Vincent hissed, his eyes widening. He turned his thumb up. Then he put his other thumb up and glanced at Matteo.

"Oh, yes," Matteo breathed, giving me a thumbs-up. "Please."

"Excellent." I looked straight at Matteo. "Do you have any objections to playing with Vincent's ass while I direct you? I have gloves if you want to use them."

There was a tiny squeak from Vincent as Matteo smiled and shook his head. "Oh no. None at all. And I don't need the gloves."

I smiled. "It may involve the use of some toys he likes."

"All right," Matteo murmured as Vincent threw me a bashful smile and lifted his thumb up into the air.

"And, Matteo, how do you feel about percussion play? Do you like crops and paddles? Floggers?"

"All the above."

"Anything other than blood, piss and shit off limits for you? Think carefully."

"I don't like medical play or extreme humiliation. I don't enjoy name calling for the purposes of degradation."

"Noted. Thank you for telling me." I wrote that down. "Okay," I said, tossing my note pad on the table. "I think I have enough to know how to begin with the two of you." I took off my glasses and gave them a stern look. "Go upstairs and strip. And I want you to kneel at the foot of the bed, one on each corner. I'll be up soon."

"Yes, Sir," they said. Vincent headed up the stairs first with Matteo following.

"Jesus Christ," I swore, trying to stay calm while my two beautiful submissives prepared themselves.

Even though I'd given Vincent and Matteo a little preview of some of the ideas I was tossing around, I knew I needed to move slowly, both because Vincent didn't have experience with men as sex partners — only with Zane as a Dominant — and because we still didn't know Matteo all that well. We liked him, and obviously trusted him enough to involve him this way, but we needed to proceed with caution.

I gathered my wits about me and formulated a plan.

By the time I opened the bedroom door to my two naked acolytes, I was horny and ready to take this to the next level. The saying was true. The submissives were in control. As their Dom, I curated the experience to their specifications, desiring a satisfactory outcome of mutual pleasure among all three of us.

The first thing I did when I went into the bedroom was ignore them. I wanted them to feel superfluous and invisible, like pieces of well-made furniture — serviceable and beautiful, yes, but otherwise inconsequential to me except as practical adornments to my space.

While I actively ignored them, letting them savor the anticipation for the scene, I changed into a pair of loosely fitting, faded jeans, pulled on an old Sex Pistols T-shirt, and laced up my scuffed Doc Marten boots. I often went barefoot in scenes, but this evening I wanted to feel powerful and extra-dominant, since I had two subs and one of them wasn't used to serving me. I looked forward to observing Matteo's submission now that he was unbound and active in the room.

After taking the riding crop from my drawer, I straddled the straight chair that I'd pulled out and placed in front of the two kneeling men.

"All right, boys," I said, snapping the crop against the leg of the chair to make a sudden *thwack*.

They looked up, Matteo quickly settling his gaze back on the floor, Vincent fixating on the crop in my hand.

Both sported healthy erections already. Matteo's cock — girthy, and, unlike Vincent's, circumcised, stood in a neatly trimmed nest of pubic hair, the head almost purple. Vincent's pink glans peeked out from his foreskin like a surreptitious spectator.

"Crawl to my feet and kiss the boot nearest you, then sit back on your heels with your hands behind your head."

I waited while they obeyed, Vincent moving with his usual grace and Matteo just as elegant in his submission. When they sat back on their heels, their cocks jutting out beautifully, I smiled.

"Very good, boys. You look wonderful."

I kept my left arm folded on the back of the chair and extended the crop to tap the bottom of Vincent's testicles.

"Spread your legs wider for me, please," I said, and he did so, his eyes fixed on mine, the pupils dilated.

I stroked his balls delicately with the end of the crop, then slid it up the underside of his cock and tapped the leaking tip, making him shudder. I gathered some fluid and traced the leather up his belly and sternum, then along his statuesque neck and over his chin, and pressed it against his lips.

"Lick," I said.

Vincent's lips moved into a smile before his tongue came out and lapped the moisture off the leather.

I returned his smile, then placed the crop under Matteo's testicles and repeated my actions, getting him to lick his pre-cum off the leather as well. No secret smile in Matteo's case, but he looked like he was going to combust and we'd only just begun.

I grinned and moved the crop toward Vincent again. "Vincent has sensitive nipples," I told Matteo, using the tip of the crop to tease the small buds on Vincent's chest.

"Matteo, I want you to go to Vincent on your knees and keep your hands behind your head. Use your tongue and your mouth on those pretty pink nipples of his. Do you think you can do that?"

Matteo sighed. "Yes, Sir."

He came around and turned his back to me so he could lean forward and press his mouth to Vincent's sweet buds. I met Vincent's gaze over Matteo's back. He seemed cautiously into it and to have abandoned any residual hesitation when faced with the clear pleasure and arousal he gained from Matteo's practiced technique.

"Very nice," I said, trailing the crop down Matteo's back and flicking it at one round buttock, making him whimper.

"Everyone okay?" I said, checking in.

"Yes…yes, Sir," Vincent gasped, his eyes closing as Matteo lapped and sucked at him. Matteo mumbled the same as he side-eyed me and kept at it.

It was unreal to see my beloved Vincent being sucked by another man. So fucking hot, especially since the experience was fresh to Vincent. My boy enjoyed doing new things and submitting to acts that initially pushed him out of his comfort zone.

I nudged at Matteo's muscular thighs with the tip of the crop. "Widen your legs and stick your ass out, Matteo. I want to see your hole."

His skin gained a rosy hue as he obeyed my command. Once he'd spread himself, I traced the leather pad up the inside of this thigh to his shadowed cleft and poked it against his hole, making him tense and gasp. I didn't try to push it inside, simply teased him with the threat of it.

He gasped and twitched in an entrancing way.

I trailed the crop over his buttock and slapped it down, *thwack*, on his ass.

"Oh!" He moaned against Vincent's chest as he continued to bite and lick at his nipples.

I repeated my action. Vincent watched the crop land and groaned, letting his head fall back as he tried to keep his hands in the correct position. He was struggling, I could tell. Having his sensitive nipples played with for so long was likely tortuous.

"All right, Matteo, that's enough," I said. "Now bend down and take his cock in your mouth. Keep your ass in the air for me — even higher now."

"Yes, Sir," he panted as Vincent's eyes flew wide.

"Vincent, you are not allowed to come, so tell Matteo if you get close so he can back off."

"Yes, Sir," Vincent panted, as Matteo bent and swallowed his cock to the root. "Oh, fuck!" he moaned, his mouth dropping open in pleasure and head falling back again.

As he sucked Vincent's cock, I tapped Matteo's ass with the crop. I started soft and increased the strength and speed of my strikes.

Matteo did his best to maintain his mouth-work while I cropped his ass, but I could tell it challenged him.

Vincent let out a shout and Matteo retreated as Vincent's cock jerked. He came with such suddenness that even he appeared to be surprised. He closed his eyes and kept muttering "Sorry, Sir. Sorry, sorry, sorry..." as the fluid oozed out of him and Matteo licked his lips and stared at Vincent's still-hard cock.

"Hmm. Well, I am disappointed, but there's nothing to be done about it right now. Matteo, clean him up while I figure out what to do about his little mishap."

"Yes, Sir," Matteo sighed, body shuddering as he bent to lick and suck the jizz off Vincent's sensitive dick.

We'd gone over risks and benefits of such intimate play, and exchanged recent test results, so I knew Matteo would be okay with what I'd commanded.

I put the crop down and watched as Vincent squirmed under Matteo's attention, gasping and whimpering as he tried to stay still.

When Matteo had licked all the fluid off him, he backed off and sat on his heels, his gaze meeting Vincent's with a shy eagerness that I found adorable. Matteo's cock stood straight up against his belly, shiny with pre-cum.

"All right, Vincent. Your turn. Let's see if Matteo is better at holding off than you. While you attend to him, I'll consider your punishment for coming early."

"Yes, Sir," Vincent said, seemingly disheartened but staring at Matteo's cock like he couldn't think of anything he'd rather do right then but go at it—which was very interesting, because I didn't think Vincent had ever sucked another guy's dick, and since he'd already come, I was surprised by his level of focus.

"Okay, Vincent. Go for it. Enthusiasm usually makes up for inexperience, you know."

He glanced at me, and I winked. He gave me a soft smile, a quick nod, then bent to press his lips to the tip of Matteo's girthy dick.

I sat up straighter and pressed myself against the chair, making a low whimper. Watching Vincent's fumbling attempts at fellatio proved incredibly arousing to me. He was really trying and doing a good job, although I could tell he felt out of his depth.

"Vincent," I murmured. He glanced up as he licked delicately at Matteo's glans. "Pretend Matteo's dick belongs to me," I said. "If I had one, how would you suck it?" My voice was husky and deep with arousal, and I knew Vincent saw the heat in my gaze.

Matteo straightened and pushed his cock out toward Vincent as if he had a very important job to do. Vincent licked his lips and closed his eyes, seeming to assemble his resources. This time, when he bent to Matteo's dick, his gaze held mine as he aggressively swiped at its length with his tongue and proceeded to use his whole mouth to much better advantage.

Matteo groaned loudly as Vincent's enthusiasm grew and he began to go at Matteo's erection as if it were connected to me.

In fact, I was starting to feel like it was. I got off the chair and approached Matteo from behind. I placed a hand on his shoulder so he knew I was there and knelt in the space between his spread knees. I snugged up against him and wrapped one arm around his waist, holding him tight against me as I slid my other hand down his belly to wrap around the base of his dick. He moaned long and loud when I fed his cock to Vincent as if it were mine.

"Give me your hand, Vincent," I said, reaching out with my left hand.

He brought one hand down to clutch mine as he began a now-frenzied attack on Matteo's cock.

Vincent's own cock was standing again as I held Matteo's dick steady so he could go at it properly.

"Oh yes, Vincent, you are such a good boy. That's excellent licking technique. Now suck it, swallow it, baby."

He met my gaze with dark, blown pupils as he held on to my hand and did as I'd asked, swallowing Matteo's cock as much as he could, gagging a bit but not stopping at all. He let saliva drip from his lips as he worked Matteo's cock hard, and Matteo gasped.

"I'm close. Oh God, Sir, I'm close..." Matteo stuttered.

"You may come," I said, pressing my body close against his as I gazed down at my boy sucking and slurping my surrogate dick.

Vincent was making whimpering noises along with sucking sounds now, as he prepared for what was coming.

"When Matteo comes, don't swallow. I want to see it all dribble out between your lips and down your chin." I figured I'd take some of the pressure off, and also that it would be fucking hot right there. Sure, it was sexy when a guy or girl swallowed, but *not* swallowing could be even more messy and dirty and delicious to see.

My words were enough to tip Matteo over the edge. He stiffened in my embrace and groaned, as Vincent continued his attack and let Matteo's jizz push out between his lips.

"Oh, fucking hell," I swore as I watched it drip down Vincent's shiny chin as Matteo trembled in my arms. It was one of the hottest fucking things I'd ever seen.

I gave Matteo a friendly squeeze and released his dick, standing and moving to the bed. I needed to come after watching that, and I knew just how I wanted to accomplish it.

"Vincent, don't wipe your mouth, but get up here and lie on your back. I need your cock, like...*now*."

Vincent scrambled up from where Matteo still knelt, recovering from his orgasm, and climbed onto the bed beside me. I peeled off my T-shirt and stripped off my pants.

"Matteo, you can relax. You don't have to stay in position," I panted, straddling Vincent as soon as I was naked. I didn't even care that Matteo could see my body. He was only an instrument to our pleasure. I could be wrong, but I thought he quite enjoyed that role.

"Touch me, Vincent," I whispered. "Help me fuck you."

He shuddered a groan as he slid his hands down my sides and his fingers between my legs, spreading me as I impaled myself on his long cock. We both cried out and rocked together as I came suddenly, which always happened when I was this turned on and I mounted my boy. Vincent stayed hard, and as I kept thrusting against him, I felt my desire build quickly again. Thoughts of him sucking Matteo and the jizz dripping out of his mouth and down his chin as I stared at his beautiful face made me hit another peak very soon, and I shuddered and collapsed on him as it happened.

"Sir...Sir..." he panted desperately, thrusting up inside me. I knew he wanted permission to come himself. Since he'd done so prematurely earlier, there was no way he'd orgasm without my leave right now. And suddenly I knew what his punishment would be.

"No, Vincent. You can't come inside me. Since you seemed to like Matteo's mouth so much, you can come inside it again."

He gasped and swallowed, stilling in an effort to hold off as I pulled up and off him and rolled to the side.

"Matteo," I said. "Come and suck my boy again, please. He's been very naughty, but since he did so well just now, he can come in your mouth again."

Matteo wasted no time but climbed onto the bed and collapsed between Vincent's spread legs, sliding his arms under Vincent's thighs and holding him tight as he took Vincent's cock into his eager mouth.

Vincent cried out and propped himself on his elbows so he could watch Matteo work his cock.

"Fuck yes, that is so hot. Come whenever you want, sweetheart," I breathed, moving in close and turning Vincent's head so I could kiss him as he erupted between Matteo's lips, making adorably sweet noises of surrender.

Matteo's more active involvement in our scene had been a resounding success. I spent some time talking to him while Vincent showered, then Matteo cleaned up and, before he left for home, I made sure to check-in with him.

As Vincent and I cuddled in bed before falling asleep, I asked him how he felt about everything.

"It was...pretty mind-blowing," he admitted, blushing sweetly.

I traced the outline of his jaw, where some late-day stubble was growing. "Seeing you with your lips around Matteo's dick was a revelation. So fucking hot."

"I was nervous at first, but I liked it. When you told me to pretend it was your cock, I just...I mean, yeah, that rocked. I loved that."

I smiled sadly. "Sometimes I wish I had been born with one."

Vincent's smile disappeared and he looked sad. "I don't wish that. I love you the way you are, Nic. You know I do."

"I know. Most of the time, I do, too." I trailed a hand down his belly to touch his flaccid cock. "But penises are so much fun."

"Hmm. You say that because you've never had to hide an erection in public."

I shook my head. "No, I say that because playing with your penis is one of my favorite things in the world to do. Imagine if I had one of my own?"

Vincent laughed loudly. "You'd never leave your room!"

"Yeah, probably."

"And you wouldn't be able to fuck me with all your fantastic dildos. See? You have lots of penises."

I laughed. "That's true. The best of both worlds."

Chapter Fifteen

Work was…work. Busy, which I enjoyed, because it made the day fly. Coming home to my crowded house was starting to seem normal, which was very, very weird. I'd always thought I enjoyed living on my own. Now I couldn't remember what it had been like.

Even Daphne and her entourage had become a regular part of my day, although she assured me she would be out of my basement by Thursday. I didn't think I'd miss the sounds of kinky adventures coming from my basement, but who knew? I was definitely looking forward to getting my dungeon back, especially since I now had two subs to manage — at least for the time being. I had no idea if Matteo would want to continue to play with us once our need for his domestic services ended. I imagined it wouldn't be on such a regular basis, but I certainly had no objection to having him involved occasionally.

As I drove home, my thoughts returned to Taylor. I was becoming more and more worried about his mental health. We all were.

His jaunty personality had yet to return, and his eating habits were questionable. He ate small bites of things at meals, but he never cleaned his plate anymore. Vincent said he slept in until noon and played video games all afternoon. He didn't initiate conversations and barely replied to queries of any kind. We had all tried and failed to engage him. The book Matteo had given him sat on his dresser. I didn't know if he was reading it or not, but it didn't seem to move from day to day. Something had to be done.

"What if the church still has his things? Is it possible it's all sitting in a room somewhere?" I said.

It was Friday and we were eating the supper Matteo had prepared. Taylor had, surprisingly, gone out for the evening with a friend who, when she'd picked him up, seemed to be as worried as all of us, although she'd pretended not to be. I was glad he was getting out of the house. Maybe seeing his friend would help.

"It's possible," Vincent said, "but unlikely."

I chewed a piece of steak. "If it's possible, I feel like we should try to get his stuff back."

Matteo stilled with his fork halfway to his mouth and nodded. "I think it's worth a try."

Vincent sighed. "We don't even know what church they go to."

I winked at him. "I'll have you know I am an amateur private detective in this Internet age. Let me see what I can find out. We have to do something. I'm honestly at the point of checking to see if any of the knives are gone from the kitchen or if any of our bondage rope had disappeared."

Vincent paled. "Nic."

Matteo cleared his throat but nodded. "I'm right there with you."

Vincent shook his head. "Taylor wouldn't do anything like that."

I didn't want to question his conviction, but Matteo and I exchanged a skeptical glance.

"I hope you're right."

After supper, I sat down with my laptop in the living room and googled churches in the neighborhood where Taylor's parents lived while Vincent and Matteo played Red Dead Redemption Two. It was Vincent's game, but since his thumb and finger were compromised he hadn't been able to play. He'd initiated Matteo into it and now Matteo was hooked, so Vincent watched Matteo play, directed him on which missions to take up and gave him hints and tips.

"Do you know what denomination Taylor's parents are?" I asked Vincent.

"Catholic."

There were two Catholic churches in the area, so I only needed to figure out which one they belonged to. I found the website for the closest and checked the blog and the calendar. I searched for their names with no results.

I glanced at the game to see Arthur Morgan in the bath. "Vincent, didn't you already have Matteo bathe him? At the beginning of the game?"

"A cowboy can never be too clean," Vincent said.

"I don't know if that's a standard in the old West, but okay."

"He needs some new clothes," Matteo commented.

"Yes! We should go to the store and get some. Good idea."

"Is this just a dress-up cowboy game for you guys or is there some serious gameplay going down?" I asked, not expecting an answer as Arthur got out of the bath and headed for town.

"Get the Fancy Pants and a nice shirt, no jacket," Vincent told Matteo. "Everyone will keep asking if you're cold, but ignore them. He's much sexier in his shirtsleeves."

"Got it," Matteo said, as Arthur Morgan strode through town on the lookout for the haberdashery.

The website for the other church was more appealing and user-friendly. After a few clicks I stumbled upon a blog entry from the past week.

Huge thanks to the following parishioners for their donation of used clothes and belongings to our fall rummage sale.
Nancy Booker
Joe and Emilia Simmons
John and Barbara Carpenter
Chloe Forman
The Lord will bless you!

"Bingo," I said. "Found them."

Vincent glanced over. "Really? You did?"

"Church of the Redeemer, 1501 Avenue LaFrance."

"Wow. You are good!"

"Did you even doubt me, Vincent?" I looked up the phone number of the church. "Looks like they're collecting items for a rummage sale. They should still have the stuff. It's a question of getting it. I don't want to wait for the sale."

"No," Vincent said. "We need to get Taylor's things back sooner rather than later."

"I'm going to call the church," I said, standing and moving into the kitchen with my phone while Matteo attempted to dress Arthur Morgan according to Vincent's instructions.

I hit Call on the number for the Church of the Redeemer and, as expected, it went to an automated answering system. I listened to several options and selected number three.

"Thank you for calling the Church of the Redeemer on Avenue LaFrance. This is Father Geoffrey. Please leave your name, phone number and the reason for your call after the beep. I will endeavor to get back to you very shortly. God bless."

"Good evening, Father Geoffrey. My name is Nic Walker and I'm calling to find out if it's possible to buy back a donation of clothes and other items that was made last week. Please return my call at 613-222-4785 when you are able. Thank you."

I hit End Call and set my phone down on the counter. I'd hoped to be able to speak to someone immediately but, of course, it was seven p.m. on a Friday evening. However, while I was pouring myself a glass of water from the fridge, my general ringtone sounded.

I answered.

"Hello. Is this Nic Walker?"

"Yes. Father Geoffrey?"

"Yes, you left a message for me?"

"I did. I'm hoping you can help me with a delicate situation," I said, leaning my elbows on the counter. "You had some items donated last week by some parishioners, and I was wondering whether they had already been separated and sorted or if they were still together?"

Father Geoffrey hesitated. "It's an unusual request."

"Yes, I'm aware."

"I'll be honest with you. The person in charge of processing donations has been off sick, so everything that was dropped off here is still in its original configuration. Can I ask who made the donation?"

"The donation was made by John and Barbara Carpenter, but they don't actually own the items that were donated."

There was a pause. "I'm sorry?"

I cleared my throat. "Those items belong to Taylor Carpenter, their son. There should be a guitar among the items?"

Another pause. "Yes, I remember seeing it. It's a nice guitar," he said. "I did wonder why they were donating such an expensive-looking instrument."

"I want to be honest with you, Father Geoffrey. I'd also like to take advantage of the policy of confidentiality put in place for delicate matters discussed between a priest and a layman."

"Yes, of course."

"Taylor is staying with my family at the moment, because he decided to leave his parents' home and seek shelter elsewhere. He's seventeen years old, and under the laws of Quebec and Ontario, is legally entitled to do so.

"Yes, I understand. That's a shame, but he is entitled to make his own decisions in that regard. I agree."

"Yes, well, the laws also dictate that he is entitled to retrieve his belongings from that home."

"I see."

"However, since all the items have been donated, he was unable to retrieve them."

"I see," said Father Geoffrey. "That doesn't seem quite fair to Taylor."

I closed my eyes and nodded, grateful that he appeared to be sensitive to the issue at hand and perhaps might help me.

"No, it isn't. I would like to get those things for Taylor, and I would purchase those items as a donation to your church, Father Geoffrey."

"But don't they already belong to Taylor?"

"They do. I'm so glad you see it that way. But I would like to make a donation in thanks to you and the church. Do you think a thousand dollars would compensate you for the loss of those items?"

There was a sudden intake of breath. "Mr. Walker, that's a lot of money," the priest said. "Are you sure?"

I smiled, because I was more than sure. "Will it be put to good use in your church? Do you have an outreach program for LGBTQ+ youth, by any remote chance?"

Father Geoffrey cleared his throat, and I did not expect to hear his reply. "We don't. However, I've been hoping to set one up, Mr. Walker. Despite what the Catholic Church officially represents, I've been trying to start one for a few years now. I understand the need because I happen to have a gay relative. Unfortunately, it's a matter of convincing my parishioners and the folks on the administrative board. That has proven to be a challenge," he admitted.

"I'm sure," I said, still rather stunned at Father Geoffrey's 'confession'. "If I donate a grand to your church and designate that it has to go to the new program, will you be able to convince them?"

"I just might," Father Geoffrey said, and I could tell he was smiling. "When would you like to collect Taylor's things, Mr. Walker?"

"As soon as possible. I'll send you an e-transfer for the money tonight if you'll give me the email address for the church finances."

"Thank you, Mr. Walker. I'm glad I could help out with this situation."

"So am I, Father Geoffrey. You have no idea how much of a difference this will make to Taylor's mental health at the moment."

"I can imagine. He's lucky to be staying with you. These young people need to grow up in a positive environment, and if they don't have one at home...well, at any rate. Are you free to pick up his things tomorrow? I can arrange to have them ready for you."

"Yes, we'll come get them tomorrow. Thank you so much, Father Geoffrey." I took down the email address. "Please let me know if you are able to set up the program. I might be able to make an annual donation in that case."

"I will, Mr. Walker. God bless you."

I hit End Call and went to my banking app, sending off a thousand dollars to the church email address. I didn't mind at all if it meant getting Taylor's things back and helping Father Geoffrey start an outreach program for LGBTQ+ youth. Whether he would be successful this time or not, he had the motivation of an annual donation now.

When I went back into the living room, Matteo and Vincent were arguing over whether to go back to Saint Denis and look for the vampire or to the swamp to look for the ghost. I had supposed this game was about outlaws in the old West, but parts of it so far had surprised me. I couldn't deny that Arthur was pretty fucking hot the way they had him dressed, though, and the game's graphics were exceptional.

I whistled. "Helloooo, Arthur. Lookin' good," I said, sitting down in the only space available on the large couch and snaking a hand up the back of Vincent's neck.

"There's supposed to be a vampire here," Vincent said. "Maybe you got here too early."

"But you said to go —" Matteo commented.

"I know, but if you don't get there at the right time, you don't find him," Vincent explained.

"I spoke to the priest at Taylor's parents' church," I said, absently.

Matteo's hands froze on the controller and they both looked at me.

"Already?" Vincent said.

"What happened?" Matteo asked.

I smiled and played with the hair at the nape of Vincent's nape. "I'm donating some money to the church and they're going to give me all his things, which are still in a separate pile in the church's basement."

They exchanged a glance. "You mean, we're getting his stuff back?" Vincent said, stunned.

I nodded.

"All of it?"

"Father Geoffrey seems to think it's all there in one spot. So, yeah."

"How much are you donating to get Taylor's things back, if you don't mind my asking?" Matteo said, regarding me with some suspicion.

"I don't mind you asking, but that's between me and Father Geoffrey. Let's just say he's promised to use the money in a very good way and I'm happy to do it. Plus, we get Taylor's things."

Matteo slowly smiled.

Vincent turned and took my face in his hands. "You are incredible. Do you know how amazing you are? You're like some kind of non-binary superhero or something. I don't know."

"Oh, come on. All I did was phone the priest," I said.

Vincent shook his head. "I didn't even think to try the church. I just assumed they'd already processed the donation. I wouldn't have thought of offering to buy Taylor's stuff back."

"I don't think I even needed to, but I'm happy to give the church the money. Father Geoffrey agreed with me that the items belonged to Taylor and that his parents had no right to donate them."

"You're kidding."

"Nope. Taylor's seventeen years old and the law says he has a right to live where he wants and the right to keep his belongings. I kind of hope Father Geoffrey tells them what happened, although I did ask for confidentiality."

"Wow."

"He's going to try to use my donation to start an outreach program for LGBTQ+ youth, which apparently he's been trying to get going for a while."

Vincent stared at me, looking stunned. "A Catholic priest in Quebec is going to try to start a program like that?"

"He told me he has a gay relative."

"Wow," Vincent said again.

Matteo smiled at me. "Well done, Nic."

I nodded at him. "Thanks, Matteo." I gazed at them both. "Now if you two can just stop playing with the sexy cowboy, maybe we can go upstairs and do some very sinful things to each other before Taylor gets home."

This time I fastened Matteo to the bed and dressed Vincent in a short red negligée and had him explore Matteo's very masculine body with his mouth. When I finally let Vincent suck Matteo's cock, the poor man begged to be allowed to come.

"Vincent, pull off and finish him with your hand. Matteo, let 'er rip."

Vincent sat back and stroked Matteo's cock until he shot with a cry and came over Vincent's fist.

"Oh God," Matteo panted. "Oh Christ," he said, placing his hand on Vincent's. "Thank you...Vincent."

They exchanged a glance as Vincent slid his fingers into Matteo's spunk and spread it over Matteo's belly.

"Use it to jerk off, Vincent. I want to see you come all over him."

Vincent whimpered, swiped up more of Matteo's release with his hand, then lifted the skirt of the negligée and grabbed his cock. Matteo's eyes just about bugged out of his head as Vincent stroked himself to orgasm, shooting spurts of semen onto Matteo's olive skin.

"Oh, fuck," I said, shaking my head in amazement. "You two are so beautiful together."

* * * *

We were back downstairs by nine, in case Taylor came home. Matteo and Vincent resumed their game and I picked up a book to read.

Before he started playing, Matteo slid a hand down Vincent's jean-clad calf and touched the anklet with his finger. "Does this mean anything, or is it simply a pretty adornment?" he asked, with a kind smile. "You don't have to tell me if you don't want to."

Vincent followed Matteo's arm and touched the anklet, sliding his fingers against Matteo's. "It's my collar. It symbolizes the connection between Nic and me — the way we are together."

Matteo nodded and withdrew his hand, but not before giving Vincent's ankle a squeeze. "I like that very much."

At about ten-thirty we heard a key in the door, and it swung open. Taylor came in, shut the door, toed off his boots and walked right past us and up the stairs without a word.

Vincent and I exchanged a glance.

"It's possible he didn't notice us in here," Matteo commented.

"But the lamps are on," I said, standing.

Then I heard a knock at the door. I walked to it and pulled it open.

Taylor's friend, Stacy, stood there with a worried expression on her face and a fountain drink in her hand.

"Taylor forgot his drink..."

I took it. "Thanks, Stacy."

"I didn't actually come to bring his drink. I just...I want to ask you to keep an eye on Taylor. He's not okay," she said, chewing her lip.

I nodded. "He went right upstairs without saying a thing."

Stacy nodded. "He barely said a word all night. I'm really worried."

"So are we, Stacy. We'll take good care of him."

Her gaze flashed up the stairs. "Please go check on him now. I'm nervous what he's going to do, Nic."

My eyes narrowed. "You think he might—" I didn't want to say it. I didn't have to.

Stacy shrugged. "Maybe. I don't know."

"Why don't you come in? I'll go talk to him right now. I might have some information that should make a difference."

Stacy blinked back tears. "Unless you're gonna tell him you got his stuff back from the church..." Her voice trailed off as she read my expression. "Wait a second. Did you?" She grabbed my arm. "Did you get his stuff back?"

"Not yet. But I have an appointment tomorrow to get it. I've already given Father Geoffrey a very generous donation and he's letting us come get Taylor's things tomorrow."

"Oh my God. Thank God. You need to tell him. I'll wait down here."

"Okay," I said, hoping Taylor wasn't about to do something drastic.

Vincent came out of the living room. "Hi, Stacy."

"I'm going upstairs. I'm hoping to bring Taylor down if I can," I said.

Chapter Sixteen

I knocked on Taylor's door, then tried the handle. It was locked.

"Taylor? Hey, I need to talk to you," I said. "Stacy's downstairs. You forgot your Coke."

No answer. My pulse started racing. I knocked again.

"Taylor? Please answer the door. I know you're upset, but I need to talk to you about something."

The door opened quickly, and Taylor stood there, staring at me with an expression of animosity I'd never seen on his face before.

"What, Nic? I'm really tired. Tell Stacy to go home. I just want to go to bed."

I blinked with relief as my pulse slowed down a bit. "Can I come in, please? I need to talk to you, Taylor."

He rolled his eyes, which comforted me in a strange way. If he could find me annoying, then maybe the old Taylor was hovering just beneath the surface.

"It's your house. Sure." He swung the door wide and loped back to the bed, where he collapsed onto his back. He stared at the ceiling, licking his lips over and over. His hands clenched and unclenched as he seemed to be trying to settle himself down.

I stepped into the room and closed the door behind me.

"It's your house too, now."

"No, it isn't. I'm just taking up space."

"Taylor."

"You're gonna kick me out eventually."

"Why do you say that?"

"Nobody wants me, not even you."

I tried to keep a level temper, even though I'd never had anyone talk to me that way before. I knew that escalating the situation by raising my voice might be what Taylor wanted, but I wasn't going to play the game.

"Oh, but I do," I said.

Taylor laughed sharply. "Why? So you can control me? Like you control Vincent and Matteo?"

I stared at him and forced myself to stay calm. "I only control them in the bedroom—and only because they ask me to." I ran a hand over my face. "Trust me. I don't want to control you like that."

He made a frustrated sound. "You don't even want to play around with me? Even a little?"

Now my eyes flew wide. "What?"

"Come on, Nic. Maybe it's just what I need," Taylor whispered, lifting the hem of his shirt up a bit and teasing the short hairs on his happy trail. "It would be a good distraction."

My composure snapped. "I'm going to pretend I didn't hear you proposition me, Taylor, because you're seventeen, a guest in my home and Vincent's cousin. Those are all reasons why this isn't up for discussion."

"Fine. I'll find some twink at a bar tomorrow and bring him home to fuck," Taylor said. "Or I'll ask Daphne to cuff me to the bench in the basement and whip the shit out of me until I can feel something besides whatever" — he stretched his arms out beside him and looked up to the ceiling — "whatever this is."

"I'm getting your stuff back."

My words hung in the air between us for a long moment, but Taylor didn't move.

"You can't get my stuff —"

"I talked to Father Geoffrey on the phone. We're going to get your stuff tomorrow."

Taylor swallowed and kept staring at the ceiling. He didn't speak for a few moments. "He won't give it to you. What makes you think he will?"

I circled Taylor's ankle with gentle fingers and applied a light pressure, so he knew I had him. I'd keep him grounded if it killed me.

"The money I sent the church as a donation. He's already accepted my e-transfer."

Taylor lay there, breathing hard, like he'd just ended a marathon. Slowly, his gaze shifted from the ceiling to my face. "You gave them a donation?"

"Yeah."

"So...so I can get my stuff back?"

I smiled. "Yeah."

He stared at me, disbelief still evident, but there was hope dawning there, too.

"Father Geoffrey's a pretty cool guy, actually. He didn't even want a donation, but I was happy to make one. He agreed with me that those things are yours and you should have them back."

Taylor blinked in confusion. "But...my parents..."

"...don't run the church, Taylor. They may think they do, but they don't. It's Father Geoffrey's church, not theirs."

Taylor nodded.

"I'm giving the church a thousand dollars for your things because that's at least what they're worth materially, and they're much more valuable than that in terms of your existence and your future. You need those things. They belong to you."

"Yeah," he said, "I need those things."

"I know you tried to act like it was nothing. But the way your parents did what they did... That was not cool. It was cruel and heartless, and the only way to make up for that was to reverse it somehow."

"Nic, I—" Taylor said, then shook as he gave up trying to hold back his emotion.

"Hey, it's okay. You know I've seen men cry before," I said with a little smile.

He nodded, letting the tears stream silently down his cheeks as I squeezed his ankle.

"Usually it's for different reasons, but it doesn't matter. You cis-guys are all the same. You try to be so tough, like nothing touches you. You bottle things up so tight you're gonna explode or you're gonna do something drastic because" —I took a deep breath and let it out in a sigh. I shook my head—"nobody can live like that."

Taylor sat up and threw his arms around me, holding tight to me like I was an anchor and he was a boat that a storm was trying to take. The relief and love I felt for this kid took me by surprise, and I realized how much it *didn't* suck to have a younger person listen to my wisdom and absorb it or that I could do something that might change a person's life—improve it, make it better.

"You know, Father Geoffrey says he's gonna use the donation to start an LGBTQ+ outreach program at the church, for youth who are struggling because their families don't understand."

Taylor snuffled into my shoulder, nodding.

"Won't that be a nice way to flip your parents off?"

His sniffles turned to laughter as he realized what I was saying.

"Can you imagine? Their own church reaching out to kids like you. It's gonna make them apoplectic."

"Thank you. Thank you for doing this, Nic."

"Hey, I just need things to get back to normal around here. I miss your wisecracks and your inappropriate interest in the kinky goings-on in this place."

Taylor nodded, smiling now. "Okay. Fine."

"But if you ever proposition me again, I will have Vincent take you over his knee and give you a spanking. and it won't be sexy at all, just very painful and embarrassing."

"Ew," Taylor said. "No thanks."

"Then behave yourself. And come down with me so I can show the others you're gonna be okay."

I let Taylor clean his face up a bit in the bathroom before we headed downstairs.

"Hey," he said, as we entered the living room and all eyes turned to him.

Stacy smiled and held out the fountain drink. "You forgot your Coke. I thought you might want to have it."

Taylor smiled back and took it. "Thanks. I'm sorry I was such a bummer tonight."

Stacy blushed and shrugged. "It's not a problem, Tay. I was just worried about you." She rubbed him gently on the arm. "Nic said he's getting your things?"

Taylor gazed at me with gratitude, then turned to the others. "Yeah. We're getting my stuff tomorrow. Right?"

I nodded. "Right."

"That's amazing. You deserve to have your stuff, Taylor. Your parents are fucking assholes."

Taylor nodded as Vincent came over and gathered him into a hug. "You okay?"

"I think so. I feel a lot better now."

"Good. Y'know, my mom never really told me how fanatical her brother was, but whenever your dad came up in conversation, she would just roll her eyes and not want to talk about him. I can see why. My mom wasn't religious at all. My dad used to say my mom was so laid back she was almost horizontal."

Taylor huffed a laugh.

"Anyway, it's too bad you got stuck with the crappy side of the family."

Vincent let go of Taylor and he sat down beside Matteo. "Sorry I missed so much of your cooking this week, Matteo. Hopefully I'll start feeling hungry again."

Matteo smiled at Taylor warmly. "I hope so, Taylor. Let me know some of your favorite meals and I'll make them."

Taylor stared at him, seeming like he might cry again, but he held it back. "Thanks, man. You're literally the best, Matteo. Are you playing Red Dead now, too?"

Matteo nodded, gesturing to where Arthur Morgan was riding his horse along a mountain trail. "Vincent's teaching me, since he can't work the controller. I have a verifiable boner for Arthur now."

Taylor smirked knowingly. "Don't we all, Matteo. Don't we all."

* * * *

I took Matteo with me to get Taylor's things at the church. Even though Saturdays were his day off from his service at my place, he wanted to help, and I thought Vincent should stay home with his cousin.

Taylor seemed much improved and more optimistic, but I didn't think he'd truly believe he was getting his stuff back until he saw it all. He'd given me a list of the really important things he wanted returned, in case there was any sort of mix-up at the church. On the list was his guitar, a PlayStation, a brown leather jacket, a MacBook Air and two sets of gaming headphones.

When Matteo and I got to the church, Father Geoffrey met us at the door.

"Nic, it's wonderful to meet you. I'm so glad you called me."

"So am I, Father," I said, shaking his offered hand. There was a blip of confusion as he took in my appearance and tried to figure out if I was a man or a woman, but it didn't last very long, and his smile was genuine.

"This is my friend, Matteo."

Father Geoffrey and Matteo exchanged greetings and the priest took us down to the basement where he had Taylor's things on a table.

"This should be all of it. If there's anything missing, tell Taylor to let me know and I'll try to find it."

I noticed the guitar and the laptop, and Matteo found the PlayStation, some controllers and the headphones. There were a couple of boxes of clothes and the jacket was on the top inside one of them.

"This looks like what we need," I said. "Thanks again, Father. You don't know how much it means to Taylor to get his things back."

"I assure you, I do. I wish all the members of my flock thought the same as me on these issues. I'm trying to make changes in this church, but there are a lot of outdated attitudes still prevalent."

I nodded. "Good luck with the program you want to start, Father. Please keep me updated and let me know if you need any help from me, either financial or practical. We don't really want to mix with your congregation for obvious reasons, but if there's anything I can do remotely for you, let me know."

Father Geoffrey shook my hand again, curling his other around it and giving me a warm look of sincere affection. "You're a good man, Nic Walker. Thank you."

"Nah, I'm just an old softie. Can't stand to see a kid upset."

Father Geoffrey laughed. "I'll help you get this stuff into your car."

The three of us loaded up the car and I drove home, stopping to pick up coffees from Tim Hortons on the way.

Taylor was ecstatic to unpack his things. Matteo and I brought everything in and took it upstairs so he could go through it in private and organize it all.

"I hope it's all there. Father Geoffrey said to let him know if you're missing anything and he'll look around for it."

"Okay, thanks. I think it's all here, though. I didn't have much, which is why I wanted it back."

"Oh, and Taylor? Whenever you're ready, we'd love to hear you play."

* * * *

Sunday passed uneventfully, and Taylor seemed more himself than he had all week. I wasn't so worried about him anymore. He even made some smart-ass remarks that made me laugh a few times. I'd told him to let me know if the anxiety didn't reduce and I would make him an appointment with my doctor.

At work on Monday, I wasn't distracted by my worry about him or Vincent, and I knew Matteo would be here to make supper and possibly come upstairs with us afterward, although I'd planned to hang out with Taylor a couple of evenings this week.

Watching Matteo and Vincent play Red Dead Redemption was not an unpleasant way to spend some time. Now that Taylor was more engaged, perhaps he could take over when Matteo found himself frustrated with the complex game controls. I had a feeling Taylor had crushed this game years ago.

It was wonderful to find Taylor and Matteo in the kitchen prepping supper when I arrived home. Matteo met my gaze and nodded with a smile. "Welcome home, Sir. How was your day?"

"Busy. Yours?"

He shrugged. "It's getting better now."

"What are you making?" I asked, putting down my messenger bag and moving into the kitchen.

"It's tacos," Taylor said cheerfully, and I was pleased to see him somewhat revived.

"Nice! Where's Vincent?"

Taylor inclined his head toward the stairs. "In the bedroom folding the laundry, even though I said I'd do it."

I rolled my eyes. "That man should be punished."

"That's what I told him you'd say when you found out. He didn't listen."

"I'll make him listen." I winked at Taylor.

"Yeah, I bet. Maybe that's why he's doing it," Taylor said with a smile.

I laughed. "Maybe. Although it's probably more that he can't sit still. That's why he enjoys bondage so much."

"TMI," Taylor said and put his hands over his ears as I laughed even louder.

I headed upstairs in a fantastic mood and found Vincent sitting on the edge of our bed beside a pile of badly folded shirts and towels. I sat beside him and took his good hand gently in mine. He let me lace our fingers together.

"You know, Vincent, it's okay that you can't fold laundry properly right now."

He regarded me out of helpless and dejected blue eyes. "Then why do I feel so useless?"

I smiled gently. "You were awfully useful to me last night."

He blushed. "I know. Thank goodness I can still do *that*." He looked at his feet, then glanced up through his lashes. "Are you going to put me to good use tonight?"

I smoothed the tawny hair from his forehead. "Oh, most definitely."

He nodded. "Good. I need to feel used. I mean, useful."

He gave me a little grin and I squeezed his hand. Vincent stared at me with a weird, emotional look on his face.

"What?" I asked.

"You. You're such a sweetheart."

I frowned. "I...really don't like that term."

Vincent laughed. "Okay, then. You're a badass, Nic Walker. A badass with a big, mushy, kinky heart."

"Fine. Have it your way."

"The sub is always in charge," he murmured, kissing my cheek.

"You don't need to tell me that," I said with emphasis.

He took my chin in his hand and pressed his lips to mine, keeping up a soft pressure that melted my resolve. I slipped my fingers behind his neck and opened my mouth to his gentle and thorough attention.

We made it downstairs eventually.

The tacos were a hit.

While we ate, Taylor dropped this bombshell.

"I said I'd help Daphne out after supper."

I stopped eating, my second taco halfway to my mouth.

Vincent put his down and stared at Taylor. "Help Daphne with what?"

Taylor shrugged. "I think just holding stuff or passing her what she needs. Nothing really involved..."

"Did she ask you to help out?" I said as Matteo watched Taylor with a curious gaze.

Taylor shook his head. "I offered. I need something to do, Nic. I'm bored out of my mind."

"I'm pretty sure there's a legal issue here," Vincent said.

Taylor sat up straighter. "I'm seventeen. The age of consent is sixteen. Besides, I'm not going to be that involved — and Daphne doesn't have sex with her clients."

I put my taco down. "The problem is, I'm probably already violating zoning regulations with this set-up. I don't want to get into trouble."

"I'm not going to tell anyone," Taylor said.

"Perhaps Taylor could wear a disguise of some kind," Matteo suggested, "so he doesn't look as young as he is — and nobody would be able to identify him."

I turned to Vincent. "What do you think?"

Vincent regarded Taylor, who stared back at him with a low-key challenge in his gaze. "I mean, it's a little weird, but I'm not gonna tell him he can't."

"I think Matteo's suggestion is a good one," I said.

"What about the pup hood?" Vincent said. "If Taylor wears that, nobody will be able to ID him. Since his face will be hidden, it won't be obvious exactly *how* young he is."

"Wait a second. You have a pup hood?" Taylor asked, sounding impressed and surprised.

"Yes. I bought if for Vincent before I realized he preferred to be a kitten when we were going to play that game."

"Good God," Matteo whispered.

"I don't think Taylor needs to know that," Vincent mumbled, his cheeks flushing.

Taylor regarded Vincent with a smile as he crossed his arms and nodded. "Meow."

"It's an expensive leather hood. I'd be glad to have someone use it," I said.

"I'd have to see it before I agree to wear it," Taylor said. "And try it on. What if I look stupid?"

"You won't look stupid," Matteo said. "You'll be adorable."

Taylor winked at Matteo. "Well, now."

Matteo stood and began to gather the plates.

"Vincent, why don't you take Taylor upstairs and let him try on the hood?" I suggested, since supper was over.

Vincent nodded. It was the best way to keep Taylor's identity a secret. There was no way I was letting Daphne's clients see him without a face covering of some kind. I wasn't quite comfortable with him helping her out, but he was an adult and could decide that for himself. I tried to shake the feeling I was corrupting an innocent, then remembered he'd seen worse on the Internet by now. I trusted Daphne wouldn't get him to do anything inappropriate. At least, I didn't think so. *Perhaps I should take her aside and set some ground rules.*

I went to the top of the basement stairs and knocked loudly on the open door. "Daphne? Sorry to disturb you, but I need to talk to you for a moment."

A man's loud squeal came before Daphne yelled up. "One second!"

I waited while she'd finished, then her pretty face appeared at the bottom of the stairs. I crooked my finger because I didn't want to shout.

Daphne turned and said, "Just you wait quietly until I get back — or I'll punish you severely."

She carefully climbed the stairs in her fancy heels. "What can I do for you, Nic? Does that boy of yours need a spanking?"

I grinned. "Probably...but that's my business." I beckoned her closer. "Taylor told me you asked him to help you out down there."

At least she had the grace to look a little guilty. "I might have."

I narrowed my eyebrows at her. "Daphne…"

"What? The poor kid needs something to take his mind off his loser parents. What better way than helping me whip some attractive men into submission?"

"I'm sure there's something better he could be doing."

Daphne put a hand on her hip. "Really? You and Vincent and Matteo are kinking it up on a regular basis, which is awesome, but poor Taylor is left to play video games or surf the Internet. Let me keep him busy and entertained, Nic. I can use the help, and he can learn about safe kink practices and respecting peoples' fetishes."

I pretended to think it over, even though I'd already decided it wasn't my decision. "I'm going to make him wear Vincent's pup hood. It's important he not be identified, especially considering his age."

Her eyes lit up like party lights. "Oh, that's a fantastic idea! I get my own little pup helper. He's going to look adorable."

"I need to set some ground rules."

"Okay. Sure."

I narrowed my eyes. "He doesn't touch them, and they don't touch him."

Daphne inclined her head. "Right. I already told him that."

"Good. He doesn't take off the hood in anyone's presence but yours."

"Makes sense," Daphne nodded.

"He doesn't let anyone know he lives here."

Daphne gave me an appraising look. "Have you and Vincent discussed having children?"

"*What?*" *How could she know we just had that conversation?*

"You're giving off major Dad vibes right now, and it looks good on you, Nic."

I narrowed my eyes. "If I were Taylor's father, I definitely wouldn't let him do this."

"He's seventeen. He can make his own choices."

I sighed and crossed my arms, leaning against the door frame. "Nevertheless. This is my home and you're already taking incredible liberties with it."

Daphne smiled kindly. "I know I am. And I appreciate you letting me use this space so much. I will be out by this weekend, I promise."

I closed my eyes. "I thought you said by Thursday."

"Well, the thing is, we need to move all this stuff back to my place, so I figured we could get everyone to help out on Saturday morning."

I held up my hand. "Fine. Okay. No problem."

She gave me the wide, dimpled smile she was known for — the reward for good behavior her clients aimed to achieve. "Nic, you are amazing. I appreciate this so much."

"Sure. Okay."

"I have to get back to Alex now. He was ready to come when you called, but now he has to wait longer, which falls perfectly into my plan." She grinned.

I saluted and turned away.

"Send Taylor down whenever he's ready," she called.

"Yep. No problem."

This had turned into a very weird day.

As I walked back to the kitchen, Vincent and Taylor came down the stairs.

"Jesus fucking Christ," I said.

"What?" Taylor said, his voice echoing inside the leather hood as his hazel eyes regarded me curiously.

"I think jeans and a tight T-shirt would have worked just fine," I said tersely.

"I would have felt overdressed," Taylor said. He wore a snug pair of fire-engine-red boxer briefs, scuffed Timberland boots with work socks and a black crop top that showed off his pierced navel.

"Whatever," I said, shaking my head.

Matteo cleared his throat. "I think you look lovely, Taylor. The men down there will eat you up."

"Aren't they mostly straight?" Taylor said.

"Perhaps, mostly," Matteo said.

"The people who engage in this kind of play often don't define their sexuality as rigidly as the rest of the world," I said. "I imagine you'll turn a few heads."

"Oh goody," Taylor said. "That's going to make it even more fun!"

"Plus, Daphne will definitely want to eat you up. But she'll behave herself because I've told her to."

"I have no issue with that," Taylor said.

"Uh-huh," I said, grinning in spite of myself. "Be a good boy, Taylor."

"I will be the very *best* boy, Nic," he remarked, as he headed for the basement stairs.

Chapter Seventeen

By Friday evening, Taylor was regaling us with tales of his adventures in my dungeon basement over Matteo's expertly cooked supper. His vibrant personality had returned, along with an undiminished curiosity about kink and related subjects, which I'd prefer any day over the morose depression that had previously taken hold.

"Daphne is the shit! The way she knows just what to do to get these guys off? It's wild."

Vincent cleared his throat and avoided Taylor's gaze. He knew exactly how good Daphne was at her job. He'd had first-hand experience.

Matteo wasn't as circumspect as Vincent. "Yes, she's good at what she does," he said, dishing salad onto his plate.

"Good?" Taylor scoffed. "She's a fucking queen. It's so much fun helping her out."

"I'm glad you're enjoying yourself," I said.

"You were right about the pup hood. They were eating me up."

"It was probably the boxer briefs and crop top," I said. "But, sure."

"Anyway, I've never seen guys come so hard, except in porn. They definitely get what they're paying for." Taylor grinned.

"Yes. Daphne does ensure her clients are satisfied."

"Do you know what she calls me?" Taylor asked with a smug grin.

I closed my eyes. "As long as it's not your real name, I'm happy."

"Oh, it's not. It's 'Sparky'."

Vincent grinned and shook his head.

"She calls you 'Sparky'?" I asked.

"Yeah. The first scene I helped with was an electro one."

I nodded. "Well, settle down and eat your dinner, Sparky. Are you helping Daphne out again tonight?"

"Are you kidding? Yeah. This beats video games any day."

I couldn't help laughing. Taylor's mood had definitely improved. If helping Daphne out made him this happy, I wouldn't complain. I caught Vincent's gaze. He shrugged and rolled his eyes, but he tried not to smile.

* * * *

Daphne confirmed that she would be moving her dungeon equipment back to her house. The renovations were more or less completed, and she was eager to set up her new space.

We convened on Saturday — Me, Vincent, Taylor, Matteo and Daphne — to move all the gear out of the basement. Vincent directed and managed the endeavor, since he couldn't help with carrying anything.

Daphne had borrowed a van from someone, and between the five of us, we got everything loaded up in the space of an hour and drove to Daphne's townhome on Besserer Street in Lower Town.

"Holy fuck, Daphne. This is incredible!" I said, when I saw the newly renovated space.

"I know, right? Worth the inconvenience of having me dungeoning out of your place for weeks?"

I cocked my head, my gaze flying around the room, landing on various spots of interest. "Hmm. I see an opportunity here. Are you willing to let me use this space sometime during your off-peak hours?"

Daphne smiled. "Of course!" She eyed Vincent and Matteo. "You three could get up to all kinds of fun stuff here. We'll arrange it. I think that would be a great way for me to pay you back for your kindness, Nic."

"Excellent," I said, clapping my hands together and grinning at my two sex partners. "What do you think? Want to try a scene or two over here sometime?"

"Sure," Vincent said, gazing at the large shower stall with hoses and nozzles coming from everywhere, his eyes like saucers.

Matteo nodded. "Whatever you like, Sir. I'm happy to accommodate you."

Daphne squeezed Matteo's arm. "I knew you'd be the perfect person for these two, Matteo. I'm so happy, considering the circumstances."

"Thank you for thinking of me, Mistress," Matteo said, bowing his head and accepting Daphne's kiss to his cheek.

After supper that evening, Vincent and I sat down with Matteo and asked him if he'd provide his domestic services for another week or two, at which point Vincent would be able to resume his regular duties on a relaxed schedule.

"Yes, of course. Service is what I live for. I can also keep making dinner for you a couple of nights a week while he's easing back into things, if you'd like."

"Matteo, that would be wonderful. Then we'd be assured of seeing you regularly." I glanced at Vincent, then at Matteo again. "How do you feel about what we're doing together upstairs, Matteo? Is it working out for you? Because I'm enjoying it very much, and I believe Vincent is as well. But we need to make sure it's working for all of us if we're going to keep going."

"Yes, that makes sense. I'm very happy with what's going on upstairs between the three of us." He leaned forward with his elbows on his knees. "Once Vincent's hand is better, he can help me prepare supper and I can teach him all my kitchen tricks, including how to chop vegetables safely."

We laughed and Vincent smiled. "I'm looking forward to that. I'm sure you can show me a few things, Matteo, in the kitchen as well as in the bedroom."

Vincent held Matteo's gaze and something meaningful passed between them. I was beginning to suspect they were developing more than a physical interest in each other.

* * * *

Sunday was Matteo's day off, so I threw together a batch of pancakes for the three of us. We sat at the kitchen table in sweatpants and T-shirts, relaxing.

"Wow, these are not that bad," Taylor commented, chewing.

"Can you even taste the pancake under all that syrup?" Vincent asked.

Taylor nodded. "I can, and it's delicious. I didn't know Nic could cook."

I raised my eyebrows. "I can do just about anything, Taylor. But it's only pancakes."

"Only pancakes, he says." Taylor rolled his eyes and swallowed, then cut himself another piece.

"I was wondering if you'd play your guitar for us sometime today, Taylor," I said, hooking another pancake with my fork and slapping it onto my plate.

His gaze went back and forth between me and Vincent. "Okay," he said, finally. "I'll get my guitar after breakfast."

Taylor brought his instrument down when we were finished and sat in the chair at the table, tuning it carefully while we waited and watched. Finally, he looked up, a flush of embarrassment in his cheeks.

"What do you want? Something lively or something soft?"

"Soft," Vincent said. "It's ten in the morning." He sipped his coffee, looking adorably rumpled and still sleepy.

"No problem," Taylor said with a smile.

He looked at his feet as he strummed a gentle melody, then began to sing. His voice came hesitantly at first, then strengthened. It took a moment for me to recognize the Leonard Cohen song, because the smooth tenor sounded so different from the gravelly bass of the original singer. Taylor's voice, so sweet and melodic, lent the song an ethereal beauty the original lacked.

Vincent stared, gobsmacked, at Taylor as the young man sang gazing at the floor.

When he'd finished, he waited a moment, then lifted his gaze and met mine with a curious expression.

"God," I said. "Taylor, that was lovely. That, right there, was worth the money I donated to the church."

Vincent clapped softly. "Taylor, that was beautiful."

Taylor blushed and shrugged. "It's just a hobby. But I love to play."

"That's evident. You're literally glowing," I said.

"Am I?"

"Yes," Vincent affirmed. "Play another. Please."

"Okay."

Taylor played a couple more songs, both as sweet and gentle as that first one, then coughed and leaned the guitar against the counter. "Is there any coffee left?"

I topped up Taylor's mug and slid the sugar and milk over.

"Have you learned any piano?" I asked Taylor as Vincent shot me a warning look.

Taylor spooned some sugar into his coffee. "No."

"Would you like to learn?"

Vincent cleared his throat as Taylor lifted the mug to his lips.

I crossed my arms and glared at Vincent. "I am perfectly capable of not turning a piano lesson into a form of sex play."

Taylor sputtered and coughed before setting his mug down. "Wait, what? *What*?"

"Fine," Vincent said mildly. "I hope so."

I smiled at Taylor. "I used Vincent's piano lessons as a gateway to getting kinky with him. And now his lessons are still a form of foreplay for us on occasion."

Taylor's gaze swung back and forth between us. "You kinky shits."

Vincent's cheeks reddened.

I smiled. "Well, Taylor, if you'd like to begin some chaste and non-kinky lessons, I'm perfectly happy to teach you."

"Seriously, Nic?" Taylor said, using a napkin to wipe coffee off his chin. "You've done so much for me already. I can't ask you to give me free piano lessons, too."

"You're not asking, Taylor. I'm offering. It's something I'd enjoy doing."

He raised his eyebrow.

"Yes, I enjoy giving regular piano lessons as well as kinky ones—in a different, but equally valid, way." I smiled innocently and sipped my coffee.

"Fine," he said, laughing. "I'd love to learn to play."

"Awesome," I said, grinning.

"Fantastic," Vincent said, rolling his eyes.

"Worried I won't have time for *kinky* lessons with you, boy?" I said archly. "Don't be concerned about that. Now that your hand is healing, I think kinky piano lessons should resume with some regularity. That kind of exercise is the perfect thing for your nerves to repair themselves."

"Fine," Vincent said with a smile.

Taylor huffed out a laugh and shook his head. "You two are insane. But you're also awesome. By the way, I told Daphne I'd help her out on the weekends in her new dungeon."

"Oh, yeah?" I said. "You really have an interest in what she does?"

He nodded. "I do. I think sex workers should be part of the health care system, honestly," he said.

I smiled. "I agree. It's a shame the job is so taboo."

"I think she's an artist," Taylor said. "There is magic in what she does."

I gave Taylor a slow, appreciative smile. "I'd have to agree with you there."

After breakfast, Taylor went upstairs and Vincent helped to tidy the kitchen.

I was excited to have my basement dungeon back and was in a great mood. The others had helped return the things we'd put in my bedroom back to their designated spots downstairs.

As we finished cleaning up, I flicked Vincent with the dish towel. "Are you up for a scene in the basement this afternoon? Just you and me?"

He flashed me a bashful smile. "I thought you'd never ask."

He followed me down the stairs, then immediately stripped and got into a submissive position.

I'd never put Vincent on the St. Andrew's cross and I'd told Daphne not to use it for her clients. He liked the spanking bench so much that we'd made do with that, then Daphne had taken over the basement.

"How do you feel about a lengthy edging session to break in the space again?" I asked as he knelt on the wood floor, naked and trembling with anticipation.

"Good, Sir."

I walked over and ran my hand across his cheek, cupping his chin in my palm and tilting his face to me. The heated floor felt nice on my bare feet, my favorite scene-jeans soft and familiar. I'd opted for a tight black tank, so Vincent could see my tiny breasts and erect nipples. It felt wonderful to have our dungeon back.

I smiled down at him. "I'm putting you on the cross."

He inhaled and began to turn his head to look at the imposing wooden structure, then remembered his place and kept his gaze on mine. "Yes, Sir."

"Stand and walk over to it," I said as I released him.

He stood gracefully and padded over to where the polished wooden beams made an X against the wall. I backed him up against it.

"Face forward," I said, moving close. "Arms up."

I attached his wrists and ankles to splay him there for my delectation. I covered his eyes with the lacy blindfold I'd brought from the bedroom and gagged him with the phallus gag.

"Comfy?" I asked with a smirk.

He groaned and pulled at his wrist cuffs.

"I thought so. If you need to safe-signal me, make a controlled noise repeatedly and hold up two fingers."

Vincent nodded, his cheeks flushed, lips slack around the gag. I knew the phallus gag made him vulnerable and the position in which I'd bound him gave me access to whatever part of him I wanted to torment.

I looked him over, admiring his smooth, pale skin and the way his lean muscles curved and defined themselves. He had shapely legs and, of course, his ass was spectacular, although mostly hidden against the cross. His erect cock jutted proudly upward.

I reached a finger out to trace the line of its underside. Vincent gasped when I made contact and whimpered as I followed its arch over his foreskin to the tip of his protruding glans, just as a bead of fluid leaked out.

"Beautiful," I whispered, bending to taste it.

Vincent cried out as I ran the flat of my tongue over him, his body tense. I smacked my lips together and moved away.

"Good boy. I'll be right back."

He whimpered as I found what I needed. I brought the long string of anal beads and the bottle of lube with me as I approached again. I slicked up the beads and slid two fingers behind Vincent's balls and into his crack.

He moaned as I rubbed the slippery liquid on his hole and pushed my fingers inside.

"Relax," I said gently as I withdrew them and pressed the top bead against him.

He did as I'd asked and relaxed, so I was able to push the first two into him. He made the most delicious noises as I introduced beads three, four and five. When he had taken six, I stopped and let the remaining four beads dangle from his ass. *What a delicious sight!*

"Oh, baby, you look so good."

I nudged the string of remaining beads so it swayed back and forth. "We'll save these for later."

Chapter Eighteen

Vincent groaned as I picked up the crop and tapped the tip against his erection.

"Still so hard." I shook my head as if I regretted how priapic Vincent was. "Always so hard. How do those beads feel?"

Vincent gasped and shuddered, his cock twitching.

"Perfect." I teased him with the crop for close to half an hour, running it along his body in all the sensitive spots and bringing it down harshly where I knew he liked the sting, talking to him about all the dirty things he enjoyed and how naughty that made him.

When I finally let up, his skin was covered in a sheen of sweat and he was breathing hard, so aroused that I knew he'd come in a second if I touched him just right.

But why on earth would I do that?

I put down the crop and moved close, taking my time to shove the remaining four beads up his rectum while he moaned with the pleasure and humiliation of it. I was careful not to touch his dick and immediately stepped back when I was done.

"Stuffed. Stuffed and horny. I'd keep you like this forever if I could," I said. "Strung out on a high of endorphins and testosterone, ready to explode from one touch, one word, one slap."

Vincent struggled and groaned, his dick reaching for something it couldn't find.

I slipped the tip of the crop under his balls, tickled them with it, slid it behind and tapped his ass.

Vincent whined in erotic agony as his body contracted around the invasive rubber. All ten beads were inside his body—only the handle was left and it fit snugly between his cheeks. The thought of how he must feel with that bead-snake inside him made me wetter than anything.

"We're gonna play a little game, Vincent."

He groaned louder. He knew what a sadist I was.

I moved in close and pressed my hand firmly on his belly behind his astonishingly erect cock, careful not to touch it.

"I'm going to pull on one bead at a time, and you are going to try not to come until the entire string is out."

He sighed, likely as he realized how difficult that would be. Although the balls on this string were smaller than some I used, each removal would cause involuntary muscle contractions that could—and would—result in an orgasm...eventually.

I wasn't going to touch his cock—at least, not with my hands. I had something up my sleeve if he made it through the first few extractions without exploding.

"Ready, sweetheart?" I asked.

He puffed out a breath and nodded slowly, his forehead creasing with the effort of retaining control of his body. And it was only going to get harder.

I snuck two fingers between his legs and grasped the handle of the bead-string. He let out a moan before I even started pulling, and when the first ball popped out, he gave a shuddering sigh. His dick seemed to surge as additional fluid pushed out of its tip.

"Good boy. Very good boy. Hold on to that orgasm. I know you can do it."

Vincent's body shook and his gasps increased as I pulled the next one out. He moaned, long and low, as his thighs tensed and he almost lost it. The same thing happened when I pulled the third bead from him. I glowed with pride as my boy held off with herculean strength and mind-over-body levels of control.

"Very nice."

But I was tired and wanted to be done. And I needed to watch him fly apart without meaning to.

Moving quickly and quietly, I grabbed the crop from the table and slapped his dick with the leather end of it, twice.

He froze, his body stiffening as his dick probably wondered what to do with this sudden sensation. Then he let out a scream and came hard, jizz shooting out of him. I reached around and pulled the remaining beads out of his body as his orgasm expanded and Vincent's hoarse cries increased in volume.

What a sight to see him come undone like this, completely overtaken by his body's need and response to me! He rocked against his restraints as more jizz oozed from his stiff cock in soft spurts of pleasure and I watched, spellbound, as he jerked his head back and hit the cushioned spot on the wall behind him. I'd installed that padded square specifically for this kind of occurrence. Vincent didn't need a concussion, after everything else that had happened. As his orgasm subsided, he breathed in short gasps and cried with release and surrender as I kissed his neck and rubbed his arms.

"Ah, what a beautiful, beautiful boy, coming for me like that," I said. "I'm so glad to have you back to myself and able to worship you in this space again."

"Sir... Oh, God, Sir... Please...do that again... tomorrow."

I laughed with glee, because I would do it tomorrow and the next day, and the next, until he begged me to do something else. I loved dominating Vincent, and I cherished the way he responded to me.

"I bet Matteo would like to be a fly on the wall for this sometime."

Vincent emitted an exhausted sigh and a shudder of agreement as I began to unbuckle his restraints.

Once he was down, I had him crawl on all fours to the spanking bench. I took off my jeans and straddled him as he obediently got me off three times with his mouth and tongue as I clutched his hair with one hand and the bench with the other.

* * * *

I had booked Monday off work so I could take Vincent to get his bandages off at the hospital.

The place was crowded and he didn't get in on time, but when he came out of the doctor's office, he appeared cheerful and lifted his hand, showing me that he could move his thumb and first finger back and forth.

"What did the doctor say?" I asked.

"She was pleased with how it's healed. Says I did a good job not using it too much and letting the skin and muscles knit properly."

"What's the prognosis?"

"I'm supposed to use it gently this week and next, and by then it should be fully functional and I can stop babying it," he explained happily.

"That's great!" I said, wrapping my arm around him.

"Yeah, it feels so good to have the bandages off."

"I'll bet."

As we walked through the hospital and exited into the sunny day, Vincent flexed his hand again and said, "It's wild what one small accident in the kitchen can do to mess up your life."

"True," I nodded, leading the way to where we'd parked the car. "But we wouldn't have met Matteo if you hadn't sliced your hand open. Right?"

Vincent stopped. "God, that's true. I'm not exactly happy it happened, because I never want to go through that again. But since it did happen, I'm glad Daphne sent us Matteo."

We walked on silently for a little while. I'd parked on a side street in order to avoid the exorbitant parking fees in the hospital lots.

"Why don't we have a scene with Matteo in the basement, now that we have it back? He's never been with us down there," Vincent suggested.

I smiled. "I was thinking the same thing. In fact, I'd like to have you kitted out in some of your sexy lingerie, if that sounds good? Matteo hasn't seen you in your fancier things yet."

Vincent blushed and smiled. "No, he hasn't."

I took Vincent's unbandaged hand gently in mine. "And that's a damn shame."

Matteo looked surprised when I answered the door to his arrival, since I was normally still at work when he got here.

"Hello, Nic. Did you take the day off?"

"Yes, I drove Vincent to get his bandages off."

"I forgot about that. How did it go?" Matteo asked, slipping off his boots and putting his slippers on.

"The doctor says his hand is healing well. Vincent is happy to have those unfashionable bandages off."

Matteo laughed softly. "He didn't like the way they made his hand look."

"Yes, our Vincent likes to be pretty, you know. Then again, you don't *really* know, do you?"

Matteo raised his eyebrows. "Well…I did pick out a pretty pair of panties for him that first scene. And I seem to remember he had a drawer full of them. Also, the negligée he wore that other time looked lovely on him."

"Vincent would like you to see how he looks in some of his more elaborate finery, if you're up for it tonight? Taylor's going over to help Daphne after supper."

Matteo closed his eyes and swallowed, nodding. When he opened them, they blazed with desire.

"Oh, yes, Sir. I can assure you I am *up* for it. Most definitely."

"Good. What were you planning for supper?"

"Just a light stir fry — chicken and vegetables."

I put my hand to my chest in shock. "But stir fry isn't Italian, Matteo!"

He grinned wryly. "I'm not a one-trick pony, you know."

I winked. "Glad to hear it. And that's perfect for tonight if we're going to have an intense scene."

"Intense?" he said, voice deep with desire.

"Oh yes. We should celebrate those ugly bandages coming off, now, shouldn't we?"

Vincent helped Matteo prepare supper, since Taylor wanted to practice a song on his guitar. He was getting something ready to play for Matteo.

Watching the love of my life and our occasional play-partner — who was becoming more of an integral member of our little family — work cheerfully to prepare dinner made my sentimental old heart happy. Vincent seemed pleased to be able to help and hadn't been scared off using knives and other kitchen gear by his unfortunate mishap. Matteo gave him some safety tips and other helpful advice as they worked.

I felt the sexual tension in the air, too, through seemingly offhand gazes and innocent touches as they moved about the room. Surprisingly, perhaps, I felt no jealousy, just an appreciation of Vincent's fluid sexuality and Matteo's kind and solicitous care.

When supper was ready to serve, we called Taylor down. He descended the stairs with a grin on his face and asked if he could play the song he'd been practicing before we sat down to eat.

"It's up to Matteo and Vincent," I said, "since they prepared the meal."

Matteo inclined his head. "That's fine, Taylor. I'm excited to hear what you have for us, since I didn't get to hear you play earlier."

Taylor nodded, pulling his chair out and sitting down with his guitar on his lap. He peeked at Matteo through his lashes. "This one's for you, Matteo. I know it's one of your favorites."

As he began to play, I recognized the melody, but it wasn't until he began to sing that I recognized the melancholy Beatles song, *While My Guitar Gently Weeps*.

Matteo seemed as impressed by Taylor's guitar and vocal talent as we had been. He blinked back emotion as he smiled and clapped when the song was over. "Amazing. And so beautiful. You have a wonderful talent, Taylor."

"Well, I wouldn't be able to express it without all of you," Taylor said, clearing his throat. "Thanks again for getting my stuff back."

"It would have been tragic not to. I'm glad I had the idea to call the church. And I'm glad Father Geoffrey surprised us all," I said.

I helped Matteo place the steaming serving dishes on the table.

"In a few months, Taylor and Vincent should be able to put on a little music concert for us."

Taylor snorted. "Yeah, I'll be in regular clothes and Vincent's going to wear pink panties and a ball gag."

Vincent smiled, I laughed and Matteo nodded.

"Sounds delightful," he said.

"I have no problem with that," I added.

"I fucking knew you wouldn't," Taylor said, shaking his head.

Vincent rolled his eyes.

Once Daphne had picked up Taylor, I took Matteo and Vincent down to the basement. I'd collected the clothes I wanted Vincent to wear and put them on top of the cabinet. I had Matteo strip and kneel in the corner with a blindfold covering his green eyes while I undressed Vincent and prepared him.

I helped Vincent get into the white frilly panties, black garter belt and purple basque, then pulled up his stockings, attached them to the garter belt, and laced the Doc Martens on his feet. I showed him the royal blue eye mask with silver sparkles all over it, accented by a tall white feather attached to the side that I had found.

"Oh...that's beautiful." He sighed.

"It will be stunning on you," I said as placed it on his face and tied the ribbons in back. "Hands behind your head."

I stepped back to admire my work and sucked in a breath. "You are a thing of beauty, Vincent, my pretty princess."

"Thank you, Sir," he whispered, his gaze flicking to where Matteo kneeled on the floor with a stiff erection and a trying-to-be-patient expression.

I followed his gaze and grinned. "A princess needs a page, you know, especially as pretty as you are."

I left Vincent standing in front of the St. Andrew's cross and walked to Matteo.

"You can look now," I said, removing the cloth from his eyes.

Matteo blinked in the dim light, trying to focus. When he caught sight of Vincent, he made a small sound.

"Pretty, isn't he?" I said.

Matteo smiled, "Yes, Sir. Stunning." He couldn't tear his eyes away from my beautiful, fancy boy. My lovely princess.

"Would you like to worship at her feet, Matteo?" I asked.

"I would like nothing more, Sir," Matteo said, swallowing thickly as his cock arched stiffly toward his belly.

"Very well, then. You may crawl on your hands and knees to Vincent and kiss her boots."

Matteo closed his eyes and nodded before he obeyed.

Vincent's intense blue eyes tracked Matteo as he crawled across the floor. I had a flashback of the two of them innocently cooking in the kitchen a short time before and thrilled to see them in this perverse tableau — such an illicit mindfuck.

Matteo kept his focus on Vincent's purple Docs as he crawled. When he reached them, he flashed up to Vincent's face, then lowered again as he leaned down to place a soft kiss on each one. When he sat back on his heels, his gaze drifted up Vincent's long, stocking-clad legs, over the frilly panties with the obscene bulge of Vincent's erection outlined clearly, along the front of the purple basque and exposed flesh of Vincent's chest and neck until their gazes met and held. I felt the heat between them and lifted my chin so my heart could absorb it. The sexual tension was so ripe that I almost saw flames rise from the floor.

"Fuck," I said.

Neither looked my way, too caught up in their incendiary connection. A sudden stab of jealousy surprised me, but it fizzled out as quickly as it came. Knowing that I controlled everything in this moment, even the volatile energy between them that would ebb or flow depending on the positions I put them in, extinguished any hint of that emotion until it was simply a burning ember that only added to my enjoyment of the scene.

I knew what I wanted to happen next, and I wasted no time.

"Vincent has another chance to prove he can control his impulses, since he performed so embarrassingly the other day. Matteo, use your hands to pull down our girl's white panties and suck her fat cock. And my princess will *not* come. Will *not* make a sound, if she knows what's good for her."

Vincent's gaze met mine as he raised his eyebrows in incredulity. I gave him a slight, self-satisfied smile to assure him that I meant what I'd said. He shut his eyes in defeat before opening them and regarding Matteo with frustration. His expression was bound to become even more pained as the scene progressed, and he had to be quiet and still while unbound and suffering the attentions of Matteo's talented mouth.

Matteo licked his lips as he brought his hands forward. He had to slide his fingers under the bottom of the basque to reach the delicate waistband of the frilly white panties. Vincent's cock was so hard that it pushed the elastic out, but Matteo pulled the fabric over and down so his dick jutted free in front of the delicate fabric of the basque.

Matteo, not under the same restrictions as Vincent, growled low in his throat as he nestled the white silk beneath the swell of Vincent's testicles and bent to his task.

"Slowly, Matteo. Tease that pretty girl," I said, meeting Vincent's gaze as Matteo ran his tongue slowly up the underside of Vincent's cock as it arched toward the basque.

Our sweet princess took great pains to be quiet as Matteo licked and kissed the length of his dick while I watched, Vincent's muscles clenching and unclenching as he fought for control.

Matteo was into this big time. His gaze kept flying to Vincent's as he used the tip of his tongue and his soft lips to give Vincent pleasure, but never enough to soothe the sparks or arousal that tormented our boy.

"Very good, Matteo," I said, sitting on the spanking bench to watch in comfort.

I was in no rush. We had all evening.

As Matteo continued, Vincent's iron grip on his responses began to break. When he opened his mouth and let a moan escape his slack lips, I hit the bench with my hand so hard that it made a loud *slap*.

Vincent froze and Matteo stilled for a split second, then continued.

"Quiet. Just because you are a pretty princess doesn't mean you can disobey me, pretty girl." I shook my head and clicked my tongue. "So, so naughty, Vincent. I'm going to take you over my knee."

Vincent took a sudden breath. That was exactly what he wanted. He loved going over my lap. With Matteo as a witness, I think he was more thrilled than ever to receive a spanking.

"Matteo, stop and back up. Pull Vincent's panties up over his cock and ass, then come and kneel on the floor at the end of the bench."

I waited as Matteo reluctantly stopped attending to Vincent's penis, arranged his frilly panties and positioned himself where I'd indicated.

"Excellent. You'll have a good view of Vincent's face while I spank him."

"Yes, Sir," Matteo responded in low tones. His cock stood tall, clearly interested in what was going on.

"Vincent. Come stand next to me," I said, giving him a smile before reverting to Dom mode. "Now."

Vincent walked slowly over and stood by my knee. "Sir?"

I reached out and traced the line of his swollen cock under the silk panties as he clenched his hands into fists, closed his eyes and tried not to groan.

"You don't have to be quiet anymore, sweetheart," I said. As soon as the words were out of my mouth, he let out a loud whine that dissolved into helpless whimpers as he quivered under my touch.

"Now, over my lap. I want to hear you while I spank you. Understand?"

"Yes, Sir," he panted.

I took his wrist and pulled him into place, so his hands were on the floor, ass in the air and the toes of his boots trailing on the wood. I loved to feel the weight of him in this position. It grounded me, soothed me and made me feel like I was home—which I was, and back in my dungeon basement, thank goodness.

I slid my fingers under the boned cloth of the basque and hooked the waistband of the panties, sliding them down to expose Vincent's pale ass—plump and firm and perfect.

"You have the nicest ass, Vincent," I said with reverence.

"Thank you, Sir," he whispered.

I smoothed my hand over it and glanced at Matteo, who watched with avid attention.

"Very good, Matteo. I want you to watch. In fact, I'm going to get you to count. First, I want you to give him a kiss while he's lying over my lap."

Matteo opened his mouth as if he were going to protest or ask a question, then closed it and nodded. "Yes, Sir," he whispered, his words barely intelligible.

"You can do it however you want. It can be quick and chaste, or it can be more. Whatever you like."

He shuffled forward on his knees so he could bring his hands up and cup Vincent's face, angling it so he could press his lips to Vincent's. At first it was soft. Then, as if unable to help himself, he moved his lips and

Vincent opened to him, sighing softly as Matteo deepened the kiss and tongues came into play. It was so erotic that I had to stop myself from making a noise as the heat between them rose again.

"Enough," I said, and Matteo backed off as if pulling against an irresistible force. I knew how he felt. Vincent's energy worked on me in a similar way.

"Very good. Hands on your thighs. I want you to count after every spank. If you miss one, he'll get extra. Got it?"

"Yes, Sir."

When Matteo had positioned his hands obediently on his thighs, I tickled Vincent's balls and asked if he was ready for his spanking.

"Oh yes, Sir. Please," he groaned, his cock pressing against me slickly.

"Right then. Here we go." I brought my hand down with a loud *thwack* as Matteo said, "One," and licked his lips, his gaze tracking my hand as I pulled back for another spank.

I wondered what it would be like to watch Matteo spank Vincent. Was that something I wanted to try in future? I pictured myself observing from a comfortable chair, with a glass of brandy or Scotch, observing Vincent writhing over Matteo's lap while he was spanked to orgasm at my command. I'd have to broach that idea with them, because I'd definitely like to set that up. It would, of course, depend on their comfort level with the subject.

I renewed my focus on what was happening in the moment and shook thoughts of future scenes out of my brain.

Matteo counted each spank as I laid it on Vincent's sweet backside, and soon the skin there was a glowing pink, his breathing fast and harsh. He began to squirm and instinctively tried to avoid the blows. I tightened my arm around his middle, holding him fast.

"There is no escape, my dear," I murmured as I amped up the force of my blows.

We were up to fifteen and Matteo was beginning to look like he was struggling as well. His cock was painfully hard and the fluid that leaked from its tip made it shiny and slick. There was an answering wetness in my crotch.

When Matteo grunted out "Twenty!" I glanced up in time to see his cock spill over. The viscous white spurts landed on the floor as Matteo moaned and tried to stay still, his eyes closed and face flush with arousal as he came from the sight of Vincent receiving a spanking.

"Don't look at Matteo," I warned Vincent, who promptly glanced up and did just that.

"Oh, no, fuck, Sir, no..." he said, then groaned as his orgasm overtook him and the warm wetness of his release soaked my thigh.

Chapter Nineteen

"Get up," I said to Vincent, giving him a swat to emphasize the directive.

"I'm so sorry. I couldn't help it," he muttered, his face as red as his bottom.

"It's too late for that. On your knees and clean this up," I said, showing him the puddle of jizz that had begun to soak into my jeans.

Immediately he bent his mouth to it and lapped like the obedient submissive he was.

"I'm so sorry, Sir," Matteo muttered from his spot on the floor.

"I'm not mad at either of you," I said calmly. "I don't think I gave instructions not to come." I looked at Vincent. "Okay, that's enough. Go get a warm cloth and clean up Matteo."

Once the two of them were presentable, I had Matteo remove Vincent's feminine finery one piece at a time. It was quite the erotic process, and they were both hard again by the end of it.

"What a shame those erections will have to go to waste," I said. "But that's enough for tonight. I accomplished what I set out to do, and I need to get some sleep."

They got dressed and we spent some time snuggling upstairs before walking Matteo to the door.

"What are you making for supper tomorrow, Matteo?" I asked, my arms crossed in front of my chest as if I hadn't just watched him orgasm while I spanked my boyfriend.

He smiled easily. "How about chicken cacciatore?"

"That sounds lovely."

He gave us a cheerful salute and was gone into the cold night. The weather had turned from early fall warmth to the first signs of a winter chill this week.

I took Vincent's hand without looking at him and twined our fingers together. "We're very lucky with that man. Whatever his personal life is at the moment, he has room for us and our weird proclivities. He's a real gentleman." I pulled Vincent close and cupped his chin. "You, however, are a dirty little slut, and I cannot wait to fuck you."

Vincent sighed happily and dropped his forehead to my shoulder. "Please."

I laughed and ruffled his hair. "Oh, you act like you're starved for it—like you didn't just come on my leg down there."

He nodded against me. "Yes, Sir."

"Come on, then. Upstairs."

When we got to our bedroom, I stripped my clothes off and lay down in the middle of the bed, splayed out.

"All right, then. Have at it."

He peered at me, confused. "Um. Are we still in the scene or not?"

"*Not.* I want you to fuck me, Vincent, however you'd like."

He smiled a slow, delicious smile that almost undid me. He was like a child who'd been given a basket of chocolates and told he could eat all of it at once.

I swallowed thickly and spread my legs, pinching my nipple with one hand. *Fuck, I want him.* I wanted my hard boy now, the man I could dress as a princess and spank until he came. I wanted my genderqueer lover to fuck the shit out of me with his thick, beautiful cock.

"Wider," he said, with a deep, purposeful tone to his voice that I hadn't really heard before.

My eyebrows shot up. "Oh, is this what we're going to do?" I said, smiling with wonder at his gumption.

"Yes. Spread your legs wider."

"You're not asking, are you?"

"No, I'm not."

I felt some unease at the sudden shift in power dynamics, but I could see how much he wanted this. "Vincent, I'm not really...very good...at being submissive."

"Please," he said softly, circling his left wrist with his right hand, like he wanted to touch me but was scared. "Let me do this. Let me try."

His begging undid me, and I nodded. "Okay."

He smiled again and stepped forward, taking my knees in his hands and forcing my legs apart with a gentle persistence I found extremely arousing.

This was *no-nonsense* Vincent, *I-know-what-I-want-and-I-want-it-now* Vincent. My beautiful boy was taking what was his—what would always be his.

When he had my legs spread, he climbed up and slid his hands under my thighs, pushing my legs up and back over me, so my cunt was laid bare in front of his face. As our gazes met between my legs, I swore. "Oh fuck." I sighed and watched Vincent bend his mouth to my wet sex.

When he made contact, all sensation zeroed in on that spot as he licked and sucked at me with a zeal that I remembered from the first time I'd ordered him to eat me. Before I knew what had happened, I was coming from his expert technique. I shook and moaned as he sucked me through it, then slid two fingers inside me and found my G-spot. I came and was climbing again as Vincent kept my legs spread with his shoulder on one thigh and free hand on the other. He thrust two fingers inside me with an insistent rhythm.

If he wanted to drive me mad, he was succeeding.

"Vincent," I panted, making soft noises as he treated me with the roughness I enjoyed. "Fuck me, goddammit—with your cock, not your fingers."

"No," he said.

I grabbed his hair and pulled his mouth off me to show him how serious I was. He gazed at me with hooded eyes and a wet face as I narrowed my focus.

"I need your cock, Vincent."

"You're not getting it yet, Nic," he said evenly, a curve to one side of his mouth as I stared in disbelief at my rebellious sub.

"What the fuck, Vincent?" I swore, forehead creasing as I knitted my brows together in frustration. "*What the fuck?*" I sounded affronted, but I didn't struggle.

"I'm calling the shots right now. And you're letting me," he said, bending to my cunt again.

"I'm...I'm...letting you," I agreed, letting go of his hair and gripping the bedsheets as he worked me to another orgasm that barreled over me almost without my consent.

I cried out and shook beneath Vincent's merciless assault, because that was what it was—a downright erotic attack that I was not prepared for in the least. I could have used my safeword, but did I really want to?

No, I fucking well did not. I was determined to ride this out and let Vincent have control for once. What was the harm in it?

"Vincent," I whined. "Please…" My pleading voice sounded strange to my ears, but Vincent clearly liked it.

With one fast movement, he climbed onto me and guided his cock to my desperate sex, pushing inside me with a self-satisfied groan as he slammed his mouth against mine.

I allowed myself to lie there and take it, this raging conquest of his. He fucked my mouth with his tongue as aggressively as he slammed my sex, and I came again, just as Vincent cried out then stilled as he emptied himself into me.

We gasped and kissed through our pleasure and slowly came down from it. His kisses became soft and soothing as we settled into a gentle embrace, but he didn't withdraw from me. Eventually, his cock shrank and slipped out on its own.

"Oh, sweetheart, that was lovely," I said, smoothing his damp hair off his forehead as he peppered my chin and cheeks and lips with soft kisses, as if to apologize for being so aggressive.

He laughed and kissed my earlobe. "I'm sorry. I'm sorry. I got carried away. You don't usually let me," he said.

"You know I prefer to be the dominant one. But you needed to take charge tonight, and I don't mind that occasionally." I laughed, cocking an eyebrow. "You really needed it, didn't you?"

"Yes. I did," he said.

I grinned and traced the muscles of his back with my finger, trailing it down his spine and over his buttock as he flinched. I scraped a short nail over his spanked flesh, just because I could.

"I think I needed that too," I said.

* * * *

The rest of the week passed quickly.

Vincent's hand felt better every day. By the weekend, he could accomplish all the normal movements without pain or stiffness. He needed to be careful, though, which was why I'd been sure to keep Matteo on to help out.

Taylor enjoyed his forays to Daphne's dungeon to assist her with the domination of the men and women who paid her. He'd gone back to being the cheerful, mischievous, smart-assed kid again, and we were relieved.

A couple of weeks after Vincent's bandages had come off, we invited Daphne to dinner. In truth, I missed her. I'd gotten used to her being around all the time, even though I'd initially been put out by the inconvenience.

Vincent and Matteo were getting dinner ready, and I was in the living room with Taylor while he played me some songs he'd been working on when the doorbell rang.

I opened the door to a spectacularly clothed Daphne, who wore a wry expression on her fresh, expertly made-up face.

"Welcome," I said with a smile and a gesture to welcome her in. "I hope you're hungry."

She waltzed in, looking every inch the wealthy socialite in her best casual suit and a pair of expensive pumps. Nobody would ever guess what Daphne did for a living in this outfit. She could have landed a prestigious office gig with her degree in political science, but it turned out the things she'd learned at university had prepared her more for domination than office work. She'd attempted a 'regular' job once and had almost died of boredom. I still thought she'd make excellent management material, except, knowing her as I did, I wouldn't be surprised if she let a few inappropriate references slip and she'd be in trouble.

"Hello, Nic. Well, I'm famished, actually," she said, peeking into the kitchen, where Vincent and Matteo were slicing and dicing the vegetables for supper. "They're hard at work, aren't they? They make a good team." She gave me a knowing smile.

"Yes, they do," I admitted, almost blushing. But then, Nic Walker never blushed.

She followed me into the living room and caught sight of Taylor.

"Sparky! Nice to see your face, since you usually have the pup hood on when you're with me."

"Hey, Daf," Taylor said, grinning and waving. "How's it going?"

Daphne sat on the sofa near him, crossing her long legs and bending to kiss him on the cheek, probably so her cleavage could be seen to its best advantage. "It's going well, Sparky. Nice technique."

Taylor smiled like a well-praised child and nodded, strumming the strings of his guitar in a casual riff. "You look super-hot, by the way," he said.

"Why, thank you. I dressed up for dinner."

"I love what you wear in the dungeon. But you look super sophisticated right now and it's kind of blowing my mind."

She smiled and leaned closer. "I like what you wear in the dungeon, too."

Taylor blushed.

Daphne had bought him a pair of latex shorts and a rubber shirt to better show off his physique to her clients, and provided him with a pair of brand-new Docs as appreciation for his assistance, since I didn't want her paying him. It was best to keep Taylor out of actual sex work for the time being.

"I hope you like lasagna, Daphne, because Matteo makes an amazing one. They're just getting ready to put it in the oven."

As if on cue, Vincent and Matteo came into the living room.

"It's in," Vincent said.

He was so happy to be able to do things again, and it was adorable. The weeks of being hobbled by an injury had been rough on him.

"That's what *she* said," Daphne joked. "Or he. Whomever." She laughed.

"Classy joke, Daphne," I commented.

She shrugged. "I think you mean *classic*."

"Sure, we'll go with that."

Daphne stood and approached Matteo, giving him a friendly hug. "How are you, Matteo, darling? Nic and Vincent treating you well?"

Matteo held Daphne close for a moment. "Very well, Mistress."

Daphne smiled and returned to her seat on the couch. "I knew you were the perfect solution when Nic told me about Vincent's injury. I'm glad it's worked out so well for all of you."

I smiled at Matteo. "It has. Matteo is a wonderful addition to our household."

"Thank you, Nic," Matteo said. He stepped away from Daphne and closer to me, bending to speak softly in my ear. "May I speak with you for a moment?" He glanced at Vincent, then back at me. "Privately?"

"Yes, of course. We can talk in the kitchen," I said.

He seemed hesitant. "Perhaps your bedroom would be best."

"Okay, sure." I wondered what he wanted to talk to me about. I shot a questioning glance at Vincent and he shrugged, looking concerned but not alarmed.

Matteo followed me upstairs. I shut the door behind us and waited for him to begin.

"I'm sorry, Nic," Matteo said. "I've been mulling this over for some time and I should have mentioned it sooner, but I didn't want to ruin what was happening between the three of us."

"Matteo, you can be honest with me," I said, folding my arms across my chest. "Are you not enjoying doing scenes with us anymore?"

"No," Matteo said, holding up his hand. "I mean, yes, I am. That's not the problem." He sat on the edge of the bed. "It's more complicated."

"How so?"

He smiled and raised his hands helplessly. "I'm starting to developing deeper feelings for both of you. And I don't know if that's...allowed."

We were silent for a long moment. "I don't have control over your feelings, Matteo. Neither do you."

He nodded. "Yes, I know. But I wasn't sure if there was the potential for this...thing...between us to go beyond a purely physical arrangement. And I want to know, because I don't want to get in too deep if it's not something you and Vincent want from me."

I stared at Matteo and felt in my heart what he was saying. Things had begun as solely a physical thing, that was true. But over the course of a few weeks, Vincent and I had begun to think of Matteo as more than simply a convenient addition to our scenes.

"I don't think we've actually re-visited our needs in that respect, but it might be a good idea to address the possibility that we're all in this a little deeper than expected and see how we feel about that," I said. I put a hand on his knee. "I'm glad you told me how you feel."

"Thank you." He peeked up at me, looking younger than the experienced older man he was. "I don't want to stop being with the two of you. But if I'm only supposed to be a sideline attraction, then it would be better for me to bow out now. That's all."

"I understand," I said.

He nodded. "Do you think you can share him? With me?"

I grinned. "I think I already am sharing him...with you."

"But I..." He swallowed. "You're very possessive of him."

"Oh, I tend to be possessive of the things I like, Matteo. Of the things I maybe, perhaps, love."

He smiled and his green gaze met mine with an honesty and vulnerability that made my knees weak.

"The three of us need to be completely honest if this is going to work. So, I'm glad you told me."

Matteo smiled, significantly relieved.

"Now we need to go downstairs and eat the very delicious lasagna you and Vincent put together."

He put a hand on my arm. "Will you explain this to Vincent? I'm a little shy to lay out my feelings for him."

"Oh, Matteo," I said, feeling such empathy for the mild-mannered submissive. "You'll take his cock in your mouth but you're too scared to tell him you really, really like him?"

Matteo laughed softly. "It does sound ridiculous."

"Of course I will." I leaned in and kissed Matteo on the mouth.

When I pulled back, he stared at me in astonishment, then smiled as though I'd given him an unexpected gift.

Chapter Twenty

Later that evening, I told Vincent about the discussion I'd had with Matteo.

"He's nervous about continuing on with us if there's no possibility of something beyond a physical relationship."

Vincent nodded, looking at the floor. He glanced up at me. "Is there?"

I had to be careful because I didn't want to influence Vincent one way or another. It wasn't my decision. I needed to know his true feelings about it.

"I don't know. Maybe. What are your thoughts?"

Vincent seemed troubled. His forehead creased and he worried his hands together. "I like Matteo."

"So do I."

"A lot." He glanced at me again.

"Enough to share me with someone else? Enough to be shared?"

He tilted his head. "Isn't that what we're doing now? I know it started off as just a physical arrangement, but

Matteo isn't the only one dealing with stronger emotions."

"I agree. The question is, where do we go from here?"

I went to stand, but Vincent grabbed my wrist. "Is our relationship strong enough to handle expanding to include Matteo? That's the only thing that gives me pause," Vincent said. "You're the best thing that's ever happened in my life, and I don't want anything or anyone to complicate that."

"Well, I'm afraid it's too late. It's already gotten complicated. But it's worked well so far. Who's to say it won't continue working out?"

A few days passed before we got together for a scene with Matteo again.

Before we dove into it, we spoke about what Matteo had told me and what Vincent and I had discussed.

"I think there's definitely the possibility of taking this to the next level," I said. "It's a question of if that's what we all want—because I think it's heading in that direction, and if anyone is in over their heads, they need to pull out now. Pun intended," I joked.

Matteo nodded.

We were in the living room. Taylor was at Daphne's again.

"What would you consider the next level?" Matteo asked, gazing at both of us.

"Well, I guess it would be acknowledging that the three of us are in a relationship—and figuring out what that means to us."

"Yes," Vincent said. "Because we can define the terms of our relationship as much as we can define any other arrangement."

"To an extent, yes, that's true," Matteo said. "But sometimes emotions don't follow along with such terms very neatly."

We were quiet for a few moments, and I was wondering what this might mean for us.

"I think," Matteo said, "that we should go ahead with more of the physical side of the...relationship...and see where that takes us? I feel better now that I've explained how I feel and you two seem to be on the same page."

"That's sounds good to me," I said. "Vincent?"

"Sure. Okay."

We went downstairs.

I wanted to do something different this time, to see how a change in my approach might shake up the dynamic between Vincent and Matteo. I wanted to gauge the flexibility we had between the three of us. If we were going to be in a relationship together, I wanted to see what kind of options we'd have in terms of changing things up to keep it interesting.

I'd told Vincent to wear his sexiest pair of lacy panties and keep his jeans on. But Matteo was naked.

"Matteo, I'm going to let Vincent dominate you tonight. Do you have any issues with that?" I asked, remembering how dominant Vincent had been with me the other night. I wanted to see if anything interesting would spark between them in this dynamic.

I could see plainly the attraction between the two of them, and I suspected they'd held back because it was only supposed to be physical. I wanted to see what came out now that we'd acknowledged it was more than that already.

I didn't want Matteo to stop being a part of our lives. I don't think Vincent did, either. Expanding a two-person relationship to include another was always risky, but so was engaging in the kind of sex play we liked.

Life was boring and sterile without risk.

Vincent looked blindsided by my announcement. "What?"

"Manners, please. Just because you're dominating Matteo doesn't mean you're not submitting to me. You are."

"Yes, Sir. I'm sorry," Vincent said.

"What's your safeword, Vincent?" I asked.

"Piano," he said quietly.

"And yours, Matteo?"

"Spaghetti."

"All right. Let's get down to business," I said cheerfully.

They both looked so serious all of a sudden. I only wanted to play a little differently.

"Matteo, come here."

I fastened Matteo to the spanking bench on his belly, cuffing his ankles and wrists to the legs. I spoke softly in his ear while I worked.

"Would you consent to me having Vincent fuck you? If he's interested in doing that? He would use a condom, of course."

Matteo sighed and made a noise in his throat. "Yes."

"Okay. I'll broach that with him."

Matteo closed his eyes and nodded silently.

When I was done securing him, I walked to Vincent, who watched intently, his gaze on Matteo's prone form and indecision on his face.

I moved in close and embraced my boy from behind, laying my hand flat on his soft-firm belly. "He looks good spread out there, doesn't he?"

"Yes," Vincent said.

"I asked him if he would consent to being fucked."

Vincent closed his eyes and whooshed out a breath. "By whom?" he asked with a tremor in his voice.

"I supposed I could fuck him, too. I'd have to check in about that, though."

Vincent shuddered in my arms. "I'd like…I'd like to see that."

"Would you want to fuck Matteo, Vincent? If I gave you the chance?"

Vincent didn't answer for a long moment. When he did, I barely heard him.

"Pardon?"

"Yes. Yes, Sir. I would."

I grinned and kissed him on the shoulder. I returned to Matteo and crouched beside him near his face, which lay sideways on the cushioned bench. His eyes were closed, his lips parted minutely, his breaths already quickening with anticipation.

"Matteo," I said softly, "Vincent *does* want to fuck you."

Matteo's expression turned pained, but he smiled.

"But he has asked me to fuck you first." I glanced at Vincent, whose gaze was fixed on Matteo. "I think he's nervous. It's quite adorable."

Matteo laughed softly. "It is."

"Would you be okay with a pegging from me?"

Matteo sighed, flushed. "Of course. Yes, please, Sir."

I smiled and leaned in to kiss his rough cheek, which was already stubbled with new beard growth after the morning's shave.

"What's your preference in dildos? Realistic or fantastical? I've got a really nice dragon dick in my collection somewhere."

His eyes widened. "I think…realistic…for now. We'll save the dragon dick for another time."

I chuckled and rubbed his shoulder. "All right then. Let's get started."

I stood and backed away from Matteo.

"Vincent."

Vincent tore his gaze from Matteo's bound form to look at me, his face flushed with excitement.

"Yes, Sir?"

"I want you to go over there and touch Matteo, anywhere you want, in whatever you want, until I tell you to stop. Your goal is to tease him and get—" I glanced down at Matteo's already substantial erection. "I mean, *keep* him hard. I know you can."

"Yes, Sir," Vincent said, biting his lower lip with determination as he moved forward. I leaned against the wall to watch what my boy would do as the rise of anticipation grew in me.

The first thing Vincent did was walk slowly past Matteo, trailing his fingers along Matteo's naked bottom and up his back. When his fingers stopped at the Matteo's nape, Vincent bent and ran his hand up through Matteo's thick hair. He did this several times while Matteo sighed with pleasure.

Vincent examined Matteo's muscular body like an antique expert assessing a valuable piece of furniture. Not that Matteo was old, but his body was more mature than Vincent's, and I think Vincent enjoyed the way it differed. Matteo had love handles where Vincent was sleek and slim. Matteo's skin was rougher and hairier, and he was beginning to show evidence of silver streaks, even though he was only in his late thirties. He was only a few years older than me.

When Vincent splayed his hands over Matteo's buttocks and moved them this way and that, exposing Matteo's vulnerable hole, sliding his thumbs along the sensitive wrinkled flesh, Matteo groaned deep in his throat.

Vincent straightened, then brought his hand back and down with a snap on Matteo's ass, causing a startled inhale, followed by a whimper.

"Oh, good idea," I commented, thrilled to see Vincent take the reins.

He smiled and shot me a coy look, like he couldn't believe he'd just spanked Matteo, and I rolled my eyes. He really wasn't a Dom at all, but that was okay. That was just fine. He was good at pretending, and that was enough for us to have some fun.

"Okay, enough playing around. Now shimmy under that spanking bench and lick Matteo's cock. No sucking, just licking. Matteo isn't allowed to come."

Vincent nodded and immediately dropped to his knees, twisting under the bench so he lay on his back with his head in the appropriate spot. He clutched the sides of the spanking bench with his hands so he could angle his face close enough to Matteo's erection to do as I'd ordered.

At the first touch of Vincent's tongue, Matteo yelped and struggled against the cuffs holding him in place.

"Don't worry. I'm going to give you something to distract you from Vincent's attentions," I said.

I walked to the cabinet that held my tools and found Vincent's favorite leather paddle. I showed it to him when I approached the bench.

"I'm going to use this on Matteo while you tease his cock. I've never paddled him before, so if he gets close to coming, you need to back off and give him a moment."

"Yes, Sir," Vincent said, meeting my gaze with a hungry look.

I mouthed, "You okay?"

He gave me a smile and a thumbs-up.

While I paddled his ass and Vincent played with his cock, Matteo made the most wonderful sounds and was able to hold back. I suspected he wasn't as much of a spanking slut as Vincent, which kept him focused.

Now it was time to get serious. I had Vincent help me with the strap-on harness and dildo I'd selected. Vincent recognized it immediately.

"Oh. That's my favorite, Sir," he said.

"I know."

"You're going to like Nic's cock, Matteo," Vincent said. "It's thick and long, with a noticeable head. It's as real as they make them, but a little more solid than a flesh-and-blood one."

"Good!" Matteo said and we laughed.

I had Vincent prepare Matteo and my silicone cock with copious amounts of lube.

"Oh," I said, closing my eyes and acting as if Vincent was touching my real dick. His motions pressed the base of the dildo against my cunt and caused sparks of pleasure to ignite. I slid my fingers into the waistband of Vincent's jeans and pulled him against me, finding his mouth with mine and opening under his eager kiss. He kept rubbing my pretend cock with one hand while the fingers of the other slid behind my neck and settled on my nape, causing a frisson of excitement on the surface of my skin.

"Oh, fuck, Vincent," I said, panting as I broke away. "I can't wait to watch you screw Matteo. I'm about to explode even imagining it. But I'm fucking him first and I'm going to get him nice and ready for you."

"Yes, Sir," Vincent said, voice husky and eyes wild.

"Take off your jeans. You can touch yourself while I fuck him, but you'd better not come."

Vincent backed away and stripped off his jeans.

"The panties stay on," I said.

"Yes, Sir."

"Good boy."

He blew me a kiss, the cheeky bastard. I gave him a withering look that made him shudder with desire.

"Never mind your sweet wiles. Watch how I fuck Matteo so you can do the same. You've never fucked another man before. I want you to see the way I move and how careful I am."

"I'm watching, Sir."

The baby blue panties Vincent had on today were the ones we'd picked out on our very first shopping trip together, back when neither of us knew where this unique connection would take us. But I put all thoughts of how fucking pretty Vincent looked in his delicate panties with a raging, leaking erection out of my mind and focused on Matteo.

I moved in close, letting my fake cock rub against the back of his thigh, so he'd get an idea of its girth and length before we started. Matteo moaned and wiggled his ass, eager for it.

I used my fingers to tease and stretch him, which he responded to with enthusiasm. Poor Matteo was desperate for a fucking. We'd involved him in our scenes, teased and tormented him, but neither of us had ever fucked him.

I slid two fingers in deep. "You ready, Matteo?"

"Yes, Sir," he gasped.

"How do you like to be fucked, boy? Soft and gentle or rough and hard?"

"Both, Sir. Start gently, if you please."

"I always do, Matteo, for I am nothing if not a gentleman," I said with a wry smile, pushing the head of my fake cock against his slick hole. As it eased inside, Matteo uttered a long groan and a curse.

I paused when I was about an inch into him, letting him become accustomed to the girth.

"How does it feel?"

"Big, but good, Sir. Very good."

"Excellent." I peered at where the toy disappeared into Matteo's ass, tilting my head to see it from several angles. "It looks amazing." I glanced at Vincent, who stood close, also mesmerized by the sight. "Doesn't it, Vincent?"

"Uh-huh," Vincent muttered. He ran the palm of his hand over the panties along his erection a couple of times and grunted. "Amazing."

"I'm going to get you all stretched and ready for Vincent," I murmured as I pushed my cock in farther, using gentle thrusts that opened Matteo up and loosened him. I listened intently to the sounds he made so I'd know if he was hurting at all. A good Dom could distinguish between sounds of pleasure and pain. But it was always wise to check in.

"You okay, Matteo?" I asked.

"Fuck. Yes... Oh, yes."

Soon I was fucking Matteo with the whole length of the dildo while he made encouraging, desperate sounds. Although I was thoroughly enjoying myself, I couldn't wait to see Vincent have his way with Matteo and I didn't want Matteo — of the alarmingly-sudden-hands-free-orgasm-reflex — to come before Vincent had penetrated him.

So I patted Matteo gently on the rump and withdrew, moving to the side and gesturing for Vincent to take over. My fake penis bobbed in front of me as I picked up the condom.

"Hands behind your back while I prepare you," I said to Vincent, who promptly obeyed.

I pulled the lacy panties down to nestle under his balls and rolled the condom onto his length while Vincent's gaze remained locked on Matteo. I peeked under the bench to see that Matteo's cock was hard and wet. I hoped they could hold out long enough for this to be worthwhile.

I squirted lube onto the condom and spread it over Vincent's erection.

"You'll both need to hold off from coming until I give you permission. I don't care how difficult it is. You need to be good for me."

They both replied in the affirmative.

I slapped Vincent on the ass. "Get in position but keep your hands behind your back. I'll help you get inside him, then you're on your own."

He sighed, his dreamy focus on Matteo's soft hole. Then he remembered himself and acknowledged my orders. "Sir," he said, as he positioned himself behind Matteo.

The tip of his cock brushed Matteo's buttock, causing Matteo to shudder and gasp. He pulled at his bindings, seemingly excited to get fucked by sweet Vincent.

I went behind my boy, sliding my fake dick between his thighs as I reached around and wrapped his condom-covered cock with my fingers, nudging the tip of it against Matteo.

"Press forward," I said as I held Vincent's cock where it needed to be as Matteo's shuddery breaths filled the space. After a moment, the head of Vincent's dick slipped inside.

Matteo groaned and Vincent's chin dropped as his gaze met mine. He made a noise of astonishment as I let go of his dick and backed away.

"Okay, sweetheart. He's all yours. But be careful and slow until he gets used to you." I shook a finger at him. "And keep control yourself."

Vincent put his hands on either side of Matteo's hips and pressed forward gently, surprised when his cock slid smoothly in halfway. He cursed and shot me a questioning glance.

I nodded. "That's why I fucked him first. He's ready for you."

I watched the absolutely delicious sight of Vincent penetrating another man for the first time with wide eyes, a lump in my throat and a surge of wetness between my legs. It was pretty much *the* hottest thing I'd ever seen. Like the softy he was, he worked his way in gently until he was balls deep in Matteo, then froze, as if recognizing the significance of this.

"Oh fuck. I'm all the way in," he said incredulously.

Matteo groaned.

"Matteo," Vincent panted, trying to stay still, "does it feel good?"

"Oh yes. Incredible, Vincent. You're perfect."

"You can fuck him properly, now," I said to Vincent. "Start slow and do whatever feels good."

"Yes, Sir," he said, his voice shaky, as he withdrew halfway and pushed inside Matteo again, eliciting a gasp.

"Good boy."

Vincent found a slow rhythm which drove Matteo mad. Matteo turned his head as much as he could to watch Vincent with desperate eyes. When Vincent tightened his fingers on Matteo's hips and his motions quickened, I told him to stop, because I was a bit of a sadist.

"Stop?" he asked desperately, trying to still his thrusts as Matteo's heat likely teased him to continue. "You mean, now? Stop fucking him? Sir?"

I almost laughed at Vincent's erotic confusion. "Sink in all the way then hold still. There's something I want to try."

Matteo made a frustrated sound, but Vincent, my obedient boy, did as he'd been told, struggling to stay still with his cock buried in Matteo's firm backside.

I went nearer and kissed Vincent on the cheek. "That was very well done. And lovely to see. Are you close?"

Vincent closed his eyes and swallowed. "Yeah," he said, grimacing. "At least, I was."

If I hadn't strapped Matteo's thighs to the bench, he would have taken over. His thigh muscles quivered with frustrated energy.

"I'm going to spank you while your cock is buried in Matteo. You're not going to move of your own volition. And you're going to come whenever you can. Got it?"

Vincent made a sound, then nodded and gritted his answer through clenched teeth. "Yes, Sir."

Matteo cried out. "Oh God. Oh God."

"You can come after Vincent, Matteo, but not before. Understand?"

Matteo whined but nodded obediently, his face the picture of distress.

Vincent closed his eyes and opened his mouth as I rubbed the flat of my hand over his buttock. When I lifted it, he clenched in anticipation, and when it came down with a *thwack*, they groaned with the agony of release so close, yet still not attainable. *Vincent being the spanking slut he is, it shouldn't take long.*

I started up a fast, hard rhythm, driving Vincent's cock deeper into Matteo each time, and giving Vincent the sting and the burn he loved while he was buried in the soft heat of Matteo's body.

Vincent lowered his head, placing his hands on the spanking bench beside Matteo while he let himself be rocked into him. On the ninth spank he stiffened and cried out, his breath coming hard. "Oh God. I'm coming!" he moaned. "God…"

Matteo made a primal sound as his cock erupted, spurting all over the floor.

Chapter Twenty-One

When I released Matteo from his bindings, he fell to his knees at our feet.

"Thank you. Thank you so much," he murmured, staring at the floor while Vincent and I glanced at each other with surprise.

I crouched down and put a hand on his shoulder. "Hey...thank *you*, Matteo. You were wonderful."

He gazed up at me and smiled, then glanced at Vincent. "*You* were wonderful. Both of you."

"How did you enjoy topping Matteo, Vincent?"

He grinned. "I liked it. A lot." He shrugged. "The spanking helped." He shuddered with remnant pleasure. "I didn't expect that. That was...hot."

I chuckled. "Yes, it was. Very."

I cocked my head, regarding my spent subjects with affection. "Let's go upstairs."

"But what about you?" Vincent asked. "You didn't get off, Sir."

I shrugged. "I'm okay for now. It was so hot watching the two of you, and I want to bask in my arousal for a bit longer."

We climbed the stairs, and while Matteo showered, Vincent and I cuddled on the bed.

"I liked that a lot. I like Matteo a lot."

I smiled. "So do I."

I rubbed my hand up and down Vincent's back while I spoke. "I think you and I are fucking incredible together. But the *three* of us? There's something special there, too. And Matteo seems to fit with us, you know?"

"Yeah."

When Matteo came out of the shower, he seemed unsure of where we wanted him.

"Would you like me to leave?" he asked. "Or should I stay here for the night?"

I glanced at Vincent. "We'd love you to stay, Matteo. There's room for three in this bed."

He smiled, relieved, and crawled onto the bed toward me.

"May I?" he said as he hovered over me, his handsome face close to mine.

"May you, what? Be specific, Matteo."

He smiled and blushed even more. "May I kiss you, Sir?"

"You don't have to call me Sir when we're in bed like this. And, yes, you can kiss me, Matteo."

He surged forward, and when his lips met mine I was surprised by their firmness and the sparks that flew up from his touch. I opened underneath his kiss and welcomed his inquisitive tongue into my mouth as he tasted and tested me.

Then Vincent's face was beside Matteo's and he turned Matteo's face to his and kissed Matteo with a tenderness that took my breath away. There was a very obvious connection between the three of us that we could no longer deny.

A few minutes later, as we lay entwined together, I heard Vincent's soft snores and assumed Matteo had joined him in sleep. I slipped out carefully to close the curtains, and when I came back to bed, Matteo's eyes were open. He watched me climb under the covers and slip in next to him.

"Hey."

"Hi."

"You okay?"

Matteo didn't say anything at first.

"I don't know," he finally admitted. "I'm feeling overwhelmed."

"That's understandable," I said. "We had a very intense session down there, and the three of us are realizing there's more to this than physical interest. That's huge."

"Yes, it is. And I'm...scared."

"Why are you scared?"

He chuckled to himself. "I don't know. It's what I wanted. It's why I told you how I felt. And now I'm not sure if I want to risk it."

"Risk what, Matteo?"

He closed his eyes. "My heart."

"Oh, honey."

He opened his eyes and in them I saw reflections of pain and loss. "It's been through a lot the last few years."

I covered his hand with mine and gave it a reassuring squeeze. "Want to tell me about it?"

He shook his head. "I can't. Not yet. Maybe someday."

"All right."

"I just...don't know if I'm ready to risk my heart again. You know?"

I smiled and lay my head back, staring at the ceiling. "Oh yeah. I know."

He shook his head, looking down at the bed, then back up. "I don't know if you do. I'm terrified that if we continue, the two of you are going to destroy me."

I blinked. "Oh. I see."

He looked behind him at Vincent, sleeping like an angel, oblivious to Matteo's discomfort. Then he returned his gaze to me.

"I love this so much. It seems like the answer to everything I've wanted. But I'm worried I'm going to do something wrong or make a mistake and it will dissolve into nothing. And I'll be alone again but with the memories to torture me every day—of what I could have had, of what I did have, for a moment."

I nodded, slipping under the covers to put my head level with his. "Do you know, I almost lost Vincent because I was scared to death of how much I did actually care for him?"

Matteo stared at me out of emotion-laden, intelligent, thoughtful eyes—eyes that I didn't want him to take far from me anytime soon.

His eyes were so different from Vincent's sky-blue, ethereal gaze. Matteo's were a rich green, deep and grounded. He knew who he was, when Vincent was only beginning to discover himself. I found it both reassuring and welcome.

"I was determined never to be hurt again, because I'd been treated so badly by someone in my past. I almost didn't give Vincent and me the chance to create what we have now, what we're willing to bring you into. Being a third coming into an already established relationship between two people must be intimidating. We want you with us, Matteo, in this emotional space," I said. "But you have to decide if you want it enough to risk losing it."

He blinked and licked his lips. "Thank you. I'm going to get dressed, go home and try to figure out what I want to do."

"Okay," I said, moving so he could get out from under the covers without disturbing Vincent. "For what it's worth, Matteo, I think you are already a wonderful addition to this household. I know Taylor regards you as a father figure. You're already enmeshed into our lives and we are the better for it."

"Thank you, Nic. That means a lot to me."

* * * *

When he woke, Vincent was surprised by Matteo's absence.

"I thought he'd spend the night," he mumbled, his forehead creasing in consternation as he splayed his hand on the empty bedsheets beside him.

"He decided to go home and think things over."

"Oh," Vincent said. "Does he regret what happened?"

I shook my head. "No. He found it very overwhelming, in a good way. But…he's unsure if he's ready to risk his heart by getting in too deep with us. Which I understand, because I felt like that with you, remember?"

Vincent smiled. "I remember."

I returned his smile. "I'm glad I rose to that challenge, because letting you into my heart was the best decision I've ever made."

"And I only had to risk hypothermia that one time," Vincent said, referring to his stint on my doorstep in a downpour while I was still trying to decide whether or not to bail on the relationship.

I raised my eyebrows. "So far."

His head fell back onto the pillow. "Oh God. You'd better not put me through that again. Why is everyone such a big chicken? You were just like that at first." He put on a face. "*Oh, Vincent, I think you're so hot, but I don't want to fall for you. So just play my piano in these frilly panties while I try to keep my heart separate from my cunt.*"

I glared at him, pressing my lips together in a firm line. "Vincent Blake, did you just make fun of me?"

"Yes," he said, sticking his tongue out. "Yes, I did."

I laughed but rolled him onto my lap and pushed the sheets down. "That's a spanking if you've ever deserved one."

He squealed and tried to escape, but I landed a few hard smacks before I let him go.

"Ow. My ass is still sore from last night," he moaned.

"*Bull. Shit.* I barely touched you last night. You came before I could really get into it."

"Okay, fine. But what do you think Matteo's going to decide? And what are we going to do if he decides he doesn't want us?"

"Then, my dear boy, we're going to thank him for the time he has given us, for all the delicious meals he's prepared and his pleasant and intelligent company, and we're going to let him go...because that's what adults do."

It was Sunday, and we didn't expect Matteo back until Monday afternoon, so Vincent and I endeavored to forget the fact that he might not show up the next day, or that he might show up solely to give us a proper goodbye. Basically, we prepared ourselves for any outcome and distracted ourselves by looking after Taylor.

Despite getting Taylor's things from the church, he still had a very limited wardrobe, so I'd promised him Vincent and I would take him shopping.

As Vincent pulled the car out of the drive I said, "Hey, remember our first shopping excursion?"

Vincent blushed. "How could I forget?"

"Oh God," Taylor moaned, putting his forehead on the back of my seat. "I'm scared to ask."

"Then don't."

"I can't help it. There's something wrong with me. I have an insistent curiosity. Was it a...kinky shopping trip?"

"Why, yes, Taylor. It *was* a kinky shopping trip," I said with a smile, glancing at Vincent's profile while Taylor sat up straight and slapped the back of my seat with his palm.

"I knew it!"

"Taylor, we're not exactly circumspect. You know Vincent and I have a very kinky relationship, so, of course, it was a kinky shopping trip."

Taylor laughed. "What about Matteo? Are you going to take him on a kinky shopping trip, too?"

Vincent glanced at me.

"What a wonderful idea. Maybe." I raised my eyebrows in a silent query to Vincent, who nodded, letting me know he thought Taylor should be in on what was going on between the three of us.

"We're not sure Matteo is going to be part of our relationship for much longer, I'm afraid," I said with a frown.

"What?" he said. "What do you mean? Are you breaking up with him?"

The horror in Taylor's voice surprised me.

"No, Taylor, of course not. But he might break up with us."

"What the fuck. Why?"

I wasn't prepared for the vehemence of Taylor's outburst, and I don't think Vincent was either, with the look he gave me. I turned around to face Taylor. His face expressed shock and unease at this possible development.

"Taylor. Why are you so upset? This is between me and Vincent and Matteo," I said gently.

Taylor regarded me as if disappointed I wasn't smarter.

"No, it's not. It's not *only* between you three. I'm a part of this family, too. At least, it feels that way."

"Is that what we are?" I said, turning to Vincent. "A family?"

He shrugged, glancing at Taylor and back at me. "I guess so. I guess we kind of are."

"Fuck, if Matteo doesn't... What if Matteo doesn't want to cook supper for us anymore?" Taylor said in a panicked voice. "He's teaching me to cook, you know. I want to learn how to cook so I can look after myself when you guys eventually kick me out."

"What?" I blurted. "We're not going to kick you out. I've told you that."

"Eventually you're not gonna want me freeloading off you, Nic."

"Well, that may be true. But once you get a part-time job, you can pay me a bit of rent and keep living there. I don't mind having you around."

He seemed surprised. "I know you're just saying that because you know I don't have anywhere else to go."

"I'm not just saying that, Taylor, and don't you dare dismiss my words so casually."

Vincent had pulled over to the side of the road so we could discuss this properly, as Taylor was becoming quite emotional.

"Sorry. It's just— I know I'm intruding. But it felt like Matteo and I were a part of something bigger."

I shared another look with Vincent, and he stepped in.

"Taylor, you're my cousin. You *are* family," he said.

"There's a difference between being family and being a part of one. My parents and I are *family*. But we're not *a family* anymore and I'm fucking thrilled. Maybe we never were."

He sat back against the bench seat and rubbed his face. "Fuck, I just don't know if I can take any more. I loved Matteo. I mean, I really loved Matteo. He was like the older brother I never had, maybe—or the father I wish I'd had."

"Don't talk about him in the past tense," Vincent said. "He hasn't made his decision yet."

Taylor's forehead creased in worry, but he said, "Okay."

"Let's hope for the best, okay?" I said, reaching back to take Taylor's hand. "Vincent and I will still be your family, no matter what happens. And don't forget about Daphne."

Taylor wiped his free hand over his eyes as if to hide sudden moisture. "Who could forget Daphne? Jesus Christ."

Vincent and I laughed.

"I'm pretty sure I'm the adopted son she never had, so, yeah, that helps." He sighed. "All right. Buy me some cool clothes to soothe my spirits, then. Please?"

I laughed. "Whatever you want, Taylor. But I'm only buying frilly panties for Vincent."

Vincent groaned and pulled out into traffic.

Taylor snorted. "Uh, that's a deal."

We got to the mall and found ourselves at The Gap. Before I knew it, Taylor had way too many pairs of pants in his arms.

"Taylor, you don't need six new pairs of jeans."

"Okay, I'll put these back." He put one pair of designer jeans back on the table. I gave him a look.

"That just made my cock hard," he said, his eyes like saucers as he held the other jeans close to his chest.

My horrified expression caused him to burst out laughing. "I'm kidding, Jesus. Vincent, can't your evil Dom take a joke?"

I grabbed Taylor by the neck of his jacket as he tried to move past me and held him firmly.

"Oh, be still my heart," he said breathily, and I couldn't hold it in. I doubled over with laughter while Taylor straightened his clothes.

"You know what? Keep the other pair of jeans," I said. "Get whatever you want, pretty boy, because I just want you to be happy."

"Whoa. And I didn't even put out," Taylor said, glancing at Vincent, who rolled his eyes.

"Can we get his stuff now so I can do my own shopping? I need a few things," Vincent said.

"I just want to check this other display," Taylor said, moving to a table full of shirts. "Be right back."

I leaned against the jean table and reached out, taking hold of Vincent's belt and pulling him close. The store was notoriously understaffed, so we were unobserved for the moment. "What do you need, lovely boy? Something frilly and pink and dainty?"

Vincent side-eyed the rest of the store. Once satisfied we were alone, he leaned close and whispered in my ear, "Always."

I turned and caught his lips in a quick kiss. "Then you shall have it, my precious darling. Always."

That night, when we went up to bed, we tried not to think about what might or might not happen with Matteo. Vincent put on the pretty underthings I'd bought him and spent almost an hour eating me out before he pulled his cock roughly out of the pastel panties and fucked me to within an inch of my life.

We lay together afterward, not saying anything, just holding hands and hoping for the best.

* * * *

On Monday, I kept dreading a text or a phone call from Matteo saying he wasn't coming to make supper that night—that he'd thought it over and he just couldn't be a part of our lives anymore. But a call didn't come.

So, when I arrived home, hoping to see him in the kitchen cheerfully making supper and he wasn't, I dropped my bag, alarmed.

"Vincent? Taylor? Where is everyone?"

Taylor appeared from the living room, holding a game controller. "Hey, Nic, how was work?"

I eyed him carefully. He seemed calm and happy, which boded well. "Fine. How was your day?"

"Oh, just peachy."

"Well? Where is everyone? Is Matteo here?" I forced myself to ask.

"Oh, he's here. Vincent's showing him just how happy he is that he's come back. They're upstairs."

I felt a lightness in my chest, as if a tight cord had relaxed. I put a hand to my forehead. "Jesus Christ. I thought he hadn't come — hadn't even let me know that he was done with us."

Taylor scoffed. "Matteo wouldn't do that. He's a gentleman. I'm going to practice my guitar. We're getting takeout, by the way."

I nodded, taking off my jacket and heading upstairs. When I knocked and opened the door, the word 'gentleman' as a descriptor for Matteo was not the first thing that came to mind.

He lay on his back on the bed, his shirt off, pants opened. Vincent was crouched over him, wearing the silver striped panties I liked while Matteo cradled his tight balls with one hand and the other moved slowly inside his pants. Matteo's face was a picture of adoration as he gazed at our boyfriend

They turned together and Vincent shot me a coy grin. "Matteo's here, Nic."

"I can see that. Thank God." I climbed onto the bed and crawled over Matteo, who seemed startled and pleased. I didn't say anything more, just caught his chin in my hand and kissed him soundly on the lips, parting his mouth with my tongue. When I drew back, he regarded me with surprise.

"What was that for?" he asked softly.

"For coming back to us."

He smiled and took our hands in his. "How could I not? I had to take the chance on it. You know?"

"I do know. We're so glad, aren't we, Vincent?"

"Yes. Matteo, you make our lives so much better."

"I feel the same about you two. Can I ask you something, though?"

"Sure," I said.

"Why did Taylor jokingly call me 'Deadbeat Dad' when I showed up?"

"Oh my God." I turned to Vincent. "I'm going to kill him."

But Vincent was laughing and so was Matteo — and soon, so was I.

Chapter Twenty-Two

"Eh, Nic, where's the whiskey?" Daphne's voice came from the kitchen. "Matteo said it was in the cabinet, but I can't find it. You need a proper liquor storage solution!" she said, slamming cupboard doors.

I decided that the next time I renovated the kitchen, I would pay for soft-close cabinets. I stood up from my spot on the sofa beside Vincent. Matteo idly stroked Vincent's hair as Vincent cuddled against him.

"Hold on a second," I said, heading her way. I stepped into the kitchen to see Daphne perched precariously on the small stool we kept to reach the high shelves. Her leather pants strained around her ass as she stretched up to peer into the top cupboard.

"Cold. So cold," I said, walking to the cabinet farthest and lowest from where she was and opening it. I reached in to pull out the bottle of Macallan we kept for special occasions and held it up with a smile.

"Fuck." She got down carefully and closed the cupboard door before walking over and taking the bottle from me. "Thanks. What are *you* having?"

I laughed. "You can't have all that, Daphne."

"Watch me."

I frowned. "That's double-cask, twelve-year-old Scotch. That bottle cost me a hundred bucks."

She twisted the cap off and smiled, bringing it to her lips. "I'm worth it."

"Fuck," I said, putting a hand to my forehead. "You are evil."

She grinned, swallowing the expensive alcohol like it was water. "You like it, baby. I know you do."

I followed her sashaying body out of the kitchen and into the living room, where I appropriated the bottle and wiped the rim with my shirt.

"Anyone want a small glass of this very expensive Scotch before Daphne drinks it all?"

"Oh, me, me!" Taylor put up his hand before anyone else.

The very attractive person standing nervously beside him, whom Taylor had introduced to us as Forrest, raised their eyebrows and smiled.

"No. Next?" I said, turning to the others.

Taylor narrowed his eyes. "What? Why can't I have some?"

"Because you're a child," I said.

Taylor approached me, ready to fight. "I'm not a fucking child."

Then I lifted the bottle and grinned, holding my hand out for his glass, since I'd been teasing. "All done with your lemonade? Ready for a grown-up drink?"

"You're an asshole. But, yes, I am." He turned to the kid he'd brought. "You want some?"

The young brown-haired individual with the carefully trimmed goatee and dark-rimmed glasses grinned. "Sure."

They held up their glass as Taylor poured some Scotch into it. "I'm a little confused. What exactly are we celebrating?" Forrest asked.

Taylor grinned as he handed the bottle of Scotch back to me. "I'll let Nic field that question."

I smiled. "We are officially welcoming both Taylor and Matteo into our little family circle," I said, winking at Vincent, who took a sip of champagne and held up his glass.

"Oh," Forrest said, "I see."

Daphne glided over to Forrest and cupped their chin in her hand. "I don't think you actually do. Let me explain." She pointed at me. "That guy, Nic, is in a romantic relationship with that pretty young man over there. Then Vincent cut his hand and couldn't do anything for weeks, so I lent them Matteo to do their cooking. But they wanted Matteo to help out with some 'other things', if you get my drift. Nudge, nudge, wink, wink."

Since Forrest looked like they'd been ambushed by our bold and voluptuous pixie of a Dominatrix, Taylor took their hand and pulled them away from Daphne. "Hold on, Daf. I've got this."

Forrest regarded Taylor with relief and something quite like adoration in their eyes as Taylor explained the dynamic somewhat more clearly, while sliding an arm around Forrest's trim middle and holding them close. "Vincent and Nic are lovey-dovey kinkster boyfriends. Matteo was invited in for some fun sex games, but things got serious and now they are an official poly unit. Got it?"

Forrest smiled. "Oh! Sure."

Taylor continued. "And tonight, we're officially acknowledging Matteo's presence in our family. Oh, and also mine — except I don't play the sex games." He glanced at Forrest, whose eyes had widened. "Well, not with them. They're like my three kinky dads." His eyebrows knit together. "No, that doesn't sound right, either."

I cleared my throat, trying not to laugh at Taylor's awkwardness.

"Taylor needed a home and now he has one. Although we're not his actual parents, Vincent and Matteo and I are looking out for his welfare as if he were our son. So, yeah. Three dads, I suppose." I raised my glass. "A little more than you bargained for when you asked for a place to stay?" I winked at Taylor.

He rolled his eyes. "Well, yeah. But I wouldn't trade it for the world."

After the party, Taylor asked if he could have the car overnight, since he needed to drive Forrest home and wanted to stay the night.

"As long as you have the car home by noon tomorrow, it's fine." It was Saturday night, and I didn't need the car for work or anything else. "Have fun. Be safe."

"Always." Taylor smiled. "Come on, Forrest," he said, taking their hand and pulling them to the entryway. "We have a party of our own to throw."

Daphne left soon after, giving each of us a hug and a kiss and a wink. "Have a lovely evening, gentlemen. Don't do anything I wouldn't do." She cackled.

"Since that is a very short list of rather dubious activities, you can rest assured, we won't. Probably," I said.

After I'd closed the door behind her, I turned to see Vincent and Matteo whispering together.

"What's going on?" I said, taking another sip of my whiskey and enjoying the pleasant burn as it slid down my throat.

Matteo stepped forward and took the glass from me as Vincent wrapped my hand in his long fingers.

"Come with us," he said, tugging me up the stairs as Matteo put the tumbler on the kitchen counter and followed.

When we got into our room, Vincent led me to the bed. "Sit down."

I did, observing them warily. "Hold on. Is this a mutiny?"

Matteo smiled. "Only if you want to play pirates."

I grinned and waggled my eyebrows. "The joke's on you, because I would *love* to play pirates. I want to be the pirate captain."

Vincent rolled his eyes. "Then, yes, this is a mutiny. We're taking you captive and having our way with you, Captain Nic."

"Oh," I said, suddenly very interested in how Vincent's hands had untucked my button-down shirt and were now working the buttons open. "Leave it on me, okay?" I said, not always comfortable being completely naked with them.

Vincent smiled at me. "Of course."

"So," I said, as Matteo kissed my neck and Vincent pushed me gently onto my back while he undid my belt and pants. "Is one of you first mate? Or are you just a couple of restless deckhands commandeering the ship for the fun of it?" My voice sounded breathless. The whiskey had relaxed me, and I was able to enjoy whatever this was.

"Just a couple of deckhands," Vincent said, pulling my pants off and throwing them into the corner.

He stood and began to unbutton his shirt. It was white with little red flowers all over it. I had bought it for him on our shopping trip with Taylor.

"We've been watching you order everyone around on this ship. And we want to give you a taste of your own medicine."

"Oh, really?" I said, grinning as heat flared in my belly and surged up my chest.

"Well, just for tonight," Matteo said, also beginning to undress. "Tomorrow you can be captain again, but tonight we're in charge, Sir."

"And we're going to steer this ship," Vincent said, kneeling on the bed and sliding his fingers into my already-wet cunt as he loomed above me.

"Fuck it, okay," I said. "I'm yours...and his. And I'll do whatever you want, as long as you promise to cuddle me after."

"Said every cruel pirate captain to his kinky mutinous crew, I'm sure," Matteo laughed, grabbing Vincent's chin as he kissed him hard, directly above me.

I watched them — one light and ethereal, the other dark and brooding — as they kissed each other in the dim light from the single lamp and descended on me, determined to steer us in the right direction.

Epilogue

The first time Vincent put on the kitty outfit for Matteo and me, we almost keeled over from the level of adorableness inherent in the costume. The gear I'd ordered online had come shortly after Vincent's accident with the kitchen knife, and he hadn't had a chance to try it out until now.

It had been worth the wait.

"Jesus," I said, as Vincent crawled toward us on all fours, the pink ears with their furry white edges nestled in his light-brown hair, a black spot painted on the tip of his nose and a delicate purple collar circling his slim neck. The tiny bell hanging from the collar rang with a dainty tone as Vincent moved sinuously forward. He had the little wrist decorations from his Tom Holland outfit on, along with white thigh-high stockings that make my mouth go dry.

"My goodness," Matteo mumbled, staring at our boyfriend with appreciation as he moved toward us, the white fluffy tail draped over his arm. I'd caged

Vincent's cock and it looked so small and benign in its steel confines.

"Here, kitty-kitty," I said, rubbing my fingers together to tempt him.

He crawled to me and sat back on his heels, staring at me with a placidity and ambivalence that was distinctly feline. When Matteo reached to stroke his hair, Vincent leaned into his touch.

I traced the purple collar with a finger, then bopped his nose. "What a pretty pussy."

Vincent smiled and advanced, encircling my waist with an arm and curling his body over my lap with his head against my chest.

"*Meow*," he said.

I laughed as I stroked his hair and kissed the top of his head, while Matteo lifted the fluffy tail from Vincent's arm and caressed its length.

"Are you a girl kitty or a boy kitty?" Matteo asked.

Vincent turned to him and gestured to his purple collar while wiggling his hips.

"What a pretty girl you are," Matteo said, then running a hand along Vincent's bare back while Vincent rested his head on its side and blinked at him. His blue eyes glowed with delight and the excitement of dressing up for us.

"You need a name, don't you, pretty girl?" I said, thrilling to the sight of my sweet Vincent in this gear that transformed him so easily into a fetching pet.

He rubbed his forehead against me and tightened his arm around my waist. He arched his pale back and wrapped his other arm around my leg.

"What about Dolly?" Matteo asked.

Vincent frowned. It was quite obvious he didn't approve.

"Okay. How about Snowball?" I suggested.

Perhaps we should have discussed his kitty name beforehand.

Vincent shook his head.

"Lucy?" I suggested, to no avail.

We went through some other names, and I was ready to get Vincent to suggest one when Matteo said, "What about Priss? Like Daryl Hannah's kick-ass character from *Bladerunner*?"

Vincent froze, then nodded enthusiastically and made a purring sound.

I glanced at Matteo. "How did you do that?"

He chuckled. "It's one of our favorite movies."

"Well," I said, dipping my head to regard Vincent's charming visage. "My lovely Priss. How about you climb onto that bed and show yourself off while Matteo and I decide what to do with you?"

Vincent — or Priss — did as they were told, and climbed onto the bed on all fours, arching their back and regarding us with a hooded gaze that plainly expressed a desire for whatever we had in mind. The sight of the long white tail emerging from between his curved buttocks and cascading down the backs of his pale thighs did wonderful things to my libido.

I turned to Matteo, leaning forward and kissing him.

"Shall we?" I said, taking his hand and leading him to the bed where we reclined on either side of our pretty pet and spent the next fifteen minutes cooing and stroking Vincent until the closeness and sexual energy between us proved way too difficult to ignore.

Want to see more from this author?
Here's a taster for you to enjoy!

We Three Kings:
A Spoonful of Sugar
AE Lister

Excerpt

Christmas was coming, and even though I didn't have a partner and children to spoil, I had to think about my parents and siblings. We didn't go overboard with gift-giving over the holidays, but the adults in the extended family were expected to provide a few thoughtful presents to the nieces and nephews.

The men I'd met at a Halloween party and subsequently gone home with in October, Jericho Griffin and Pascal Olejatz, hadn't been available to meet up in person much this month, although we'd kept in touch via Facetime and text. I was busy, too, with marking and assessments.

I mentioned to Pascal on one of our phone calls that I had gift shopping to do, and he said he did as well and that maybe we could meet up on a weekday when the stores weren't crowded and go together. He said Jericho did most of his shopping online, but he liked to see what he was buying then bring it home to wrap.

So, Pascal booked off the following Thursday, and we went Christmas shopping at St. Laurent Center. I swung by their place, and Pascal was waiting on the front step, wearing jeans that showed off his muscular legs and bubble butt, black leather boots, and a short wool jacket, with a gray scarf wrapped casually around his neck.

"Hello!" he said cheerily as he got into the passenger side. He leaned in and kissed my cheek. "How are you, Scott?"

"Good! You ready to face the masses at St. Laurent Center in December?"

"It shouldn't be too bad, since it's a weekday."

I reversed out of the driveway and headed east. "Oh, it'll be bad — but hopefully tolerable."

I was right. Even on a weekday, Ottawa's favorite mall was full of shoppers looking for exactly the right gift or loading up with several. I had to search for a parking spot but found one fairly close to the entrance. The crowds would be worse on the weekend, so I was grateful we had a window of opportunity.

"Where do you want to start?" I asked Pascal as we entered the large, modern shopping center in Ottawa's east end. The giant Toys R Us sign shone blue and yellow above us.

"I have some things I need to get there. At least most kids will be in school, so there should only be parents with babies shopping."

"Sounds like a plan," I said, and followed him into the cavernous and fully stocked store.

There were a number of moms and dads carting their little ones around and trying to score gifts, but it wasn't too bad. The occasional toddler went into tantrum mode, but Pascal and I efficiently managed to get what we were looking for and book it out of there.

"Next?" I asked, after we'd dropped our packages back at the car.

"Is there a gaming store here? I want to get Jericho a couple of the new releases," Pascal said.

We popped into The Source, and he found the games he needed.

"Right. Now, how about a clothes store?" I suggested.

"Sure."

We made our way along the concourse and were about to pass La Senza when Pascal shouted out, "Hey! Vincent!" and lifted his arm in a wave.

A charming young man with light brown hair and intense blue eyes, who was dressed in tight jeans and a soft T-shirt looked over and smiled. He was holding a folded jacket over his arm and a blush-pink La Senza bag by the corded handles.

"Pascal. Hi."

He waved, and nudged the arm of the arresting shorter guy who was accompanying him.

"Hi, Nic. What are you two shopping for? Oh wait, let me guess," Pascal said as we approached.

Vincent held up his pretty bag and blushed a lovely shade as Nic chuckled and raised his eyebrows.

"Oh, just a little something pretty for my favorite boy, that's all. Who's your friend?" he said, scanning me from head to foot.

Nic embodied the spirit of pure androgyny, although dressed toward the male side, but I'd have to be careful about what pronoun I used. I thought he was a guy, but I couldn't be entirely certain. Luckily, Pascal had the courtesy to assist me.

"This is Scott. Scott, this is Nic. He's a friend of mine, and Vincent's partner-slash-Dom."

Nic inclined his head, evidently pleased with this description. "Nice to meet you, Scott."

"Same." I shook his hand.

"And this cutie-pie is Vincent."

"Oh, come on," Vincent said, rolling his eyes at Pascal and shaking his head in embarrassment but still smiling. "Nice to meet you, Scott."

"You as well."

"Doing some Christmas shopping?" Nic asked. He wore clunky motorcycle boots, loose black jeans and a soft leather jacket over a black button-down shirt. A pair of mirrored sunglasses were pushed back on his short, untidy hair, the sides of which were shaved close. His hazel eyes pierced mine with intelligence and curiosity.

I liked the look of him, and Vincent was adorable.

"Yeah," I said. "I don't have much to get, but I don't want to be anywhere near the malls in a few weeks."

"I hear you," Nic said. "We got most of ours done last month. But Vincent decided he needed some more lacy underthings, and I couldn't say no."

"Ha-ha," Vincent said.

"Okay, that's not entirely true," Nic admitted. "The fact is, I enjoy buying him beautiful things to wear for me, and he enjoys indulging my eccentricities. And he looks so pretty in them." Nic gave Vincent a sweet look, and Vincent bloomed with obvious pride under his gaze.

I tried not to picture this beautiful man standing in front of me in pink and baby-blue lace. I failed.

"Where's Jericho?" Nic asked.

"Working hard, as usual. I booked the day off to do some shopping and brought our new *patient* with me."

"Oh-ho! How nice. And what exactly is ailing Scott here?" Nic asked. He seemed fully aware of Jericho's sideline as a *pretend* medical practitioner. "What prompted him to, ahem, seek treatment?"

Now Vincent was looking me over and awaiting my answer with obvious interest.

"Pure desperation and a chance meeting," I said. "I was literally on death's door. Luckily, I fell into very good hands."

"Yes," Pascal agreed. "I'm happy to say his treatment is going superbly well. But there will need to be follow-up visits for quite some time, I'm sure."

I laughed. "Yeah, I'm counting on it. Can never be too careful."

"We were going to get some lunch," Nic said. "Would you boys like to join us?"

I glanced at Pascal for cues.

"Sure," he said. "Scott?"

"Absolutely."

"All right," Nic smiled. "Why don't we get a table at Moxie's? It's just down the road. It's Vincent's favorite." He shot Vincent a loaded gaze, which made the young man's cheeks darken even more.

Vincent whispered "Sir…" and ducked his head.

Hmm. I'm missing some kinky subtext here.

"Okay with you, Scott?" Pascal checked.

"Sure. Anything but the food court, honestly."

Pascal laughed. "I hear you."

We drove the short distance to Moxie's and found Vincent waiting for us inside the door.

"Nic has a table. Come on."

He led us to a booth, where Nic was sprawled on the bench, checking his phone. He put it away and stood, motioning for Vincent to slide in beside him.

Pascal slid in across from Vincent, and I sat beside him, facing Nic.

Nic leaned back and folded his arms. He'd removed his leather jacket and rolled up the sleeves of the black shirt, revealing slim forearms dusted with light hair and delicate wrists, one of which sported the latest in Apple watch technology on a brown leather strap.

"So, Scott, have you always been interested in medical kink or only since hooking up with Mutt and Jeff?"

"Nic, Jesus. Cut right to the chase, don't you?" Pascal snorted.

"Why not? I don't see any point in prevaricating. Vincent and I are as kinky as you and Dr. Jekyll."

My eyebrows flew up. "Oh no. Does that mean there's a Mr. Hyde that's going to appear sometime soon?" I glanced at Pascal, who was shaking his head with good humor.

Pascal said, "Don't listen to Nic, Scott. He's only trying to get a rise out of you."

Nic gave me a slow, sexy smile, and I knew exactly what kind of rise he was after. My dick began to swell in obedience to that dominant sneer.

I cleared my throat. "I've always had an interest but Jericho is the first person to, uh, exploit it."

"I see. And how did you meet? Craigslist? ChristianMingle?"

I liked Nic. He was funny and forthright.

I laughed. "Sonny's, actually."

"The Leather bar? *Really*."

"I went for the Halloween party. I almost turned around and walked out because it was so awful. But then I went upstairs, and that's where I met Jericho." I glanced at Pascal. "I had no idea he was a dog owner."

"Hardy-har," Pascal commented. "I've been showing Scott the basics of pup play. He used to be a skeptic, but now —"

"I'm definitely a convert. Not that I want my own or anything. But I get to play with Digger on occasion, and

I must admit, I'm starting to appreciate that particular lifestyle."

"Ah. Vincent, why don't you tell Scott what we like to do when you're in the mood for some pet play?" Nic said, maintaining eye contact with me. The charismatic intensity of the slim Dom was entrancing.

Vincent opened the menu and scanned it for something to order. He glanced at me and smiled sweetly. "*Meow*," he said, with a wink.

"Huh?" I asked.

"Vincent's been experimenting with some kitten play. And I must say, it's going extremely well. Isn't it, darling?"

"Mm-hmm."

Nic leaned toward me.

"When he climbs into my lap and wraps his fluffy white tail around my neck, grinding his cock against my belly and whispering naughty things into my ear, with those cute kitty ears on a headband and a pretty little bell collar around his neck…" Nic bit his bottom lip. "Well, there's nothing else quite like it, Scott."

I pictured the lovely Vincent dressed as a sweet white kitten and couldn't deny it made an intriguing image.

"I imagine that's true," I said, licking my lips.

Nic sat back. "What do you do for a living, Scott?"

"I teach anthropology courses at the college level."

Nic inclined his head. "Nice. I teach music theory and composition."

"Oh? Really?"

"Yes."

"Nic's teaching me piano," Vincent commented.

Nic winked at Vincent and bumped his shoulder. "It started as a kinky game, but Vincent's quite talented —

so now he has regular lessons, rather than only opportunities for kinky foreplay."

I imagined Nic having Vincent sit for a lesson and teasing him with the possibility of punishments for a lack of finesse or energy and swallowed thickly.

"I bet Vincent is an excellent student."

"Oh, he is…in so many ways."

We eventually stopped talking about sex and enjoyed a lovely lunch. Nic and Vincent were intelligent and pleasant company. Nic was charismatic and alluring, and Vincent sweet and attentive. I imagined the young, blue-eyed man made an excellent service-slash-sexual submissive. I had no doubt Nic was a stern but caring and creative Dom, and I got the feeling they were well-matched.

After lunch, Pascal and I drove back to the mall and finished our shopping before heading back toward his and Jericho's place.

"I haven't seen you much over the last couple of weeks because of school, and I'm having a really good time hanging out. Do you want to come in for a cup of coffee or some hot chocolate?"

"Sure, I'll come in for a bit, as long as I'm not disturbing you."

"Nope. I finished my big essay. Now I only have to study for the last test before the final exam in January. It's next week, so once that's done, I'll be free to enjoy the holidays."

"That's great," I said as Pascal keyed us inside. "I have some final marking to do this weekend, then my workload will ease up too." I followed Pascal in and toed off my boots, then hung up my jacket. "Hopefully Dr. Griffin will have some appointments available in the near future."

"Don't worry, he will. Things are always a little intense right before the holidays. Christmas is in two weeks, right? Another week, and he should be able to fit you in."

"I can't wait."

As we sat in Pascal and Jericho's snug living room and sipped our coffee, I asked Pascal how long the two of them had been a unit and how they'd met.

He told me they'd been together for four years, living with each other for three of those, and that they'd met at a pup night event when Pascal had been starting to get into the lifestyle.

"I was so nervous, and I didn't have any gear except a cheap dog collar with a tag with my pup name on it. I found myself in a pup mosh with all these experienced guys who had the full hoods and butt plug tails. And while it was awesome and I pretty much knew I was where I needed to be, it was also intimidating and intense. I was completely overwhelmed and kind of freaking out. Then this super-hot guy leaned over the gate and talked softy to me, got me to come over, gave me pets and scratches and made me feel like I was the cutest and most adorable puppy in the pit. And that was that. I've been his ever since."

"Wow."

"I'm so lucky to have met him, and the medical kink setup was an added bonus. I hadn't really explored it before and I don't think I'm as into it as you are, but I'll submit to anything to see Jericho's doctor persona in play. And being his assistant with others is a natural fit for me. It's pretty fucking hot when the patient is totally into it, like you are, Scott."

I laughed. "Ah, thanks."

We fell into a companionable silence, then both started speaking at once.

Pascal said, "Want to watch a movie?"

"Well, I guess I should be— What?"

Pascal laughed, blushing. "I just— But if you really have to leave, I get it."

"Did you ask me to watch a movie with you?"

"Yeah. But I understand if you're too busy."

"I'm not too busy. I simply didn't want to overstay my welcome."

"Well, you're not."

"Okay. Sure. I'd love to watch a movie with you."

"And cuddle on the couch? It helps me relax."

I smiled. "I'd love to."

We snuggled up on the sofa together, the way I'd seen Pascal do with Jericho many times—me underneath with Pascal between my legs and his head on my shoulder. Even though he was bigger than I was, it felt right, and I found my own seasonal stress dissipating as we laughed through the first half of *The Devil Wears Prada*. He smelled of clean cotton and fruity shampoo.

We must have fallen asleep, because the next thing I knew, the front door shut loudly, and Jericho's voice announced, "Hey, sweetie, I'm home!"

I blinked and tried to focus, swiveling my head to see Jericho step into the living room and take in the scene.

"Oh. Hey, Scott."

He peered around the room. "I thought you were going shopping."

I cleared my throat and jiggled Pascal, who lay snoring softly against my shoulder. "The stuff's still in the car. We came in to have a cup of coffee and ended up watching *The Devil Wear's Prada*. Well, part of it."

I nudged Pascal again.

Jericho laughed. "You won't wake him up like that. He's a deep sleeper." He walked over to us and gaze fondly on his boyfriend. "He's really in dreamland right now."

"Hmm, I don't think so. Wouldn't he be twitching and jerking?"

"True. Pups tend to do that when they dream." Jericho leaned down and kissed me on the lips, then pulled back. "Nice to see you."

"You, too. How was work?"

Jericho shrugged. "Busy. It always is at this time of year. I have a few things to do tonight, but at least I don't have to go in."

"I should get going."

"You could stay for supper?" Jericho suggested.

I smiled. "Thank you. But I should get back, sort out the gifts I bought and figure out if there's anyone left to buy for." I looked Jericho over. "Theoretically, if someone were to buy you a Christmas gift, what should they get?"

He rolled his eyes. "You don't have to get me a gift."

"I know. But I want to."

"Why don't you get me something to use in the 'office'?" he said, gesturing toward the spare room.

"I could," I said, blushing. "I thought of that. But then it would be a gift for me, honestly."

"True."

"Come on. What do you want for Christmas, Jericho?"

"Honestly? I want you to come spend Christmas week with us."

I blinked. The invitation surprised me. "The whole week?"

"Yeah. But you've probably got familial responsibilities…"

"No. Well, yeah, but I can do those visits in one afternoon, probably. I can spend most of the week with you two."

"Oh yeah?"

Jericho knelt down beside the couch and kissed me again, taking his time. When he pulled back, he said, "Maybe we can make up for lost time. I hate not seeing you. And I think Pascal has missed you, too."

It was settled. We'd have another week apart, but then I'd pack a bag and stay with the two of them over the holiday.

Although Jericho had said my company was the only thing he needed for Christmas, I wanted to get both him and Pascal something small to put under their tree. I simply had to figure out what.

I didn't want to get him anything for his medical 'practice', even though it was tempting. For one thing, I hadn't yet seen his entire inventory of instruments and supplies, so I was likely to duplicate something he already had. And for another thing, as I'd mentioned, that would be more of a gift for me, since I would be getting it for him to use during our medical play scenes.

I needed to think of something meaningful but nothing overly romantic or expensive. There was a delicate balance at the beginning of any relationship, in order to let a partner know you cared and thought of the relationship as potentially serious and long-term but that you weren't trying to jump ahead of them in the game. It could be tricky. And in *my* situation, where we'd already stepped outside the bounds of conventionality, it could be even more difficult to navigate those early weeks.

I settled on a gift card to the Sweet Basil Thai restaurant in South Ottawa, addressed to both of them. It seemed a good way to reinforce that I valued and respected the relationship they had with each other, even as I wanted to be a part of it. I liked them both equally, and their commitment to each other was part of the attraction.

I taped it to the bottom of an empty box and wrapped it up with some brown craft paper and a pretty green ribbon. I even went to the pet store and paid for a blue dog tag in the shape of a bone, engraved with 'To Jericho and Pascal' to attach. It looked beautiful, and I couldn't wait to present the gift to them.